A
Deeper
Sense
of
Loyalty

C. James Gilbert

C. James Gilbert

A Deeper Sense of Loyalty

FIRST SUNBURY PRESS EDITION
Printed in the United States of America
November 2012

Trade Paperback ISBN: 978-1-62006-152-7
Mobipocket format (Kindle) ISBN: 978-1- 62006-153-4
ePub format (Nook) ISBN: 978-1-62006-154-1

Published by:
Sunbury Press
Mechanicsburg, PA
www.sunburypress.com

Mechanicsburg, Pennsylvania   USA

This book is dedicated to Susanne Marie Alwine; a spirited lady who without ever knowing it, has taught me the true meaning of the word. . . courage!

Acknowledgments

I would like to express my appreciation to Lawrence Knorr and Sunbury Press, for helping to make a lifelong dream come true.

I would like to thank my editor, Jennifer Melendrez, for the splendid job she has done editing this book.

A special, "Thank You," to my wife Cyndee for her help and for listening to my dream so graciously for many years.

Finally, for their loving support, I would like to thank my children, James, Jeremy, and Sarah.

ONE

James Becomes a Man

Irony is a true enemy of those who believe they live in a perfect world because reality can bring about their undoing. It could be considered a case in point that the end of said perfect world, as young James Langdon knew it, came about on what he anticipated to be the best day of his life.

A recurring nightmare that had haunted him as a child began to play through his mind. It all started when he was seven years old. One night, long after everyone had gone to sleep, the silence was broken when several gunshots rang out from somewhere near the barn. The sounds of the gunshots were followed by a dog's frantic barking. The commotion awakened James, luring him out of bed and over to the window. He looked out and saw only darkness, but he heard what sounded like something or someone running through the lawn. About that time, he heard his father coming down the hallway. He stopped just outside James's door and James heard him say in an audible whisper, "Go back to bed, Mary, we must not wake the children." Then he continued along the hallway and down the stairs.

When James heard the front door close, he quickly dressed himself and crept to the bedroom door. Slowly, he opened it a few inches and stood, listening. There was no sound from his parents' room or from the room his two sisters shared across the hall. Slowly, quietly, he went out into the dark hall, leaving the bedroom door ajar. On tiptoe, he made his way downstairs, fearful that his father might return and find him out of bed. When he reached the bottom of the stairs he stopped again to listen but heard nothing. Easing open the big front door, he stepped out on the veranda and pulled the door shut behind him.

It was late November and the night air was chilled and damp. Dew covered the lawn; he could see the grass glistening in the hazy moonlight. All was still quiet so he walked down the steps and headed for the barn, which stood fifty yards in the distance. As he reached the board fence that enclosed the barnyard he could hear muffled voices coming from around the back. Nearly holding his breath, he sneaked to the rear corner of the barn and stood with his back to the wall. He could see light coming from behind the barn, flickering in an eerie sort of way. As he stood there quietly, shivering slightly, he could distinguish the voice of his father, and then he recognized the voice of Farley Tabor: his father's crude, intimidating overseer; an ugly man with an eye patch whose very appearance scared James to death. They seemed to be arguing. It was difficult to make out complete sentences because they were intentionally keeping their voices low. In spite of this handicap, James was sure he heard his father say, "Never anywhere near this house."

He desperately wanted to peek around the corner but was terrified of being caught. He also decided that he could not stand there much longer lest his father should suddenly return to the house. While the obscured sound of conversation continued, he summoned all of his courage and looked around the corner. There, maybe thirty feet away stood three men: his father, holding a lantern in his right hand; Farley Tabor, who was holding a torch; and a third man whose face James could not see. The third man also had a torch in one hand and was holding a dog by the leash with the other. They were standing beneath the spreading limbs of a huge live Oak tree. And there in the tree, right in front of James's eyes, silhouetted against the night sky, hung the body of a black man. There was a rope tied to a low branch and the other end was tied around the man's neck. James did not scream; in fact, he was so gripped by terror that he could hardly breathe. He wanted to run but his legs felt like rubber. All he could do was stand there with his back pressed to the barn and wait for his heartbeat to slow down.

After a few minutes that seemed more like a few hours, James slowly got down on his hands and knees in an attempt to make himself small, then started crawling towards the house as fast as he could go. He never looked back until he reached the veranda, and there he stopped to catch his breath. The only sound aside from the thumping of his heart was that of a night owl somewhere in the distance.

His shoes were soaked, as were his trousers to the knees. He removed the dripping footwear, climbed the steps to the front door, and went inside. Quickly, he made his way up to his room, got undressed, dumped his clothes in a heap on the floor, and got into bed.

The house was still quiet but James was sure that his pounding heart could be heard from a mile away. He was trembling as though submerged in ice water and the image of what he'd witnessed was like a photograph etched permanently in his mind's eye. If only he could turn back time and reverse the decision to go outside when he heard the noise. If only he'd stayed in bed.

As the clock on the fireplace mantle ticked away the minutes, James slowly regained enough self-control to ponder what had happened. Never in his short life had he seen anything so ghastly. Never had he seen death in human form. And second to that horrible vision was the involvement of his father. What had actually happened? Did the three of them really hang that man and if so . . . why?

James realized that tears were streaming down his face and he felt sick to his stomach. Just when he wouldn't have believed he could feel any worse, he heard the front door open; footsteps entered the house. His father was back and James could feel a new surge of fear course through his body. The footsteps ascended the stairs slowly, almost cautiously. All James could do was pray that they continued until his father had reached his own bedroom. He lay still and waited. All of his hope was in vain. The footsteps stopped in front of his door.

He rolled to his stomach and buried his face in the pillow just as the door opened. His father walked in and stood beside the bed. Then he bent over and picked up the pile of clothing James had left on the floor. Several minutes passed while he pretended to be asleep. Then a new thought struck hard: his shoes and trousers were wet. There was no doubt that his father would know that he'd been outside. What would happen now? Would his father be angry? Would he be forced to talk about this night and the whole grisly business?

Perhaps God *was* answering his prayer; perhaps, all things considered, his father, too, was entirely unsure of what to do because he laid the clothing back on the floor and quietly left the room.

The rest of the night was one long series of tosses and turns. Sleep would overcome from time to time, but when it did the image of what James had seen behind the barn returned as well. At times he felt like he was swimming in cold sweat; other times he felt like he was burning up.

At the moment it seemed that time had ceased and eternity had begun, he opened his eyes. Sunlight was bursting through the window and the room was so bright that it took a few minutes for his eyes to focus. At the same time, he labored to collect his thoughts.

Standing at the foot of the bed were his mother and father. Sitting in a chair near his side was old Dr. Mead. When his parents saw that he was awake, their faces broke into a mixture of smiles and tears as they explained what had happened. They told James that he had come down with a fever; he had been delirious for two days. They told him he had ranted about the most dreadful things imaginable. Dr. Mead said that when someone is in the grip of such a fever the mind can produce abnormal thought processes; things that are extremely farfetched can seem like reality.

When James told everyone he was hungry, Dr. Mead assured his parents that the boy was going to be fine. His mother told him to rest and that she would have Olivia make him something special. "I will bring it up as soon as it is ready," she said.

Dr. Mead told him to eat hardy, and then maybe some fresh air might do him good. His father told him if he felt up to it they would take a buggy ride into Macon. Then his mother kissed him on the forehead, his father smiled affectionately, and Dr. Mead bade him goodbye. They left the room never knowing how confused but how relieved he was.

The minute the door was closed, he was out of bed and at the window, looking over towards the barn. He could see

4

the limbs of the big live Oak tree towering above the roof. He stared for a long moment, expecting to see evidence of what he'd thought was perfectly real. Then, in his mind a voice said, "Can you believe it? It was a dream." The entire episode had been nothing but a dream.

A large flock of geese flew over the house and their loud, intermittent honking broke James's concentration. He thought how strange it was that his mind had gone back to that fever inspired nightmare and he couldn't help wondering what had triggered it. For a year or so after that night, he had been revisited by the bad dream on occasion but he had thought by now it was gone for good. No matter, he thought. It was such a beautiful day and there were so many *pleasant* things to think about.

The front door opened and his oldest sister, Ashton, came out to the veranda with Kate, the youngest, right behind her. They showered him with birthday greetings then sat down on the swing, Ashton on his right and Kate on his left. "Why, look at me," said James. "I'm a rose between two . . . other roses." The remark inspired laughter and lively conversation among the three of them.

"How does it feel to be eighteen, James?" asked Ashton.

"I can hardly believe it. I thought becoming an adult would feel different somehow, but I don't notice any change from yesterday. I guess you have to experience it for a while."

"I suppose that's true."

"I can't wait until *I* turn eighteen," said Kate. "I'll stay up late and entertain boys and—"

"And get yourself in all kinds of trouble," said Ashton.

"Shows what you know, smarty," Kate replied.

Then the older girl said, "Are you glad to be finished with school, James? You've been gone an awful lot the past few years."

"Yes, I believe I am. New York was exciting at times; Lord knows it is very different from life on a big plantation. But I am looking forward to helping Father run the business; that's what I went to school for."

"You'll work here in the office, I suppose?"

"Yes. You know that Father forbids us to go to the compound. Of course, I'm eighteen now so it might be all right for *me* to go."

"You'd better ask Father first. It seems pretty important to him that we stay away from there. My friend, Laura Picket, says it's because we are of the genteel class and it wouldn't be proper to be subjected to the Negro workers. She says that's why Father is so strict about it, so much so that our servants are poor whites and not Negroes like most plantation homes."

"I don't know if I'd put much stock in what Laura Picket says, Ashton. Her father owns his Negroes; they are slaves. Our Negroes work as sharecroppers. Father explained that to me years ago. We are Christians and good Christians do not own other people. Father knows that isn't right. Negroes are just people the same as we are. Remember that, Ashton. What others do is no reflection on us."

"Yes," said Kate. "Now let's talk about the party."

"I hope you like the gift I have for you, James," said Ashton. "I made it for you myself."

"Well," he said, "if you made it for me that will make it even more special."

"I didn't make my gift," said Kate. "But I know you'll like it just the same. It is something that you've been wanting; I've heard you mention it to Father."

James put an arm around each of his sisters and said, "I am sure that I will be delighted with whatever I receive."

"Oh, I do love parties," said Ashton. "We should have a party every day."

"That wouldn't do," said Kate. "Parties would become boring if there were no occasions. That's what makes them so special."

"Just the same," Ashton replied, "parties are just grand and I never get enough of them. I cannot wait to see Jenny and Bret. Are you anxious to see the boys, James?"

"I am, for a fact. When they are here I know what it feels like to have brothers," he teased.

"Well!" said Kate, in mock indignation. "Perhaps you could persuade Father to make a trade with Uncle Stanley or Uncle Joseph."

James suppressed laughter and said, "Well, let me see now. Do you suppose that Father could trade one for one or would it take you both just to get one brother?" All was quiet for about five seconds, and then they both attacked with fingers prodding his ribs until he jumped to his feet and exclaimed, "White flag, white flag. I guess I'll have to settle for having cousins instead of brothers."

At that, they all had a good laugh, and then Ashton said, "I wish Father would get home. Our guests will be here in a few hours. Let's go see if Mother needs anything, Kate." They got up from the swing, delivered another hug and kiss to their big brother, and then went inside.

James sat down again and realized that he was feeling a bit restless. This was the first time he had been home since last Christmas, which was also the last time he had seen the other families. Uncle Stanley's son, Clark, was two years older than James. Clark's brother, Jessie, was the same age as James. Uncle Joseph's son, Franklin, was sixteen, and his younger brother, Jefferson, was fourteen. Uncle Joseph's daughter, Jenny, was Ashton's age, fifteen. Her sister, Bret, was the youngest of all at age twelve. The three families were a close knit group; when they were together, they were as one. Maybe, thought James, he could ask his father to persuade his uncles to spend the night and extend the festivities. He was in the mood for a good long visit.

It was then he realized he was also in the mood for something else: a ride. It would be just the thing to pass the time before the party. He got up and headed for the barn to find George Lynch. George took care of all the animals and usually saddled James's horse for him. It wasn't that he couldn't do it himself, but since George had performed the task ever since James started riding, it had simply become a habit.

When he reached the barn he called out, but George didn't answer. Without hesitation, James picked up his saddle, blanket, and bridle and carried them down to the stall occupied by his horse, Star. Star was a beautiful Chestnut mare, three years old, and sixteen hands. The horse nickered softly as James approached. He led her out of the stall, and within minutes she was saddled and ready to go. When James climbed up, he could tell that Star was as ready for a run as he was. "Which way should we head, girl?" he asked. Then he had a thought—a very daring thought. Why not ride down the road to the compound? He actually shivered a bit. Was he being foolish or downright stupid? His father's only rule had always been that his family was never to go there. It was in their best interest, he said. James had occasionally wondered what harm there could be but never had his curiosity driven him to consider breaking this rule. Suddenly, it seemed almost silly. He knew that his father had nothing to hide. It was just that he was overprotective and probably thought it best to keep his family away from men the likes of Farley Tabor. In a way it made perfect sense. His father simply wanted his family life separated from the working environment.

There was, however, one significant difference now. James was a grown man. That would make his decision all right. Perhaps even his father felt differently now. After all, James had just turned eighteen that very day and his father hadn't had a chance to talk to him as a man yet. He was grown now and his father would want him to act as if he were grown; James was sure of that.

TWO

The Revelation

James spurred Star out of the barn and down to the main road heading in the direction of the compound. The excitement was building inside him. If he met his father on the road he would have to turn back. If not, he would see the compound for himself.

Star was an excellent example of horse flesh and she covered the miles in no time. James could see the buildings in the distance, and for an instant he nearly pulled the horse to a stop. But he had come this far and he would have felt weak in nature to change his mind.

When he reached the lane leading from the main road, he slowed Star to a walk. No need to go busting in, he thought. Just ride back casually as if he went there every day. The lane weaved its way back through a heavily wooded area that ended about fifty yards from the fence surrounding the compound. When he reached the edge of the woods, he turned his horse into the trees and stopped.

After dismounting and tying the reins to a sapling, he walked a few steps and stood just short of the clearing. He could easily survey the sprawling layout from his vantage point. In the foreground was a single-story building; well maintained with two windows in front, a porch closed in by a railing, and a chimney climbing up the right side. Going on comments he'd heard from his father, James figured it to be the field office. He could see his father's horse tied at the hitching rail out front. About thirty feet to the left was a similar looking structure except that there were two large wooden chairs on the porch and it was surrounded by a white picket fence with a gate. It appeared to have a pen attached to the back of it and James could hear the sound of dogs coming from inside. That, he thought, would be where Farley Tabor lives. In the distance and to the right were the machinery and ginning sheds next to the mule barn.

There were many wagons in sight, some empty, some loaded, and some partially loaded with bales of cotton. In the distance to the left, he could see four rows of small cabins, which, even from where he stood, appeared to be crude and hastily constructed. He could see several small black children playing near the cabins. Over by the sheds there were a few black men and at least one white man, but apparently most of the workers were out in the fields.

The compound covered about five acres altogether. Outside the surrounding fence, the cotton fields stretched far beyond the horizon. James was glad that everything seemed on the quiet side around the field office. If he *was* to be reprimanded for his disobedience, he preferred not to have an audience.

Still a bit nervous but nonetheless resolute, he was ready to ride in and surprise his father. Just as he turned toward his waiting horse, he heard a commotion coming from the office building. He turned back in time to see a black man seemingly catapulted through the doorway. His momentum carried him across the porch and ended with a hard landing on the ground. The man was naked from the waist up; his hands were tied behind his back. An instant later, two white men emerged from the office. They crossed the porch and went down the steps to stand on either side of the black man who was lying on his back in the dirt. One of the men was Farley Tabor. In a rough manner, Tabor reached down, grabbed the man by the head, and jerked him to his feet. With both hands he began pushing him towards two posts that stood about six feet high and maybe three or four feet apart. When Tabor had the man standing between the posts, he untied his hands. Then he re-tied one wrist to each post so that the man stood spread eagled with his hands above his head.

When this was done, James's father, who had followed along, handed something to Tabor that looked like a coil of rope. But when Tabor shook it out, James could see that it was a bullwhip. James watched in horror as his father stood with arms folded while Tabor began to use the whip on the defenseless man's back. Lash after lash was applied until the victim's knees buckled and he hung by his wrists from the posts. Thinking the two men were satisfied, James thanked God when the barbaric display ended. But it was not so. After a few minutes, Tabor began to kick the man in the side and in the back. Finally, the bloodied man struggled to his feet. And then, for James, the absolutely unthinkable happened. He saw Tabor hand the whip over to his father. In complete and utter disbelief, he watched as his father took his turn whipping the prisoner. James felt a warm, nauseating sensation come up from his stomach to his throat. For an instant he wanted to scream at the top of his lungs for his father to stop. Instead he turned, fell to his knees, and vomited until the dry heaves were all that was left. Tears streamed down his cheeks and he felt weak and unable to rise. All he wanted to do was to climb up on Star and get away from that awful place.

As soon as he was able to stand, without looking back, he walked over to his horse, pulled himself astride and rode slowly back down the lane. As she had on the way out, Star wanted to run, but James made the effort to hold her back. He felt drained by his upset stomach and his head was spinning. So many thoughts were swirling in his mind that he couldn't think straight. The reality of what he'd just witnessed jumped up and smacked him square in the face. There was no getting around the fact: his father had been lying to him, apparently for as long as he could remember. The blacks that worked for his father were slaves. They were bought and paid for, worked-to-death human beings just like everywhere else in the South. They were captives, held against their will—denied their freedom. Then another thought occurred to him and his blood ran cold. He thought about the nightmare that happened when he was seven years old. Was it real? It must have been. His father had stood by while a black man was hanged from the tree behind the barn. How convenient was the fever that had afflicted him?

Then he thought about his mother. What did she know about it all? Had she gone all these years keeping ugly secrets or was she as innocent of it as James had been? What was he to do?

His birthday party came to mind. How could he face everyone and act as if nothing was wrong? At that point, he didn't give a damn about a party. All he really cared about was that slave; the unfortunate man who was being whipped by his father and that despicable Farley Tabor.

Suddenly, from behind him he could hear hoof beats on the road. James was sure that it must be his father. His first instinct was to spur his horse and stay far enough ahead that he wouldn't be seen. Then he thought about getting off the road and hiding in the bushes until his father rode past. Finally, he decided to do what he never would have guessed he'd do. He would just sit, wait, and confront his father.

It took just a short time before the horse and rider slowed down, pulling to a stop beside him. James looked up and found himself eye to eye with the man he loved and respected most in the world; the man whose face was now covered in panic. He spoke his son's name, then his chin dropped to his chest, and for several minutes, the two sat in silence. When he raised his head again James was sure his father could read the whole story written plainly on his face.

"Were you down the road, James?" he asked. James nodded his head. "Did you see?" James nodded again. More time passed in silence. James did not know what to expect. He had always imagined that if something like this ever happened his father would lose his temper and the punishment would be more severe than he'd ever experienced. So it came as a complete surprise when James realized that his father's demeanor was one of uncertainty.

"We have to talk about this, son," he said. "Climb down and I'll try to explain."

James wasn't sure he wanted to talk about anything, but when his father got off his horse and looked up at him, he simply couldn't refuse. They secured their horses and walked over to a fallen tree lying just off the edge of the road and sat down. At first it seemed that his father did not know how to begin. Finally, he took a deep breath and started talking.

"I want you to try to understand that I am a man who loves his family more than anything else in the world. I want you to understand that there is nothing that I would not do to guarantee their happiness and wellbeing. And I want you to understand that I was born into this way of life. Ever since I can remember, the Langdon family has owned slaves. If a man wants to be anything more than a broken back farmer then he has to accept the fact that slavery is essential to our southern way of life. I am not responsible for how things came to be James; I am just carrying on tradition. My father taught me at an early age that we live in a hard world, and if we are to survive we have to be hard as well. I wish now that I had taught you the same. I can see now that I have been a fool; a fool to think that I could make it possible for my family to live in a perfect world, sparing them from the harsh realities. I am full of regret for having lied to you, son, but I guess I always hoped that having provided well would absolve me of that sin." Then he paused and James sensed that he was looking for a response, so he obliged.

"I have always defended you, Father," he said. "I believed that the blacks were here to make a living the same as George Lynch, Darcy Davis, and all the white folks who work for us. There were times when I was in school in New York, when almost to the point of violence I denied the accusations that we were slave owners like the rest of the South. I could accept the fact that others mistreat the blacks because I realize that we cannot control what other people do. I could accept it because I believed that it had no reflection on our family. But I don't know that I could ever accept what I have seen today."

Then it was James's turn to wait for a response. When his father started speaking again, James could clearly hear the frustration in his voice. Maybe it was because he thought he'd failed in his attempt to convince James to see the situation his way. Maybe it was because he didn't really think he should have to. James had to admit, it was probably true for most people that being safe and well provided for was what counted the most; if heads should roll to make it possible, so be it. It was obvious that his father felt that way. But James simply did not.

13

"Do you believe that a righteous man obeys the law, James? If it is the law of the land, established by responsible authority, does a virtuous man comply?"

"Yes, Father," James answered.

"Then let me ask you, have you heard of the Dred Scott Decision?"

James knew where this was going but he answered, "Yes, Father. I read about it in the northern newspapers. It was handed down on March 6, 1857."

"Yes, that is very good. According to Chief Justice Roger Taney, a slave is the property of his master. It *is* the law of the land. We are not outlaws down here, James. We are only living as did our fathers and their fathers before them."

James was not satisfied nor would he ever be. He was sorely tempted to tell his father that he was taught at Sunday worship that there were two kinds of laws: those of man and those of God. If a righteous man had a conscience he would be more prone to following the latter. He was tempted to ask him what the bible had to say on the subject, and how did the Constitution read? But James did not wish to call his father down in such a way, especially since he knew it would do no good. Instead he said, "Why, Father, does it have to necessitate such brutality?"

This question seemed to raise his father's spirits. It was as if he thought he might be getting his point across; his son might be beginning to accept it by way of trying to better understand. "Well, son," he began. "I do not agree that brutality, as you say, is any intended part of the system that we have here. We simply depend on these workers to accomplish what has to be done, and in return their needs are satisfied. But the one essential part of this is authority and who controls it. We have five hundred working age males and females here, and not counting myself, there are four men to keep them in line. If not for the establishment of absolute authority we could never handle a workforce that large. It is regrettable, to be sure, but there are times when examples have got to be made. What you saw this afternoon was just that. The black man we punished is called Bo Sampson, and the truth is that he is nothing but trouble. Twice in the last six months he has run off. Last night he tried again. This time he took two others with him. When the blacks come in from the field this evening, they will all walk past Sampson. They will see once again that an attempt to run away has failed and that it is not wise to try. That is what it takes to keep order and I ask for nothing more. Most of the blacks understand that and they accept what life has given them. And that is why the ones like Bo Sampson must be subdued. It is really an effort to maintain a peaceful co-existence."

James listened to the facts of life according to John Langdon, but he was not impressed. As his father's words and twisted rationalizations fell upon his ears, his own opinions stood their ground. How, he wondered, could this man, whom he had loved and admired since he was a small boy, attempt to justify this way of life? Had he never put himself in the place of a slave? What would he do if his freedom was taken away, if he was forced to live as his master saw fit? What would he do if his wife or his children were taken from him and sold, never to be seen again? Wouldn't he do the same as Bo Sampson? James knew that he would. And yet, his father saw Sampson as a trouble maker and had whipped him for trying to exercise the same right that God had given all men.

Now that James was painfully aware of the truth, he wondered what his own life would become. Inside, he felt torn, split down the middle as though with an axe. His love for his father reached to his very core. But to be expected to carry on the so-called Langdon family tradition was something he knew he could never do. It seemed impossible that in the space of perhaps an hour his life had gone from wonderfully set to terribly unsettled. For now, it seemed that he only had one choice. He would pretend to try to understand the reasoning his father gave him until he had more time to think. But for the time being, there was only one other question that he had to ask. "Does Mother understand what is necessary?"

"You never knew your Grandpa Barrett, but you know that he was a lawyer in Macon. He never owned slaves. He employed a few servants, but they were white. Truthfully, he did not object to slavery. He considered blacks to be an inferior race and he did not want them in his house or around his family. I guess you could say that he was indifferent to the practice. It is probably a good thing that he felt the way he did about having slaves. I'm sure it would have caused a problem between him and your mother, the same as it has between you and me. If there is anything to genetics, and I believe there is, surely you take after your mother in many ways. I never had to ask her how she felt about slavery. That was something I could figure out for myself just by getting to know her. After we were married, we lived with Grandma and Grandpa Barrett until our house was built. From that point on, things were as they still are to this day. That is why I don't have slaves working at the house. I wanted to keep things the same as they have always been in her life. It may be true that I deceived your mother. But I did it for her because I love her."

"Hasn't it been difficult, deceiving her I mean?"

"No. She understands that business is something that men and women do not discuss. Women leave business and politics to the men; men leave social events and all things concerning the home to the women. Speaking of social events, we should be getting back to get ready for your party."

Ordinarily, his father's last remark would have sparked great excitement in him, but not today. But he knew that the rest of his family, not to mention his uncles and their families, were looking forward to the get together. So he had no choice except to pull himself together for their sakes and feign enthusiasm. In his mind, the revelation of the day was far from being put to rest; he wondered if his father felt the same way.

"You're right, Father. We should be getting home." They mounted their horses and rode the rest of the way in silence.

It was almost noon when they reached the barn. George was cleaning stalls when they arrived; he took their horses, unsaddled them, and gave them a rubdown. James and his father went straight to the house to get ready for the party.

By one o'clock, the guests had arrived and a very lively gathering it was. Even James's mood had improved in spite of himself as he greeted relatives he had not seen in months. Naturally, he was especially glad to see his cousins, enjoying the company of young men close to his age. Ashton and Kate had looked forward to seeing Jenny and Bret; the older folks were elated as well.

After a meal that would have pleased royalty, Olivia, the family's cook, brought in a beautiful birthday cake with eighteen candles and set it on the table in front of James. At that moment he had almost forgotten the unpleasant experience he had gone through earlier that day. But when his father said, "Make a wish, son," it all came flooding back. He looked up, and for an uncomfortable instant their eyes locked, and the smile slowly disappeared from his father's face. Grateful that birthday wishes were never spoken, James blew out the candles in one breath, hoping that it meant his wish would come true.

When the gifts had all been opened, which included, among some other very nice things, a new saddle and a .45 caliber revolver, the gathering broke up into smaller groups for the purpose of deep conversation. The ladies and the girls settled themselves in the parlor. James and the rest of the young men gathered out on the veranda. John took his brothers, who were also plantation owners, out to the barn for a smoke and a look at a handsome stallion he'd just purchased from a farm in Kentucky.

Although a smoke and the new horse were of legitimate interest, the three men had more important things that they were anxious to discuss.

Once inside the barn, Stanley and Joseph found some empty nail kegs, put them side by side, and sat down. John did likewise, placing his makeshift seat in front of his brothers. Then he handed each of them a cigar and lit one for himself. John took the first turn to speak. "I feel that there is no need to say it, but the future is very uncertain for us all. If Abraham Lincoln is elected in November, I would bet all I own that secession will follow."

"And that will be followed by war," said Stanley.

"I don't know," replied Joseph. "I still think if it comes to secession the North might let us leave peacefully. Why, I've read in the papers that Lincoln is not exactly what you would call a nigger lover. He opposes the expansion of slavery but that might be just a political move to placate those damn abolitionists."

"Maybe," said Stanley. "But if he does get elected, who knows what he'll do. Of course going to war would be a pretty radical step to take for the likes of a race of inferiors like these niggers."

"I'm afraid I have to disagree with you, Joseph," said John. "Slavery be damned. It will be the dissolution of the Union that will cause the war. There isn't any way Lincoln will let that happen without a fight. The chances are better that the South will choose not to secede, and I don't think there is any chance of that at all. No, brothers. I think our only hope is if Lincoln fails to get elected. But I don't think we should concern ourselves with that. We need to look beyond it and stay one step ahead. What we must do is prepare as if we know that it is inevitable. We must devise a plan to keep our plantations running no matter what. If war comes, we must keep the economy strong and that means business must continue as usual."

"How do we do that?" asked Stanley.

"The first thing," John replied, "will be to talk to our overseers and the rest of our men and find out what their intentions are. If war breaks out, will they go off to fight or will they stay at their jobs? I think that Farley will probably stay but Thomas, Milo, and Sam are younger and are more likely to be up to the adventure; you both employ young men as well. It is not always easy now to keep the niggers in line. We can't afford to lose anybody. We might even need to consider hiring some men. A war could give the niggers ideas."

"I almost wish I could find someone to take *my* place," said Stanley. "I wouldn't mind taking a shot at a Yankee myself."

"I know how you feel," John answered. "But if war is declared men will be climbing over each other to join up. I think they can handle the job without us. Besides, if there is a war, I don't believe that it would last more than a month or so."

"You're right, John," said Joseph. "I'll wager that if we bloody their noses good and proper they'll head north as fast as they can and stay there."

"I hope that you're right, Joseph," said Stanley. "But I think we need to consider the strengths of the North compared to our own. They have long since industrialized while we have remained with our traditional system. How long could we defend ourselves against invasion?"

"And I say it will not happen that way," Joseph retorted. "If we show them we mean business they'll leave us alone. Besides, I've heard that there is a possibility that England will intervene on our behalf. Our cotton is very important to their mills."

"What if they don't?" argued Stanley. "What if the war drags on longer than we think? What if the North gets the idea to block our port cities? If we couldn't ship and we couldn't receive they could choke us to death."

"Then we will run the blockade," answered Joseph.

"Well," John interrupted, "for now we cannot count on anything or assume anything. That is why we have to take any precautions that we can and then wait to see what happens in November. To make one thing perfectly clear, like you boys, I would stop at nothing to protect my family and my interests."

In unison, John's brothers voiced their agreement with his statement.

"I can tell you one thing," said Stanley. "If there is a war, I won't be able to keep Clark and Jessie out of it."

"I know what you mean," Joseph replied. "Neither Franklin or Jefferson would be old enough for the army, but if it comes to war, they will find a way."

Then, looking at John, he asked. "How does James feel about it all?" John wanted nothing more than to assure his brothers that James would be ready at the first bugle call, but he thought about what had happened that morning and said, "You've both heard me talk about Bo Sampson?" They nodded in reply.

"Well, he ran off again last night—or at least he tried to. What's worse, he took two other nigger men with him, two that had never given me trouble before. Anyway, Farley and the boys caught up with them a couple of hours later. This morning, we bullwhipped Sampson until he couldn't stand up. James saw it happen. He's never disobeyed me before but he's eighteen now and I guess he figured everything has changed."

"Well, I guess you could hardly give him hell on his birthday," Joseph said.

"I don't know that I would have anyway," John replied. "I guess I do feel a little shame, keeping secrets from him all these years."

"Forgive me, brother," said Stanley. "But you're a damn fool. I've been telling you for years that it was a big mistake not only to keep it from James, but from your entire family. What was his reaction?"

"It wasn't good, I'm afraid. He was pretty upset."

"I'm not surprised," said Stanley. "I told you that if he ever found out the truth it would be far worse than if he had known from the beginning. Maybe you could keep such a secret from Mary and the girls. But how did you think you were going to keep James from ever finding out? Someday he will take your place. What did you think would happen then? That he would have accepted the facts of life just like my boys have, and Joseph's? They understand that we have our place in life and the niggers have theirs. I've wondered why I ever agreed to help you keep the truth from James, not to mention telling my sons to do the same. You should have taught him the difference between whites and niggers. He's a Southerner for Christ sake. Now it comes as a shock."

John knew that Stanley was right but it was very difficult to admit it. "I can't apologize for what I've done. Mary didn't grow up around slaves and it is not in her to harm a fly. And you know what James went through when he was seven. The boy and his mother are a lot alike. I've heard of worse things than lying to protect your family. Maybe I thought that slavery would die out before this ever happened."

"You know better than that," said Stanley. "Slavery will never die out. The South depends on it the way it depends on the rain and the sunshine. Are you ashamed of the way you live your life? Are you ashamed of owning slaves?"

John felt his temper rising. The way in which he chose to appear before his family had nothing to do with how he personally felt about slavery. "I am not ashamed of anything, Stanley," John retorted. "I do what has to be done and if I answer to anyone it will be to God Almighty. But even you will have to admit that what has to be done is not always pleasant or pretty."

"Sure, John, I agree," said Stanley. "It's a little bit like having to shoot a lame horse. You hate to do it, but it has to be done. James would have understood that and he would have understood why a nigger would have to be whipped. Like I said, someday he will have to handle such things."

"And he will," John replied. "We talked about what he'd seen, and although it wasn't easy, I believe that he understands now. I believe in my son. He is a Langdon and he is a Southerner. Mark my words: if there is a war, the South and I will be able to depend on him."

"You can bet on it," said Joseph. "We don't doubt it for a minute, do we, Stanley?"

"No," said Stanley. "We don't." John relaxed his posture. He felt better having gotten the load off his chest. He knew that James would be fine and what had happened that morning would have no lasting effect, no discord between himself and his son—he was sure of it. "Prepare as much as you can, brothers," said John. "Then we wait for the election in November."

All were in agreement and that put an end to the discussion for the time being. Each man extinguished his cigar, and forgetting about John's new stallion, they returned to the house to join their families.

Everyone did spend the night, and following a hearty breakfast the next morning, they all went to worship together. Little did John know that during the services his son was praying that God would help him do the right thing. To go against his family seemed impossible, but to live as a slave owner was deeply sinful. Although he could never be sure, James didn't believe that he would feel any different if he had known the truth all along. He thought of the possibility of the country splitting apart. If that happened, maybe it would put an end to slavery. But if it did, it would almost certainly mean that the South would have to be defeated. How could he pray for such a thing? What would happen to his family? Could the Almighty himself provide an answer to his problem? He must think it through. It would take time, but he must think it through very carefully.

When worship ended, the families said an affectionate farewell and everyone left for their respective homes. That evening at home, James's father called him into his office and immediately James was overcome by an uneasy feeling. He was sure that the conversation they'd had the day before would be resurrected. But to his surprise, his father acted as though nothing had happened. The purpose, ostensibly, was to finalize a few details concerning his new position. The following day, he was supposed to take over the bookkeeping. In part, he was grateful for the opportunity to get involved in his work. It would help to keep his mind off his problem, at least during the day. But sometimes, in the evening, he would saddle Star and ride to some lonely place to sit and contemplate the future.

He kept his distance from the compound and tried to erase the image of the whipping he'd witnessed. But it was no use. The spectacle was etched indelibly in his mind and he believed that only by trying to put a stop to such things would it ever go away.

Then came the day when something happened that would change his life and the lives of everyone in the country. On November 6, 1860, came the news that struck like a bolt of lightning into the very heart of the South. Abraham Lincoln had been elected as the 16th President of the United States.

THREE

Words of War

At one-thirty in the afternoon on December 20th, 1860, the South Carolina Legislature voted unanimously to secede from the union. There was little doubt that more southern states would do the same. Many southerners rejoiced, some wept.

On January 9th, 1861, Mississippi followed South Carolina. The next day, Florida left the Union and Alabama the day after that. On January 19th, Georgia seceded, then Louisiana and Texas. By the first week of February, a new constitution had been adopted and on February 18th, Jefferson Davis of Mississippi was inaugurated as president; Georgia's own Alexander Stephens was chosen to serve as vice president. The Confederate States of America was born. James took it as a sign, believing that God had indeed shown him the way. Now it was time to make plans.

When the news that a new government had been established reached the Langdon home, John was quick to gather his family into the parlor. As he had advised his brothers months earlier, he had done all he could to prepare for a crisis should it come to pass. The time had come to prepare his wife and children. James had never seen his father in such a state of excitement. It was difficult to tell if his behavior was born out of elation or of fear. It was not, however, difficult to see the panic that covered his mother's face and the faces of his sisters.

In spite of the circumstances, his father spoke in a steady voice designed to inspire confidence in his words. "I am afraid that the years of talk have finally evolved into action. We are now part of the Confederate States of America. What will happen next is unclear, but I believe that war is not far off. If we do fight, I do not believe it will be a long, drawn out affair. Furthermore, in my opinion, the war will never reach Georgia. Still, we are part of a new country now and we must all support the cause in any way we can. Until further developments, we will conduct ourselves and our lives as usual with one notable exception. Miss Ambrose wishes to return to Portsmouth, which will leave Ashton and Kate without a teacher. For the time being, Mother will help them to continue with their studies. Let us put our trust in God that he might see us through whatever lies ahead."

When he was finished, he got up and motioned for James to follow him out of the room. They walked down the hallway to the office; when they were inside, his father closed the door. "Sit down, James," he said. Then he reached for a decanter of bourbon, and to James's surprise, poured two glasses. "Sip this. It will strengthen your resolve." Then, seating himself facing his son, he said, "I did not wish to alarm your mother and your sisters any more than necessary, but I know that I can be more candid with you. We *will* soon be at war with the North. I feel it in my bones. I know something of Abraham Lincoln and a great deal more about Jefferson Davis. I do not believe that two more resolute gentlemen have ever squared off before. The atmosphere is at a fever pitch and more intoxicating than this bourbon. You know that I met with your uncles and a few other men in Macon yesterday. I can tell you that the South, generally speaking, is not contemplating a fight, but anticipating one. I am afraid that right now it would be difficult to find a level head, North or South. One of the biggest topics of conversation is about Fort Sumter in Charleston Harbor. The fort sits in Confederate territory but it still flies the United States flag. The people of South Carolina are in a rage over it and the rage is spreading like a prairie fire. The Confederate authorities have tried to induce the North to evacuate the fort but to no avail. The fort is surrounded by Southern gun emplacements and soldiers, but Lincoln says that he will run supplies to Major Andersen. Now it is only a matter of time. In addition to our state militias, military units are being raised all over the South. I am sure that you have considered the matter and I would like to know what your intentions are."

James knew what his father was leading up to; and of course, he was right. The time had come for every man to place his loyalty. In the mess and confusion that becomes part of a divided country there would no doubt be a few Southerners who would fight for the North and a few Northerners who would fight for the South. James had no trouble deciding what was most important to him. He would fight if necessary, but not for either army. What he wanted most was freedom for the slaves. Therefore, he would never join the Confederate army because their cause would protect the institution. And even though slavery had been abolished in the North, the Yankees only cared about preserving the Union. So James vowed that he would follow in the footsteps of the only hero he had left—John Brown. To do so would require self sacrifice because the choice he'd made might very well destroy him in the end.

James did not intend to enlist followers as John Brown had; he did not plan to incite an uprising. It was, instead, his intention to work alone, taking a few slaves at a time and somehow helping them to reach freedom.

When he thought of how much he loved his father and how his heart would break if he ever found out, a lump formed in his throat and threatened to choke him. All he could do was pray that in the end understanding would be a savior to all.

The risks would be numerous. If caught by the South, he could be shot or hanged as a traitor. If he were caught by the North, his deep Southern accent and civilian clothing could get him shot or hanged as a spy. It would take daring and a constant reminder to trust no one. The only thing he really had on his side was a very willing spirit. He had some idea of how his plans would be executed, but the smaller details would have to be made up as he went along. The thought of helping a fellow human being gain his freedom somehow helped to minimize the risks, at least in his mind. It also made it easier to deceive his father, and when asked about his intentions, without hesitation he said, "I intend to fight for the Confederacy."

With a smile that mirrored his deep felt pride, James's father lifted his glass and said, "Hurrah! Hurrah for the Southern Confederacy!"

They joined their glasses and swallowed the contents in one gulp. The fire of the alcohol burned James's throat the whole way down making him cough. Laughing, his father got up and smacked him on the back and said, "There now, soldier. Even those Yankees can't pack a wallop like Kentucky bourbon can."

"I'm glad to hear it," said James, after regaining his voice.

"So what will it be, James?" his father asked. "I was thinking you should consider the cavalry. You're an excellent horseman and I think you could gain rank quickly."

"I think that the cavalry is a wonderful suggestion, Father. I don't really see myself as a foot soldier and I think Star would make a terrific cavalry mount."

"Indeed she would, son. Your cousins, Clark and Jessie, want to join a Georgia artillery regiment. Joseph's sons are too young to join but I wouldn't be surprised if they find a way. I wish now that I'd sent you to VMI. Then you could begin as an officer. I've already tried calling in some favors in order to get you a commission but since you've had no military training they wouldn't budge."

"I don't mind, Father," said James. "I prefer to earn my way."

"Spoken like a true Langdon, son. We always earn our way. I think I know just how you should go about it. I was reading in the Macon paper about a man named Wade Hampton. He is one of the biggest plantation owners in South Carolina. Word has it that he is organizing and equipping a legion of cavalry. They say that he has no military training so perhaps it would be easier for you to learn under a man like him."

"It's settled then, Father. I will travel to South Carolina and join up with Hampton's legion."

"This is outstanding, son. You probably won't be gone long enough to get homesick. You may not even see action, but it will be a good experience nonetheless. Have you thought about when you might leave?"

"I thought that I would wait for an official declaration, Father. After the first shot is fired I will be on my way."

"I agree with your thinking, James. It will come, I assure you. Still, it wouldn't do to have you halfway to South Carolina if the Yankees should come to their senses."

So the population waited for the opening guns. To the surprise of most people, a month passed in relative quiet. Finally, Jefferson Davis ordered General P.G.T. Beauregard to shell Fort Sumter until the fort surrendered. At four-thirty on the morning of April 12th, South Carolina fired the first shot of the war. After a thirty-four hour bombardment, at two-thirty in the afternoon of April 13th, Major Robert Andersen surrendered Fort Sumter. With the beginning of hostilities past, it was decided that James would leave for South Carolina on April 15th.

One week earlier, James had made an excuse to be out of the office for the day. He used that time to take his first step towards the secret life he intended to lead. He rode to the small town of Dry Branch to rent a house. Even though the town was not more than forty miles from home, James and his family were not known there. As an added precaution, he rented the house in the name of William Mason.

The house would serve as a base of operations; a quiet place where he could rest between trips to the North; a place to keep extra clothing as well as other necessities.

After some careful thought, James realized that his pretense of joining Hampton's legion could not last for long. Writing letters to his family would not pose a problem. A cavalry unit would move around quite a bit but since he *would* be traveling to accomplish his true mission, he could mail his letters from areas where Hampton's unit might likely be. But receiving letters would be a different matter. James could not have his family sending him mail to a unit he did not belong to. It would also be necessary for him to have a Confederate trooper's uniform to wear when, ostensibly, he visited home on furlough. So he formulated a new plan that would simplify the situation.

James decided that he would write a letter to his family explaining that on his way to join up with Hampton, he had chanced to meet and converse with an operative of the Confederate Signal Service. He would explain that so fascinating was the conversation, so alluring was the challenge—and since he had not as yet made a commitment—he volunteered his services.

He knew if his father believed he was working as a spy for the government he would be more proud than if James became a general in the cavalry. He would mail his letter from South Carolina on his first trip north. James was very pleased with his idea and about how well it would cover his activities. His true endeavors had to be kept secret and his fictitious new vocation would give him the perfect cover. He would not be required to wear a uniform, his family would understand why he could not divulge details about his work, and since a secret agent should be a loner, a very obscure person, even receiving correspondence could be dangerous. Instead, he would promise to write occasionally and get home as often as possible—a promise he intended to keep.

James passed April 14th by preparing to leave the following morning. But the feeling was not what it might have been. He could imagine what was going through the minds of other Southern boys as they were getting ready to leave home. He thought they were enjoying a sense of pride; a determination to do great things for their families and their country. In the Langdon home, James's mother, his sisters, and certainly his father, treated him more special than usual because they believed that he was already a hero. Even though he felt like nothing of the sort, he had no choice but to go along with their perception.

But that night, alone in his room, lying on the bed staring at the ceiling, he tried to ease his conscience by searching for the merit in what he was about to do. Maybe once he had actually helped even one slave gain his freedom he would feel better about himself. He tried to picture the scene: the expression on the faces of people taken from a life of misery, delivered into a world without slavery. Their joy would be a handsome reward.

The following morning he was awake before dawn. The house was still quiet and ordinarily it was the perfect moment to stretch a few dozen times before rising. But James was restless; the same as the night he'd just passed. He dressed quickly and went downstairs. Instead of heading to the kitchen to see if Olivia was preparing breakfast, he went out to the veranda and sat down on the swing. There was not time to get comfortable before his father came out to join him. James looked up and said, "Just wanted a last look at the sun coming up over the trees. It could be a while before I see it again."

"But you will see it again," his father replied. "This war will not last long. You'll see. But regardless, you keep safe. Above all else, you keep safe."

"I will, Father. You take care of yourself and keep Mother's spirits up; Ashton's and Kate's, too."

"We'll be fine, James, as long as we hear from you regularly."

"Are there any foreseeable problems concerning the plantation?"

"No. Not for now at least. Thomas and Sam went into Macon to join the army but they were sent home because the quota for this district has already been filled. Milo is originally from South Carolina so he left for Charleston to join up there if he can. But I found another man to take his place so you need not worry about anything here. When this foolishness is over we can get on with our lives under a new government . . . a Southern one.

The front door opened and Ashton appeared looking as if she was still half asleep. "Please come in for breakfast," she said.

"Come on, son. Let's eat and get you on your way. You have a long ride ahead of you." Then he winked at James and said, "The sooner we have a Langdon in the ranks, the sooner we'll have those Yanks running for cover."

Breakfast was eaten in complete silence. James knew that his mother was trying hard to hide her anxiety, but it was apparent in spite of her efforts. When breakfast was over and he was ready to leave, her tears became unstoppable.

The entire household, including all of the hired help, lined up on the lawn to bid him goodbye and good luck. Darcy Davis shook his hand and said, "Keep your wits about you, James. It shouldn't be too hard to run those Yankees back to where they came from. If you should run into that boy of mine, say hello for me." Darcy's son, Tyler, had left a week earlier to join the 1st Georgia Infantry Regiment.

Then James accepted hugs from all the women of the house: Olivia, Millie, and Lucy, who added a kiss on his cheek. Even cantankerous old Martha MacGruder managed a smile, but instead of a hug she extended her hand and said, "Take the luck o' the Irish with you, boy. It's never failed a living soul." James shook her hand and thanked her.

Then it was his family's turn to say farewell. He hugged his sisters in turn, kissed them, and then turned his attention to his mother. It was difficult to see the painful expression on her face when she said, "I believe in you, James, you know that. Stay in touch with God and with your family, in that order, and remember how much you're loved." James hugged her a little tighter than usual, kissed a tear from her cheek, and told her to remember the same.

Lastly, he stood before his father. Somehow, it turned out to be the most difficult goodbye. Surely it was because his father trusted him, and he was about to betray that trust. James might have equaled his father by height, but at that moment he felt very small. But he knew that he had to be true to his inner self so he stood up straight, shook his father's hand firmly, and said goodbye.

George Lynch stood by holding Star by her bridle. As James prepared to mount his horse, George slapped him on the back and said, "Give 'em hell, boy."

James nodded and climbed into the saddle. With one last look, and a prayer that he would see them all again, he turned Star toward the main road and headed for Dry Branch.

FOUR

The Beginning

After putting a few miles behind him, James began to feel a little less depressed. He already made a promise to himself that he would make no attempts to take any slaves from his father or from his uncles. It seemed important somehow to draw a line with his actions to spare his family any trouble he could. Of course, James was sure that if his father knew the truth, freeing Langdon slaves would be the least painful part of it all. Besides, there were many plantations in the South owning thousands of slaves, and it was certain that he could not free them all.

It was his intention to start small; probably no more than two or three on the first trip. He hoped that experience would allow him to guide larger numbers in the future.

The first place he intended to strike was Live Oak Plantation. James had played there several times as a boy when his family attended picnics, so he was familiar with the layout. He even had in mind the best way to approach the slave quarters, which in reverse would be the best way to take the slaves out.

When James reached Dry Branch he stopped at the house he had rented and went inside. Sitting at the kitchen table, he spread out the map he would use to plan his route north. He had traveled back and forth to New York for four years while he was going to school, but that had been by train. This would be much different. He believed that to be sure his purpose was accomplished he would have to deliver his runaways to Canada. There was no slavery above the Mason and Dixon's Line but there was also no guarantee that slaves would be free once they crossed it. James had read that there were slave catchers operating as far north as Boston, Massachusetts. The only way to be sure was to get the runaways to Canada.

So he mapped out a route that would end in Erie, Pennsylvania. From there he could hire a boat and cross Lake Erie to Ontario. James studied his map in order to commit his route to memory. He thought it best to keep the map concealed as much as possible. He made no marks on the map so that it would in no way implicate him if it were found in his possession. This, he thought, would at least serve as a beginning. After completing his study there were a few more things to attend to. The first was to find a place in the house where he could hide some money.

When James was born, a bank account was opened in his name. Over the years, his parents had made deposits for various reasons. Reaching the age of eighteen had transferred authority over the account to James, giving him access to nearly six thousand dollars. A week earlier he had drawn twenty-five hundred from the account to take with him when he left home. Now he needed to hide a large part of it. He was not foolish enough to carry that amount of money on his person.

After a thorough search of the stone foundation wall in the cellar, he discovered a sizable stone that was loose and easy to remove. After placing twenty-two hundred and fifty dollars in a sturdy leather pouch, he put the pouch at the back of the cavity and replaced the stone. By this time the hour had reached noon and James was hungry.

Dry Branch was a small town; one street with houses and places of business lining each side for maybe a quarter of a mile. Still, it seemed to have most of what was necessary: a hotel, sheriff's office, doctor's office, livery stable, two small taverns, and a dry goods store. In addition, there was a bank and a barber shop. James walked down the boardwalk to the nearest tavern; a well-kept place called Baxter's. The bartender extended a friendly greeting as James walked through the door.

"What'll you have, sir?" he asked.

"A meal and a beer would do fine," James replied.

"Today I got some beef stew and I got some fresh baked bread. If you like catfish I got that, too."

"Stew and bread sounds good," said James.

"Sit yourself at a table and Polly will bring it over to you."

James took a table in the front corner and hung his wide brimmed slouch hat on an empty chair. There were a few other patrons, most of whom were eating or talking, paying little or no attention to the young stranger.

After just a few minutes, a young girl came through the doorway behind the bar carrying a tray loaded with a glass of beer, a large steaming bowl of stew, and a plate of bread. She smiled as she approached. She put the tray on the table then set the meal and the drink in front of him. From an apron pocket she took a fork, knife, and a spoon, handed them to James, and asked if there was anything else she could get for him. "No, miss. But could you tell me if there is a place in town where I could rent a horse and wagon?" Instantly he thought the question sounded stupid because he already knew that there was such a place just down the street. But it just popped out and he realized it was an attempt to keep her at the table a little longer.

In Polly, James saw a lovely girl about his age, with blonde hair, blue eyes, and a captivating smile. Her dark green cotton dress covered a slight but shapely figure and it was all James could do to remember who he was and why he was in Dry Branch. When she told him that the livery would rent a horse and wagon and gave him the location, he said, "What . . . oh, yes. Thank you."

"I take it that you are new in Dry Branch," she said.

He did not enjoy the idea of lying to such a lovely girl, but he knew that with so much to hide lying would have to become a practical talent. "Yes, I am," he replied. "I grew up in an orphanage in Atlanta and I wanted to put the city and the orphanage behind me."

Her face took on a sympathetic expression and she said, "I am sorry to hear that, Mister . . ."

"Mason. William Mason."

"Mr. Mason. What happened to your folks?"

"Well I only know what I was told, but it isn't something I like to talk about."

"I'm sorry, Mr. Mason. I didn't mean to pry."

"I don't mind. And please, call me William."

"Very well, William. My name is Polly."

"Yes, I know. I mean, the bartender mentioned it. I'm happy to make your acquaintance. Are you from Dry Branch?"

"Yes, I am. It isn't much of a place to be from, but I've lived here all of my life. I live with my mother in the last house down the street on the right," and she motioned with her hand, indicating the same side of the street as the tavern. "I work here to support us. My mother is in poor health."

"Oh," said James. "It is my turn to be sorry."

The conversation had become so pleasant; James had gotten so involved, that he didn't realize the stew wasn't steaming any more. And if his interest in this lovely girl wasn't enough to make him lose his appetite, what happened next was.

"What do you do for a living, William?"

"I work as a slave catcher," he answered. James had decided to pass himself off as such. It seemed like a good way to explain why he was in the company of slaves, if the need arose, at least while traveling through the Southern states. However, when he told Polly what his occupation was, it had roughly the same effect as pouring his bowl of stew over her head. She didn't say a word. The most awful expression covered her pretty face; she turned abruptly and walked away, disappearing through the doorway she'd come from.

James was fairly stunned and angry at the same time. The last thing he wanted to do was chase her away and yet he had done just that without so much as a clue as to how or why. As he rapidly sank into a deep sulk, he began to eat his stew, which had gotten cold, adding to his bitter mood. When the meal was over, or at least enough to satisfy his hunger, he got up, left some money on the table and headed for the door. He was hoping to see Polly again and maybe try to find out what he'd done wrong. But she didn't reappear and he was in no mood to pursue the matter any further.

A few doors down was the dry goods store. Although there really wasn't anything he needed, he decided to go in and look around. The store keeper, a short, balding man named Isaac Casper, was the perfect sort for his chosen line of work. He was friendly, helpful, and as James quickly learned, would talk your ear off if given the chance. While James wandered around the store, Mr. Casper talked about the weather, the war—even though it was as yet nothing to talk about—and anything else that came to his mind.

In the midst of the verbal barrage, the door opened and in walked a man who reminded James quite a bit of Farley Tabor. His faded overalls and sun baked skin suggested that he was a farmer. He walked over to the counter, beckoned Mr. Casper's attention, and said, "Got them cabbage and taters ya wanted, Casper."

"Good," said the storekeeper. "Take them through the side door and put them in the storeroom."

"Got the niggers workin' on it. I best go see to it." Then he left the store, slamming the door behind him. By that time, James had worked his way up front.

"That's old Silas Turner," said Mr. Casper. "I've known him for twenty years and never once have I seen him in a pleasant mood. He has a truck farm about five miles north of here. I buy vegetables from him. Yes sir, he is a real cantankerous sort, even worse right now than usual. He has a boil on his ass the size of a silver dollar but he won't let the doctor do anything for him. Stubborn, just plain stubborn. He has a couple of niggers that work on his place. I'll bet *they* wish he'd let the doctor do something. Now then, young fellow, what can I do for you?"

"Well, I really came in just to look around, but if you have any jerked beef I'll take a couple pounds of that and maybe a pound of coffee."

"Comin' right up."

As he waited for Mr. Casper to package his goods he noticed something of interest hanging on a wooden peg behind the counter. There were four sets of manacles but they didn't appear to be new. "Are they for sale?" James asked, pointing to the peg in the wall.

"You mean those bracelets?" James nodded. "Well sure, if you're interested. I mean, they aren't a stock item. This fellow came in a few months ago needing provisions but he had no money. He asked me if I would take them in trade. I don't usually do business that way but I like to help a body when I can so I took them in exchange for some beans and coffee. If you want them for what I got in them, they're yours."

"How much is that?"

"Four dollars."

"I'll take them."

It seemed strange that a strong social type like Mr. Casper didn't question James about his interest in the manacles. Apparently he was just happy to get his money out of them. James thought that if he were going to pass himself off as a slave catcher the manacles could come in mighty handy as a prop.

With his goods in hand, he thanked Mr. Casper and left the store. When he got out to the boardwalk, he stopped to watch for a moment as the farmer's slaves unloaded the wagon that was parked along the street. There were two men dressed in ragged clothing, both bare footed, probably about forty years of age. They worked in silence, in almost a mechanical fashion as if their chore was the only purpose for living. Perhaps it was because they were constantly under the watchful eye of Mr. Turner, who stood leisurely on the boardwalk smoking a cigar.

As the wagon emptied out and the baskets could not be reached from the ground, one man climbed up and started moving them closer to the back. But when he set one of the baskets down he had the misfortune of setting it too close to the edge of the wagon bed and it fell to the ground, spilling the contents everywhere. Surprisingly agile, the farmer jumped down from the boardwalk in a flash and grabbed the man, tearing his already tattered shirt. The slave was shoved to the ground hard, landing on his back in the street. The farmer stood over the poor wretch, cursing and threatening all sorts of physical punishment. James thought for an instant that he was going to burn the man with his cigar. After a few swift kicks the farmer stepped away, promising a whipping when they got to the farm. Then he ordered his victim to get the mess picked up.

For a moment, as he lay there in the dirt, the slave looked up and locked eyes with James. The look of despair and humiliation on his face filled James with pity. He turned away and headed back to his house with a resolution forming in his head. "By tomorrow," he said to himself, "old Mr. Turner is going to be missing a couple of slaves."

When he got to the house he put his packages on the table and then went back outside. Star was still tied to the hitching post. Trying to be as inconspicuous as possible he kept an eye on the wagon down the street, and when the farmer and his slaves climbed into it, James mounted his horse. He was not an expert at tailing someone without being noticed, but he let the wagon get some distance ahead, then he followed along at a slow, steady pace.

By and by, he could see a farmhouse along the right side of the road with a barn and a few smaller buildings. When the wagon turned in at the little farm, James turned Star around and rode back to town.

Before going back to the house he stopped at the livery to do a little business. He made arrangements to board his own horse, and then he rented a wagon and a good stout mare to pull it. After procuring the rig, he drove up the street, turned left between two buildings, and parked it behind the house. It was three o'clock in the afternoon.

James sat at the table and began writing the letter that he would send to his family when he reached South Carolina. It surprised him at how easily the words came as he explained how his plans to join the cavalry had changed. In about an hour, the letter was finished and the only thing left to do was to wait for darkness. James was ready to get some sleep in preparation for a long night.

FIVE

Point of No Return

When James awakened he was confused by his surroundings. Then, as his mind caught up with his eyesight, he remembered where he was and why he was there. He got out of bed and went over to the table where he'd left his pocket watch. It was just after ten p.m.

As he sat at the table going over a mental list of everything he would need to take along, he was beginning to feel the tension seeping into his body. The fingers of his right hand quietly drummed the top of the table as he mulled over the problems that could arise.

It would be difficult to ascertain the safest hour when he might catch everyone sleeping. However, country people worked hard and usually went to bed early. But some of the larger plantations, like his father's, patrolled the grounds at night to prevent escapes; not to mention the threat of dogs, which even a small farmer like Mr. Turner was likely to own.

James got up and began to pace the floor. Once or twice he stopped to look out the window. Irritated by the feeling of restlessness, he sat down again and started cleaning his revolver. His mind was racing.

He realized, of course, he had no idea how the slaves themselves might react to his presence and his purpose. He could not take it for granted that they would just quietly go along with him. James knew that, in spite of the situation, some slaves became very loyal to their masters. Others might be afraid to attempt escape; still others might just think that he was crazy.

James understood that he could never, ever, fail to keep in mind how the slave owners, and southern people in general, would feel about what he was doing. Without question, it was a serious undertaking. Still, it would be important not to dwell on the danger. He must not lose his respect for the risks but he must lose his fear of them.

It was eleven o'clock at night; time to go. James extinguished the table light and left the house carrying a sack of food, two canteens of water, and the manacles he'd purchased at the dry goods store. In his pockets he had a knife, a compass, his watch, and extra ammunition for the revolver he had stuck in his waistband. He climbed into the wagon and stored his provisions down by his feet. Then he drove out to the street and headed north.

The town appeared to be fast asleep. There was no sound and not a single light was visible from any window. When he reached the edge of town, he glanced over at the last house on the right. He could not help but think about Polly and her mother asleep inside. What a lovely girl she was. James promised himself that he would try to see her when he got back to Dry Branch.

As with the town, the countryside was dark and quiet except for some thousands of lightning bugs and the clip-clop of the horse's hooves on the road. Approaching the Turner farm, he slowed the horse to a walk so that he could get a good look as he passed. The house was peaceful and so were the two small cabins that sat out away from the left side of it. To the left of the cabins was a field of tall grass. He drove past the farm then stopped the wagon on the road about fifty yards away.

After hobbling the horse so she would stay put, he picked up some small stones from the road and put them in his pocket. Bending slightly at the waist, he started off through the tall grass towards the nearest cabin. When he reached the edge of the field, he was only about ten feet from the crude little dwelling. He had hoped that there would be a window on that side, and as luck would have it, there was. He reached into his pocket, extracted the stones he'd picked up, and tossed them at the window one by one.

In a few minutes James saw a light flickering from inside, then the front door opened and a black man came out carrying a lantern. He walked around the corner to the window, and after finding nothing, turned toward the field. He held the lantern out in front of him, then in a worried whisper he said, "Who's dare?"

James stood up with his hands in the air, trying to show that he meant no harm. He could hear the fear in the man's voice when he asked, "Who is you? What is you wantin here?"

James didn't know any other way to answer except to whisper, "Who I am is not important. Do you wish to be free?"

"Free?" the man whispered back.

"Yes," said James.

For a moment the man stood as if frozen. No doubt, he was completely stunned. James could certainly understand that, but there just wasn't time to stand around. "I know you must find this hard to believe," James told him. "But I will help you escape to freedom if you want to go. I will take the other black man who lives here, too." As unbelievable as it must have seemed, the man seemed to begin to accept the idea. He blew out the lantern; a light was unsafe. Then he said, "Me and Buck will go wit you but I gots me a wife. Buck gots one, too."

"Then they must go with us. Wake Buck and tell him to bring his wife and as many belongings as they can get together in about two minutes. Then wake your wife and you do the same. Go out through the field. I have a wagon just up the road. I'll be waiting there. Be careful, but hurry. If you wake the farmer your chance will be lost. I will leave the second I hear signs of trouble."

"I gets your meanin, sir. We be there quick."

James turned and headed for the wagon. When he got there he removed the hobbles and stood still, watching, listening. He pulled out his revolver; it made him feel a little safer.

It seemed like an eternity until he saw movement coming through the tall grass. Sure enough, the two men and their wives came out into the open about twenty feet behind the wagon. "Hurry," James whispered. "Climb in."

The two men carried a few possessions wrapped in blankets. They hurled their bundles into the back, helped the women up, and then climbed in beside them. James stirred up the horse and started off at a slow trot. After they were a mile down the road he sped up a bit. He knew that they must cover as much distance as possible before morning, but it was important to pace the horse to get the most from her endurance. Getting the slaves away from the farm seemed easy. He knew he'd been lucky. But there were hundreds of miles between them and their ultimate destination and he was sure that they would not all pass as smoothly.

He was now a criminal and his passengers were fugitives. He could only imagine the fury of the farmer, Mr. Turner, when he discovered that his slaves were gone. The law would be notified and that could put trouble on their trail. At all cost, James meant to stay as far ahead of any pursuit as possible, and the most precious time was now—before the discovery. One thing was certain; he was past the point of no return.

After driving for about two hours and covering perhaps forty miles, James pulled to the side of the road to rest the horse. It was one forty-five a.m. He calculated that he had maybe a little over four hours before Mr. Turner would be wise. By then, they could be more than a hundred miles from the farm. He hoped it would be difficult for the law to catch up to them with such a good head start. The only thing that any would-be pursuers could count on was that the slaves would head north. That would still leave a lot of territory to search. The chances were good that they would assume the runaways were on foot.

Back at the farm, James had parked the horse and wagon on the road for a reason. There would be no tracks leaving the road and then returning to it. If the law did assume the slaves were on foot and tried to track them with dogs, they would never catch up. Most likely, the biggest threat would be the telegraph line. A description of the slaves would surely be sent to points ahead of them and the telegraph was something they could not outrun. Hopefully, James could offset that disadvantage. If he was stopped and questioned by anyone, he hoped to bluff his way through by explaining that he had picked up the information, captured the fugitives, and was returning them himself. After all, he was posing as a slave catcher. He needed to learn to act like one.

While the horse rested, James turned to his passengers and said, "Are you folks all right back there?" The man he had first awakened at the farm looked up and replied, "We is fine, mister."

"My name is William," James told them. "Call me Bill."

"Yes sir, Mr. Bill."

"We'll be leaving in a few minutes. We have to get as far away as we can before Mr. Turner knows you're gone."

"We understands, Mr. Bill. Ole Turner will most have hiself a real bad angry when he find out. He will surely come a runnin with his whip."

"Well, I will do all I can to make sure that you never see that whip again. I have to ask you to do something now that I really don't care for, but I think it's a good idea."

"What is dat, Mr. Bill?"

James handed him two sets of manacles and said, "Put these on. If anyone stops us I want them to think that you are in my custody."

"Cusadee?"

"Yes. That means that I caught you."

"Oh, I understands, and you is right, sir."

"Cuff yourself to your wife and have the other man do the same. We have to get started again." James steered the horse back onto the road and got her moving at a quick but steady pace. After another four hours of traveling, and one more stop to water the animal and let her graze by the road's edge, the sun was on its way up. James was hungry and his eyelids had become very heavy. They were passing through an area with woods on both sides of the road.

Just ahead on the left, James could see a rutted trail leading into the trees. Hoping that it did not lead to a dwelling, he left the road and started slowly down the trail. It led a few hundred yards to an open field enclosed by woods on all four sides. He turned right along the edge of the trees and stopped a short distance from the trail. Turning around in his seat, he got a good look at all of the slaves for the first time. The two men, James learned, were called Buck and Darnell. The two women, Tisha, Buck's wife, and Emmy, Darnell's wife, looked to be in their thirties. Both were thin and calloused, no doubt from years of hard work and neglect. They stared at James as wide eyed as children. He suspected that they were as frightened as they were amazed to find themselves runaways in the company of some strange white man. "We'll stay here for part of the day," said James. "I didn't bring a lot to eat; I planned to pick up supplies along the way as we need them. I have some dried beef and coffee."

"Don't worry bout dat, Mr. Bill," said Darnell. "Vittles is mostly what we done brought along. We gots bread and pone; we gots dried peas, some salt pork, and some little bitty cakes Emmy done made. We be glad to share."

"Sure would," said Buck.

"That sounds fine," James replied. "Can you get a fire started while I tend to the mare and we'll have some breakfast?"

"We gonna get it all ready," Darnell assured him.

James removed the manacles, then unhitched the horse and tied her so that she could reach plenty of grass. He got a bucket from the wagon and filled it with water from a partially dry creek that ran through the woods.

By the time he had the horse taken care of, the coffee was hot and there was food on the tin plates that Buck and Tisha brought with them. From time to time, James could hear traffic on the road, but their camp could not be seen from that far away. Of course, he didn't know who owned the property they were on; he just hoped that the owners would have no reason to come there until they could rest and move on.

As they ate their meal, James could not help noticing that Emmy was staring at him. Finally she spoke her mind. "Mr. Bill, when I thinks about bein a slave and when I thinks about goin to a place where I can live free, I feel like my heart might bust right outta my chest. I hopes you knows how much we is obliged. But I prays you won't hold nuthin agin me if I ax you, why is you doin this for us?" Emmy's comments touched James very deeply.

"I can understand how you feel, Emmy. It is simple and yet difficult at the same time. It is simple to tell you why, but difficult for you to believe. My family owns a large plantation near Macon. I grew up believing that the Negroes that worked there did so as any white man would; by their own choice and under the same conditions. I believed it because my father convinced me that it was so. When I found out they were slaves and were treated as such; when I found out they were mistreated even when they did what was expected of them, sometimes beaten or even killed because they wanted to be free, I could not accept it. It was hard enough to see how other whites treated their slaves. When I saw with my own eyes that it was no different on my family's plantation, I made up my mind that I was going to do something about it. You may not have ever heard of the United States Constitution, but it is a document written by the people who started this country. It is a document by which we live, and the Constitution says that all men are created equal and that freedom is for all men. I guess you could say that I intend to hold the Constitution to its promise. No man or woman should be a slave, and God willing, someday no man or woman will be."

"May God bless you, Mr. Bill. Even ifn we don't make it, God bless you."

"We'll make it, Emmy. Well, let's clean this up now and get some rest."

"We all did some sleepin in da wagon, Mr. Bill," said Darnell. "When we is in da wagon we sleep some more. Now it be your turn. You sleep and we keep watch for trouble."

"All right, that is a good plan. When the sun is straight up over our heads, you wake me."

"I promise dat," said Darnell. James crawled into the back of the wagon, made himself as comfortable as possible, and quickly fell asleep.

It seemed like just a short time later that Darnell was waking him, but checking his watch, he saw that he had slept for more than six hours. They wasted no time hitching up the wagon and clearing the campsite so that no one could tell they'd been there. When all was ready, James cuffed the couples together again and they started through the woods to the main road.

They hadn't gone far before James saw a horse and rider approaching. When the rider got closer, James stopped the wagon and raised his left hand into the air. The stranger complied with the signal and reined in beside them. "Afternoon," said the man as he touched a finger to the brim of his hat. "Where are you heading?"

"I'm heading to Virginia," James replied.

"Virginia? Damn, but you got a long way to go."

"You bet," said James. "But the money is good and we all need money."

"No question about it, young fellow. But if you want to sell those niggers, you don't have to go the whole way to Virginia."

"I'm not selling them, I'm delivering them. They ran off from their owner and they managed to get a fair piece away. The only trouble was they ran in the wrong direction. I caught up with them hiding out near Atlanta." James thought the man would fall off his horse from laughing so hard.

"I do believe that's the funniest thing I ever heard. Is it any wonder that they're slaves? Anything that stupid couldn't be nothing else. So they ran the wrong way." Then he broke into a hardy laugh again, which was beginning to get on James's nerves.

"How far is it to the South Carolina line?"

"Not so far," said the stranger. "Maybe fifteen miles or so. Barnesville is just up the road a piece if you're looking for a town."

"No," said James. "I'm not figuring on stopping until I reach Greenville."

"Well I'll say good luck to you, young fellow. I gotta be going." With that, the man rode off, still laughing to himself.

James continued up the road. Soon after, they rolled through Barnesville, then a few smaller villages, and by five o'clock that afternoon, they were just outside Greenville.

James knew that Greenville was much larger than most of the other towns along the way and he felt uneasy about taking the slaves through until he had a look around. Greenville would have a telegraph office and might have received news of the escape by now. He pulled the wagon to the side of the road to think it over.

To their right was a hayfield with a small grove of trees about a hundred yards from the road. It looked like a good spot for four people to hide.

"Darnell."

"Yes sir, Mr. Bill."

"I want you and Buck to take your wives and hide in that clump of trees over there. I'm going into town alone. I'll only be gone about an hour, maybe a little more. Take some dried beef and a canteen with you. It might be a while before we have another meal." The two men helped their wives out of the wagon. James removed the manacles and said, "I'll drive the wagon over and pick you up when I get back. Now hurry over there before someone comes along." He waited until the slaves had safely disappeared into the trees, then he headed into town.

SIX

Learning Experience

Greenville was alive with activity; the streets were filled with horses, wagons, carriages, and people. James noticed Confederate soldiers standing in front of the recruiting office. It was his first reminder of the war. Then he saw the Confederate flag flying atop the courthouse. He kept walking; it was the sheriff's office and a dry goods store that he was interested in.

He located the sheriff's office first. After tying the mare to the hitching rail, he stepped up onto the boardwalk. Hanging on the front wall of the building was a posting board covered with wanted posters and other notices of public interest. James scanned the board looking for information concerning runaway slaves. There were several such notices, and after reading a few, much to his dismay, he found what he was hoping he wouldn't.

He read a notice carrying a reward for four escaped slaves, two males and two females. It gave a description of each one and even included their names. The owner, Silas Turner, was listed as well as the location they had escaped from. The only good news was that there was no mention of an accomplice or that they might be traveling by wagon. But his companions had made the wanted list, and surely, there would be those who would be trying to collect the reward.

When he was through absorbing the information he turned and collided with a large, bearded ruffian who had been standing right behind him, peering over his shoulder. "Pardon me, mister," said James. "I didn't know you were there."

The man smiled, but not in the interest of being friendly, revealing a partial set of teeth that were stained as brown as mud. His hair was long and greasy and he had a deep scar above his left eye that ran down along his nose almost to the end. He wore ragged buckskin clothing and moccasins. A holstered pistol and a sheath holding a large knife hung on a belt around his bulging middle.

"You seem mighty interested in that paper," he said. "Makes me think you might know where them niggers is."

James tried to appear calm and make his voice sound tough when he said, "Wish to hell I did. I'd drag them back to Georgia quick and collect that money."

"You don't look like no slave catcher to me, boy," the ruffian replied.

"Things don't always look like what they really are, mister." Then James turned quickly and walked away before the unkempt giant could say another word. He did not wish to have the man see him get into his wagon. Fortunately, the post office was only two doors down from the sheriff's office and James had the letter to his family that he needed to send. He took his time inside, and when he returned to the boardwalk the rough looking man was nowhere to be seen.

James got into the wagon and drove down the crowded street until he located a store where he could buy some supplies. As he tied up the horse again he heard the sound of distant thunder. The sun was still shining but a strong breeze was coming up, blowing swirls of dust around in the street. He went into the store and recited a short list of goods to one of the clerks behind the counter. He looked around while he waited, and after a few minutes he heard thunder again; this time much closer. Aside from the food supplies, James purchased a rain slicker and a piece of canvas, ten feet long and six feet wide. It took two trips to get his goods loaded in the wagon, and when he was finished, he climbed in and headed out of town in the direction from which he'd come.

By now it was only half past six, but under the heavy cloud cover that had moved in it was getting dark fast. The thunder rumbled, the lightning flashed, and the wind blew harder.

James was not far out of town when he thought he could hear hoof beats somewhere behind him. But the impending storm made so much noise that it was difficult to tell for sure. It was no more than three miles to the spot where he'd left the slaves hiding in the grove of trees. The storm was turning violent now: the thunder crashed directly overhead, the lightning lit up the heavens, but as yet, it was not raining.

About two miles from town, James looked ahead for the hayfield and the grove of trees. Slowing his speed a bit, he looked back towards town just as the lightning lit the area like midday. A scare ran through him as if he'd been struck by the bolt when he saw that he was indeed being followed. He did not need to wonder who it was. He was sure it would have to be the tough looking customer he'd literally run into at the sheriff's office and he was pretty sure that there was more than one horse and rider behind him.

He didn't know what to do and he had very little time to decide. If he went to the grove he would lead trouble directly to the slaves. If he kept going he wasn't sure what might happen. Whoever was behind him wouldn't keep following forever. Sooner or later they would figure they'd been spotted and that James was just leading them away. When that happened they would catch up and deal with him. He could never outrun them in a wagon, so he could not lose the pursuit and then double back. Quickly, he made his plan, and it was a poor one at best.

When he recognized the grove of trees, he drove off the road and crossed the field as fast as he could. Reaching the edge of the grove, he pulled to a stop, grabbed a lantern from the back of the wagon, lit it, and jumped down calling Darnell's name. The storm was raising the devil and it had started to rain. James quickly explained the situation to the slaves and told them what he wanted them to do. Then he hung the lantern from a tree limb so that it would illuminate the tiny clearing surrounded by the trees.

About one minute later, two men on horseback came through the trees and into the light. As James had figured, it was the rough man from Greenville and another man who, even in the dim light, looked every bit as unkempt and uncouth as the first. With their pistols drawn, they dismounted and stood menacingly before James, Darnell, and the two women.

"Now ain't that a sight, Henry," said the man in buckskin.

"It sure is, Virgil. Black gold," said the second man.

"Maybe you'll have more respect for my hunches after this," Virgil told his partner. To James he said, "I knew you was lying, boy. You ain't no slave catcher, no sir. Looks to me like you're tryin to help these niggers escape. Check that boy to see if he's armed." James stood still; biting his lower lip while the miscreant called Henry searched him, located his revolver, and jerked it from his waistband. Then he walked back to his spot beside Virgil. Then Virgil said, "What do ya think we oughta do with him, Henry?"

"I think we should lash that boy to a tree, tie our horses behind that wagon, and head for Georgia with these here niggers."

"Mighty good thinkin, pard—wait just a damn minute. Where's the other one?"

"Other one?" said Henry.

"Yeah, the other one. It's supposed to be two bucks and two bitches. Where's that other black son of a bitch?" From behind them, two things happened at the same time. A voice hollered, "Here!" And a club came down on Henry's head, driving him to the ground. Virgil swung around and fired a shot into the darkness. Darnell, Tisha, and Emmy scampered back out of the light, James dashed across the clearing, drove his right shoulder into Virgil, and knocked him flat on his face. Quick as a cat, he gathered himself and found Virgil's pistol, which had fallen from his grasp. Then he backed up a few steps and said, "On your feet, Virgil."

Cursing as he got up, Virgil faced James, pointed a finger and said, "You got the guts to use that thing, boy?" James cocked the hammer and replied, "One step will answer that question for you."

Virgil took the warning seriously and stood still. With the danger thwarted for the moment, Buck walked into the light and the others came back and stood behind James.

"Good job, Buck," James told him. "I'll cover these fellas. Look them over and take every weapon you can find." Buck did as he was told, finding a total of three pistols and two knives. Then James told Virgil to stir his partner and get him to his feet. It took a couple of minutes before Henry moaned and struggled to stand up. "Darnell," said James. "There is some rope in the wagon under the seat. Get it."

Darnell was back in a hurry, and while James kept the revolver trained on the two ruffians, he instructed Darnell to tie Virgil's right wrist to Henry's left.

"Now walk over to that tree," he told them, motioning with his gun. "Face it on opposite sides and wrap your arms around it." This done, James said, "Now tie their other wrists together, Darnell, and make sure you tie them tight."

By this time, the storm was going full force. The rain was falling heavily, dripping through the trees, soaking everything underneath. "We have to move," James told the slaves. "Go out to the wagon and spread that piece of canvas over the supplies and get under it yourselves. I'll be right there." He took the reins of the villains' horses and Virgil growled, "You gonna leave us here to starve?"

"I'll tie your horses to a tree out there where they can be seen from the road. I'm sure they'll be spotted some time tomorrow and somebody will cut you lose."

"I guess you know ifn I ever see you again you're as good as dead, you nigger lovin son of a bitch."

"I figured as much," James replied. Then he took the lantern and left the two of them cursing in the dark.

He tied the horses as promised; put on the rain slicker he'd purchased in town, then climbed into the wagon and started off. It was hard not to let Virgil's threat bother him, but it was also a huge relief to have escaped. "This," James told himself, "is what it will be like from now on."

Greenville was very quiet when they passed through. It was pitch dark and the rain had driven everyone inside. The piece of canvas covered the back of the wagon, concealing the slaves underneath. All was peaceful as he drove on through the night. He wondered if Virgil and Henry would make a point of trying to follow. But the rain would wash away James's tracks almost as soon as they were made. If the two of them had no chance of trying to pick up their trail until the next day, James and his companions would already be many miles away.

By eleven o'clock that night, they had left South Carolina behind and were rolling through Asheville, North Carolina. The rain had stopped and the sky overhead was clear. If they didn't run into any trouble they could reach the eastern tip of Tennessee in a few hours more. From there they would travel along the foot of the Appalachian Mountains into western Virginia.

They had covered nearly two hundred miles since leaving Turner's farm, and James was pleased by their progress; but he had pushed very hard and the miles had taken their toll on the mare. If he wanted her to hold up she would need a long rest soon. He made up his mind that when they reached Tennessee he would find a suitable site in the foothills of the mountain and they would all rest for a day.

By three o'clock in the morning, James had let the horse slow down to a walk. She was tired and he was famished. All he had eaten since the previous morning was some dried beef, and the slaves had had the same.

When the sun finally came up over the mountain James was sure that they were in Tennessee. The road had long since become more of a path and the going was rough. At length, they came to a little valley nestled between two grassy knolls. Where the valley sloped upward to the tree line there was an area inundated by thick undergrowth. James got the wagon under cover as best he could and came to a stop. He climbed down from the seat and stretched his aching muscles. His passengers were awake and he could see that they were equally happy to get out of the wagon. Immediately they busied themselves with setting up camp while James tended to the weary mare. He told them to use whatever was necessary to prepare a hearty breakfast. Then he retrieved a bucket and an empty canteen from the wagon and started off in search of water. He was hoping to find a mountain spring or a stream nearby.

When he was halfway up the far knoll that formed one side of the valley they were camped in, he looked back and noticed that he could not see the wagon. He was glad of that. He figured that they should be safe there until they were ready to move on. James's legs got heavier with every step he took. Perhaps he was learning another lesson: not to push himself to the limit, thereby dulling his senses to the point of vulnerability. As he stumbled to the top, to a spot where he could see into the next valley, he was dismayed to find what was there. Down below him was a small army camp comprised of about two dozen tents. He could also see a picket line holding thirty or forty horses and at least four supply wagons. In front of one of the tents, which was situated a short distance from the others, he could see a Confederate flag and a flag with a symbol that he didn't recognize.

Before he could react, he heard a galloping horse approaching from his left. His first instinct was to run, but he knew he'd already been spotted, so he stood still, holding onto his bucket and canteen. His revolver was still in the waistband of his trousers, but this did not appear to be a situation that he could fight his way out of. When the horse pulled up in front of him the soldier already had a pistol pointed at James—a scenario that was fast becoming routine, he thought. The man in the saddle was not much older than he was, and from the look of the homespun uniform, James knew that he was being confronted by a Confederate cavalryman. "Who are you?" asked the soldier. "And what the hell are you doing here?"

"Name's William Mason," said James. "I'm looking for water."

"So you're out in the middle of nowhere carrying a bucket and a canteen?"

"I have a camp back yonder a little ways," said James, pointing behind him. "My wife and I are heading to Lynchburg, Virginia."

Then James could have kicked himself. Inventing a fictitious wife could prove to be a big mistake. If he were forced to go back to the campsite, he may not be able to talk his way out of a hanging. He had only wanted his explanation to sound as innocent as possible so as not to arouse suspicion. "We don't mean any harm," said James.

"I reckon that will be up to the captain to decide. Now you just hand over your pistol and walk on down that hill ahead of me." James surrendered his weapon, and then started down the hill with the soldier following so close that he could feel the horse's breath on the back of his neck.

When they reached the camp, he was taken to the tent with the flags, told to drop the canteen and bucket, then to remove his hat and step inside. Sitting at a field desk was a Confederate officer with coal black hair and a long black beard. His wire rimmed spectacles rested on the end of his nose as he labored at a ledger with a quill pen. When James entered the tent with the soldier and his drawn pistol behind him, the officer stopped writing and looked up with an inquisitive expression. The trooper saluted and said, "I found this man all alone on top of the hill, sir. Says his name is William Mason and he's headin to Lynchburg with his wife. Says he was huntin for some water."

The captain returned the salute and told the trooper to wait outside.

"Yes sir, Captain. Here's his pistol," he said, handing the weapon to his superior. The soldier withdrew, and James was left standing alone before the captain.

"Well now, Mr. Mason, is it?"

"Yes, sir," James replied.

"I am Captain Robert Blackwell, commanding a detachment of the 1st Virginia Cavalry. No need to explain our presence here but I would like to know about yours."

"Well, sir, as I told the trooper, I was out looking for water. My wife and I are traveling to Lynchburg and we are camped in the valley over the hill where he found me."

"I see," said the captain. "May I ask why you are heading to Lynchburg?"

"Certainly, sir. I am from Atlanta and my wife is from Lynchburg. I met her last summer when she came to Atlanta with her father on a business trip. I guess you could say that it was love at first sight. We married just two weeks after we met. We've been living in Atlanta, but now that we're at war with the North, I intend to join the Southern army." At this, a pleasant smile crossed the captain's face. "So I am taking my wife to Lynchburg to stay with her parents and I will enlist there."

It was obvious that James had made a wonderful impression with his story. The captain seemed very pleased, even telling James that if he considered joining

54

the cavalry, he would be most welcome in the 1st Virginia. But just when it looked as though he might get through the tight spot he was in, the captain said, "I guess you should be getting back Mr. Mason, before your wife starts to worry. You may help yourself to all the water you need from the supply wagon, then my orderly will escort you back to your camp."

The captain's last remark cut him like a knife. He knew that it would be dangerous to protest, but if the slaves were discovered, and no wife, there would be serious consequences. "I thank you for your generosity, Captain." The officer waved his hand as if to say that thanks were not necessary. Then he handed James the confiscated revolver and shouted for his orderly. The trooper entered the tent, stood at attention, and saluted. "See to it that Mr. Mason gets the water he needs, Sergeant; then escort him back to his camp. And before you leave, pass the word that we'll be moving out in two hours."

"Yes, sir." The sergeant saluted again and held the tent flap open so James could leave. "Good luck, Mr. Mason," said Captain Blackwell. "Perhaps we'll meet again."

"Perhaps we will, sir. Good luck to you."

James left the tent and picked up his bucket and canteen. "This way," said the sergeant. When James had gotten the water, the sergeant mounted his horse and said, "I'd give you a lift but you'd lose most of your water along the way."

"It's OK," said James. "I don't mind."

James prayed hard as he made his way up the long hill. Once again, he thanked God for listening. When they reached the top where they had first met, the sergeant stopped his horse. "You're camped down there?" he said, pointing to the valley. "I don't see your wagon."

"It's hidden in the bushes," James replied.

"Well if it's all the same to you, I'll just head back from here."

James wanted to shake his hand and recommend him for a promotion. "Certainly, and thank you, Sergeant." With a nod, he turned his horse and galloped back to his camp. James heaved a sigh of relief. If not for the bucket of water, he would have been on the horse with the sergeant and they'd have gone the whole way back to the wagon.

He hurried down the hill as fast as he could without spilling the water. When he reached his own camp he could see the panic on the faces of the slaves. But after James explained what had happened, they, too, were much relieved, especially when they heard that the soldiers would soon be gone.

It was after nine o'clock in the morning by the time James had finally eaten. He instructed Darnell and Buck to take turns sleeping while the other stood watch. "I believe we are pretty safe here," he told them. "But I don't want to take any chances. Let me sleep until I wake up. I'm dead tired."

Then he spread the canvas under the wagon to escape the heat of the sun; he fell asleep, and didn't awaken until after eight o'clock that evening.

The long rest was just what he needed. When he awoke, he lay still for a few moments and listened. All was quiet. He crawled out from under the wagon and walked back to the camp the slaves had set up. There was a low burning fire and a semicircle of logs pulled up close to provide something to sit on. Darnell and Emmy were sitting together, talking, while Buck and Tisha slept. When they saw him coming Emmy poured him coffee from a pot hanging over the fire.

"Thank you, Emmy. This will taste real good about now."

"If you is hungry, I has some stew ready, Mr. Bill."

"That sounds good, too." While James ate his stew, the couple talked about what they were going to do after they found a new home on free land. They also talked about the past. James offered his sympathy when they told him about two sons they had, whom old Mr. Turner sold when they were just eight and ten years of age. "Yes sir, Mr. Bill. I don't spect we ever see dem boys again."

Emmy started to cry and Darnell did his best to comfort her. James was more determined than ever to get them all to freedom.

At ten o'clock, Buck and Tisha woke up and Darnell and Emmy went to sleep. James sat until two a.m., then after telling Buck to wake everybody at sunrise, he crawled back under the wagon and went to sleep again.

At daybreak they consumed a quick breakfast and packed the wagon. Then James cuffed the men to their wives and they started off again. It really was a preference to travel at night, but until they could find a good road again, it would be too hazardous. For hours the wagon bounced along at a snail's pace until finally, they came out to a road that led in a northeasterly direction. At noon they stopped for an hour to eat, and by six o'clock that evening they were near a town called Beckley in western Virginia. Considering that they were in good shape for supplies, James decided they would roll on through the town and look for a likely spot on the other side to stop until nightfall. They would eat and rest a while, then travel hard to reach their first real safe haven: the state of Pennsylvania.

When Beckley was about five miles behind them, James started searching for that next campsite. Suddenly, he heard a sound that was not welcome. There was a loud crack followed by the sound of wood splitting. The front right corner of the wagon dropped, causing him to grab the side of the seat to keep from falling off. He brought the horse to a stop and carefully climbed to the ground. Everything in the wagon, including his passengers, had slid to the side and the two women were being badly squeezed. Quickly, James moved the cargo to the back and helped everyone out. Fortunately, except for a few scratches, no one was hurt. The rough going in Tennessee had taken its toll and the wheel was broken. As they all stood there staring at the shattered wheel, a team of horses pulling a hay wagon with a portly farmer at the reins was approaching from the north. Having no other choice, James waved the driver down.

He was a friendly looking man, mid-fifties, dressed in overalls and a big straw hat. Sporting a broad smile, he pulled off his hat, wiped a bead of sweat from his forehead, and said, "Howdy, neighbor. Looks like you could use a little help."

"I'd be grateful," said James, returning the smile. "This wheel is done for and I have no spare."

"We'll you're in luck, neighbor. I have everything you need to get fixed up. My name is Crawford, Tyson Crawford. I'm on my way home from delivering a load of hay. My farm is about a mile down the road. Lest you're blind, you had to have seen it."

"Do you mean the place with the big white barn and the windmill?"

"That's the one. Now let's see if we can get you fixed up."

James couldn't believe the luck. The last thing he needed was to be stranded along the road. Why couldn't the wheel have let go on the way through Beckley? Instead, James thought, the Lord had provided Mr. Crawford and they would soon be on their way.

Their benefactor got down from his wagon and walked over to have a look at the broken wheel. When he got to the sagging corner of the wagon, he looked at the slaves standing there in silence. When he saw the manacles on their wrists, his mood changed instantly. "Are those Negroes your slaves?" he demanded.

Caught off guard, James was about to go into his story about taking them back to their owner, but he didn't get the chance. Mr. Crawford cut him off, saying, "Because if they are, I'd like to give you a piece of my mind, mister. Virginia may have seceded and Virginia might hold with slavery, but in this part of the state we are loyal to the Union. We are not rebels here and we are not slave owners and the people in these western counties are making plans to secede from Virginia. No, sir! I'll not lift a finger to help a man who puts irons on another man unless he's broken the law. And wanting to be free ain't breaking the law."

With that, he stomped to his wagon and started to climb aboard. James had to make a quick decision. "Mr. Crawford, please wait." The farmer turned and glared at James. "This isn't what you think. These people are not my property . . . in fact," James took a deep breath, "they are runaways. I'm trying to get them up North so they can be free." Mr. Crawford's expression softened.

"Are you being truthful with me, mister?"

"Yes, sir, I am. I helped these people escape from their owner. We started out from Georgia about five days ago."

"Then what about those irons?"

"Just for appearances," said James. "They wear the manacles in case were stopped by the authorities. I hope to make people think that they are in my custody." By this time Mr. Crawford was smiling again.

"Well, I'll be switched. So you're an abolitionist, and from Georgia, too. I will be switched. Of course I'll help you, but on one condition."

"What is that?" James asked.

"That you come back to my farm for a spell and let me and my misses show you a little hospitality."

"That's very kind of you, sir. We *were* about to stop for a rest and some food before this happened. My name is William Mason."

"Wonderful, Mr. Mason. Let's get this wheel replaced."

James removed the manacles, and with four men to help, the wheel was replaced in no time. He offered to pay for the wheel, but Mr. Crawford wouldn't hear of it. So he turned the wagon around and followed the good samaritan back to his farm.

After unhitching the horse, James filled the depleted canteens with water. By that time, Mr. Crawford's wife, Betty, had prepared a sumptuous meal of fried chicken, peas, potatoes, and biscuits. It was a warm evening; instead of eating in the house, the Crawfords set their guests up at a large wooden table that sat beneath a shade tree. It was quite a picnic and Betty Crawford was just as congenial as her husband. They treated the slaves as friends, if not family, providing the first relaxed and enjoyable moments since leaving Georgia.

After they had all eaten, Betty went to the house to fetch two cherry pies she had baked that morning. It all seemed too good to be true. But then Mr. Crawford asked a question that bothered James a little at first.

"So, I guess they've got rewards out for your capture by now."

"Yes, they do," said James. "I saw a notice at the sheriff's office in Greenville, South Carolina. I really didn't pay any attention to the amount."

"Well, no one will ever collect it," said Crawford. "By some time tomorrow you can be in Pennsylvania. I suppose you'll head due north from here."

"Yes." James replied, relieved at the man's simple curiosity. "As they say, the shortest distance between two points is a straight line."

"You know," said the farmer. "If you're so inclined, you are welcome to rest here for a while before taking the road again. I have some cots in the barn there. Sometimes I hire temporary help and I let them sleep out there. It's mighty comfortable, so they tell me."

"That sounds inviting, Mr. Crawford. We might just do that. We *had* planned to sleep a few hours before moving on."

After eating the delicious pie that Mr. Crawford's wife served, the table was cleared and Betty went to the house to wash the dishes. Then the farmer got up and said, "I best go give her a hand. If you decide to stay a while, you'll find those cots just inside the barn door."

"You know," said James, "I think we will stay for a while." The kind farmer displayed that huge smile again and said, "Wonderful. You stay as long as you like, and in case I don't see you before you leave, good luck to all of you."

Again, James offered to pay for the wagon wheel and the terrific meal, but the farmer would take no money. Mr. Crawford headed to the house and James and the slaves headed for the barn.

The cots were easy enough to find, but as he lay there in the darkness of the barn, James began to get the uneasy suspicion that something was wrong. Maybe he was just getting anxious to reach the end of the journey or maybe he still couldn't quite believe the good fortune of the day. In any case, he decided to trust his instincts and get back on the road again. He did feel guilty about disturbing the others. He knew that they, too, could use a few hours of sleep in something with a little more resemblance to a bed.

James got up quietly to go tell Mr. Crawford that he had changed his mind and to take one last opportunity to thank him. When he got near the house he could see the farmer and his wife through a window, sitting at the kitchen table. The window was open on that warm evening, and although he felt a little ashamed at first, he stopped for a moment to listen. James could hear every word. Betty was talking and he heard her say, "Then you had to offer those fresh cherry pies I just baked."

"Would you forget about those damn pies?" Her husband retorted. "Those four niggers must be worth hundreds of dollars, maybe thousands. The reward has got to be pretty big, not to mention what they'd pay to get their hands on Mason for helpin them escape. I tell you, we'll make enough money to buy a lot of wagon wheels and you can bake as many pies as you want. Just wait a little while, let them fall asleep. Then I'll go into Beckley and get the law. We'll claim the reward."

James didn't know which was worse; what he had just heard, or how badly he had been taken in. But the farmer had been so convincing. Then he noticed that Crawford's horse and wagon was hitched and sitting in front of the house.

James hurried back to the barn and woke Darnell. "Wake the others and tell them not to make a sound. This farmer has set a trap for us. I'll get the wagon hitched up. Quickly and quietly now."

As cautiously as possible, James backed the horse up to the wagon and fastened the harness. When everything was ready, he led the horse out to the road very slowly. *Thank God it's dark*, thought James. After walking for about a quarter of a mile, he climbed into the seat and snapped the reins. Now it was up to luck.

A few miles down the road they came to a y-intersection. Now he had another quick decision to make. Should he go straight or take the other road that headed almost due east? He had told the farmer he would head directly north, but that was before he knew that Crawford was planning a double cross. The only things that James could be sure of were that Crawford didn't know the conversation between him and his wife had been overheard, and it was understood that James and his companions would not be staying all night. Of course, it was a safe assumption that a search party would be sent in both directions. He turned the horse to the right and got her moving as fast as he could. As he sped down the road, one thought kept echoing through his mind and it reminded him of the basic rule he had established before he started: trust no one!

SEVEN

The Freedom Line

If everything fell into place the way James prayed it would it might amount to as much as a three hour head start on the despicable Mr. Crawford and his posse. However, it complicated matters to be heading east rather than north. It would be much longer before they could reach Pennsylvania; longer that they would remain in the slave state of Virginia.

They stopped to rest under a bridge that crossed a shallow creek. A small group of riders on horseback clattered over their heads heading east. There was no way of knowing if they were following James's wagon or if their business was something else. It was a relief when James came to an intersection and could turn north.

There was one more problem that was beginning to make life a bit uncomfortable. The farther north they got, the more the temperature dropped. It was something that James had failed to take into consideration. In the Deep South, the weather could be quite nice in late April, but in Pennsylvania there was still a possibility of snow. He was upset with himself for not remembering what northern weather was like during his years of school in New York. James estimated the temperature to be about fifty degrees and it was only three o'clock in the morning. It would be hours before the sun was up far enough to provide a little warmth. For the time being, the important thing was to just keep moving.

At about six-thirty, James was able to see how far off course they'd gotten, thanks to the treachery of Mr. Crawford. A road sign indicated that they were three miles from Morgantown. They were somewhat east of where James wanted to be. It had been his plan to head for a small town called Mount Morris, which was just across the Pennsylvania line. From there, Erie was due north. But it

63

was no time to worry about small details, and in spite of everything they still were not far from the border. When they'd crossed it he would turn northwest for a short while to put them back on a course for Erie.

It was time to stop again and rest the mare. James climbed down and stretched his tired limbs. It had been about ten hours since leaving Crawford's farm and he was getting hungry as well as sleepy. But he felt that something more than mere fatigue was setting in. It wasn't just the soreness in his back, but more of an aching feeling all over. His eyes were watery and his throat felt a bit sore when he swallowed. The early morning air was chilly and he was shivering.

There was no sound from the back of the wagon; James assumed that the slaves were asleep. Fortunately, with the four of them close together and covered by the canvas, they would generate enough body heat to stay relatively warm.

As James was becoming slightly impatient and a little irritable, he cut the rest stop short and climbed back in the wagon. The mare walked along at an easy speed while James dozed in the seat. An hour later, he perked up considerably when he opened his eyes and saw a sign along the road that said: Mason-Dixon Line. He drove across it and stopped the wagon again—this time on Pennsylvania soil. Then he turned in the seat and woke his passengers with a gleeful shout. The canvas was thrown back; the startled slaves sat up and looked around as if they expected to be surrounded by a lynch mob. "I am sorry if I scared you, my friends," said James. "But I thought that you might like to have your first look at freedom." The announcement seemed to startle them even more, and then Darnell finally spoke up and said, "Do you mean, sir—"

"I mean, sir," James interrupted, "that we have crossed the line and are now in Pennsylvania. We have officially left the South behind and slavery along with it."

For the first time, the sound of unbridled joy burst forth from the four ex-slaves and they acted like children on the last day of school. "I gots ta feel dat ground under my feet," shouted Darnell. And truly he did when he jumped from the wagon because he was still without shoes. Then Buck joined him, then Emmy and Tisha. They danced and sang with such spirit that James thought God himself must have whispered an invitation to heaven in their ears. At length, James broke up the celebration and asked them to get a fire started for breakfast. "We still have some ground to cover before you reach your new home."

It was a meal with all the gaiety of a party, with thanksgiving and homage thrown in for good measure. The only dark shadow that was cast upon it was the fact that James was feeling worse by the minute. His appetite had faded and he ate very little. In spite of the cooler climate he was sweating profusely and he felt unsteady on his feet. He did his best to keep his condition from the others because he did not wish to throw a damper on their excitement. By the time they were ready to move on very sharp pains had begun to invade his lower abdomen. As he attempted to climb up to the wagon seat he turned suddenly, claiming that he had to relieve himself, ran off the road, found privacy behind a large evergreen tree, and vomited.

When he got back to the wagon they noticed he was very pale and he could no longer hide the truth from them.

"You looks mighty, ill, Mr. Bill," said Buck. "You gots to lie down and rest, sir." James didn't say so, but he felt that if he did lie down he might not get back up again.

"No," said James. "We'll see if the next town we come to has a doctor."

Somehow, he managed to get into the wagon, but as they started down the road he nearly doubled over in pain.

After an agonizing five miles, they came to a peaceful looking little village called Mapletown. Barely conscious, James held on long enough to pull the horse to a stop in front of the first building on the right side of the road, and then everything went black.

When James regained consciousness, he lay very still and allowed his eyes to roam the surroundings, searching for a clue that might tell him where he was. The room he was in was small and immaculate, with pure white walls and a matching ceiling with a very steep pitch. He was lying in a real bed with a thick pillow, covered by a wool blanket, atop a mattress that felt as if it were stuffed with cotton. To his left was a small table with a pitcher and bowl; to his right was a large leather chair. The room had one window and one door over top of which hung a crucifix.

When he felt like he was fully awake he tried to sit up, which proved to be a big mistake. His right side was very sore as if he'd been kicked by a mule. Once he realized that he could not rise, his next thought was of the slaves. Where were they and were they safe?

Consistent with someone who has blacked out, James tried to retrace his steps in order to figure out what had happened. He remembered making it into Pennsylvania and he remembered feeling very sick. But he didn't remember stopping anywhere or anything that had happened since. As his anxiety increased he tried to call out in an attempt to get someone's attention. But the pain in his side was so severe that he could not take a breath deep enough to put any volume into his voice.

Fortunately, it was not long before the door opened and in walked a middle aged woman wearing a lovely print dress with a white collar and something resembling a little white doily on her head. She also wore a spotless white apron and she carried a pot holder with a steaming bowl sitting on it. She had a comforting smile and looked very pleased when she saw that James was awake. After seating herself in the big leather chair she said, "I have some nourishing soup for you, son, but I'd better let it cool for a bit. How are you feeling today?"

"I feel a bit stiff and my right side is very sore. But that isn't what's bothering me most. What happened and where are the people who came here with me?"

"You were deathly ill when you got here, son," she explained. "When my husband and I saw the condition you were in, we sent for Dr. Pierce immediately. Thanks be to God that he is also a skilled surgeon because you were sick with an acute appendicitis. He told us that if you had gotten here any later you would have died because your appendix was about to burst. It was, I believe, your friend Darnell who came pounding on our door begging for assistance."

"Yes," said James. "Where are Darnell and Buck and Emmy and Tisha? Are they all right?"

"Yes," she replied. They are in very good hands."

"Can I see them?"

"Oh, no, son. I'm afraid that they are gone."

Panic hit James like a sledge hammer. He tried again to rise but the pain caused him to drop like a rock.

"Gone!" he shrieked. "Gone where! What have you done with them?"

"Please, son. There is no need to worry. By now your friends are halfway to Canada."

"Canada?"

"Yes. My husband made the arrangements."

"And who might your husband be?"

"My husband is the Reverend Percy Pyle. I am Mrs. Pyle. You are in the parsonage of the Mapletown Community Church."

"I can't believe that they are gone," said James. "It was my intention to take them to Canada myself."

"Yes, I know," said the reverend's wife. "Darnell told us the whole story. It was a most wonderful thing that you did for those people. They will never forget you, Mr. Mason."

"You say that they are halfway there? How long have I been here?"

"Two days," she replied.

James was calming down a little. He was glad that their journey had not been delayed because of him but he was very sad that he did not get the chance to say goodbye. Surely good fortune had brought them to Reverend Pyle and his wife. Then he began to reflect on the trip and he thought about the farmer, Tyson Crawford. He remembered how he had misplaced his trust in that man. "I want to see your husband," said James. "I want to see him now."

"At this time, the reverend would be in the middle of his morning service. He will be here as soon as he is through. He wishes to see you also. For now, this soup has cooled and you must try to eat."

James was becoming anxious again but he was in no shape to be obstinate. He was in a fix and he could not help *himself* let alone try to be sure that his friends were indeed on their way to Canada. He would try Mrs. Pyle's soup and wait for her husband.

In a little while, the door opened again, and a tall man in a black suit entered the room carrying a stovepipe hat in one hand and a bible in the other. Like his wife, he wore a pleasant smile and his manner was quite congenial.

"Mrs. Pyle tells me that you were able to finish a sizable bowl of soup," he said as he seated himself in the leather chair.

"Yes, sir. The soup was very good."

"Mrs. Pyle is a wonderful cook. That isn't why I married her, but it certainly has made our relationship more enjoyable," he said, showing another smile. "She also tells me that you are worried about your Negro friends."

"I am, for a fact," said James. "I apologize if I seem a bit irritable and I *am* very grateful for all you've done. But during our trip I learned that trusting people can get you into a lot of trouble."

"Sadly, that can be the case. It was a courageous and selfless act that you performed and you are to be commended for your effort. I can assure you that your friends are in the very best of company. When you are able to get out of bed I will show you something that will put your mind at ease, but for now I have a letter I want to read. It is a letter to you, dictated by your friends before they left. I helped them with some of the words but the sentiments are purely their own." The reverend took a piece of paper from his pocket, unfolded it, and began to read.

"Dear Mr. Bill,

As overjoyed as we are that we will soon be free men and women, we are very sad to be leaving you while you are so sick and without a proper chance to say goodbye. We owe our lives and what the future might bring to you and your kindness of heart. We must face the fact that it is unlikely we will ever meet again. But remember that you will always have our undying gratitude and that you will never be forgotten. May God bless you.

Sincerely,

Darnell, Buck, Emmy & Tisha"

By the time the reverend had finished reading the letter, James could feel a lump in his throat and a single tear was sliding down his cheek. He thanked Reverend Pyle for helping with the letter but when he tried to give it to James to keep, he said, "No, sir. I want to, but I'd better not. I couldn't risk the possibility of it being found in my possession."

"I understand," said the reverend. "It could be difficult to explain. Now you rest, Mr. Mason. Mrs. Pyle will bring you some supper a little later."

After a week of peaceful rest and blissful slumber, not to mention Mrs. Pyle's cooking, James was out of bed and getting around with only slight discomfort. As usual, when Reverend Pyle concluded his morning service, he stopped to pay a visit.

"It's good to see you back on your feet, William. I promised to show you something. Would you care to take a little walk with me?"

Together, they left the parsonage and strolled next door to the church. It was a lovely day and James was feeling strong and anxious to be on his way. The reverend led the way inside and James followed him back behind the pulpit. Pointing to the floor he said, "How do you like this rug? It is thick and very comfortable to stand on when I deliver my sermon."

"Yes, sir, it is nice," said James, wondering if the rug was what the reverend had promised to show him. Then the reverend bent over, took hold of the rug, and pulled it aside to reveal a trapdoor in the hardwood floor. With James's help the door was opened. The reverend lit a coal oil lamp and led the way down a set of steps to a cellar. To James's surprise, he could see by the light of the lamp that the entire area under the church was one large room. The floor was covered by bricks laid tightly together to form a smooth, clean surface. In the center of the room was a large wooden table with benches on either side. Along both side walls there were beds sitting end to end complete with stuffed mattresses, blankets, and pillows. Against the front wall were wooden shelves piled high with clothing.

"This is what I wanted you to see, William. This church was a station on the Underground Railroad for years. You've heard of the Underground Railroad?"

"Yes, sir. I have read about it, stories in New York newspapers," said James.

"For the most part, the railroad has ceased to operate. It has been more than six months since I have had runaways in the church. I was very surprised when you showed up here with your friends. I realize, of course, that it was by accident. But I am still prepared to lend assistance if I am called upon. I have a friend who owns a covered wagon. He would transport the slaves to Erie to the home of another man who took them by boat across Lake Erie to Ontario. I made those same arrangements for your people."

James was impressed. He was satisfied that he no longer had to worry about Darnell, Buck, Emmy, and Tisha. They climbed back up the stairs, lowered the trapdoor, and replaced the heavy rug. Outside again, James told his gracious host, "I would like to be heading back to Georgia. There is so much more to be done."

"I take it," said Reverend Pyle, "that I will be seeing you again?"

"Yes, sir, you will. Until I'm caught and hanged or until slavery is wiped out of existence I will continue to do what I can."

"You are a rare find, William. To care so much about your fellow man; to be willing to sacrifice your own life for your cause; it is becoming rare in this world. Dr. Pierce will be here tomorrow morning to see you. Please wait for his opinion. If he says you are ready to travel you can be on your way."

Early the next morning, Dr. Pierce gave James a thorough examination. When the doctor was finished he declared James fit to leave. James thanked Mrs. Pyle for the wonderful care and told her that, God willing, he would be back again. Reverend Pyle walked with James to the barn behind the parsonage where he helped to hitch up the wagon. Then he handed him a piece of paper and said, "This is a list of other stations between here and Georgia. There is no certainty that they are still operating or that the same people live there, so be sure to use the verification method I taught you. If nothing has changed I am sure you can still count on these locations for assistance. If you find yourself near one of them and in need of help, don't hesitate to go there. But please memorize the list as quickly as possible and then destroy it. It would be dangerous to a lot of people if it fell into the wrong hands. Be ever so careful as you travel back and forth. There are many hands against you."

James thanked the good man and said, "I am so taken with your trust and with the fact that you have revealed so much to me. I would like to prove that I am worthy of that trust. My name is not William Mason. I used an assumed name for whatever protection it might offer. My real name is James Langdon. I grew up on a large cotton plantation that my father owns near Macon, Georgia."

Reverend Pyle was visibly moved. "For a young man to turn his back on such a prosperous life, to go against everything that he was raised to be, is a true inspiration." He shook James's hand and said, "God bless you, James, and may He be by your side always."

James climbed into the wagon and headed south out of Mapletown.

EIGHT

Escape from Live Oak

It took just over two weeks for James to get back to Dry Branch as he was not pressed to travel quickly on the return trip, nor did he use the same route he had taken going up. He decided it might be wise to be familiar with more than one way to Mapletown; and he purposely drove by a few of the other stations on the list, after having destroyed it, so they could easily be located if necessary. His mission would now be a little easier, having stumbled into the hands of Reverend Pyle and his wife. He had established a definite destination for his trips north, and he would not have as far to travel to be sure that the slaves he delivered would make it to freedom.

The first thing James had to do upon his return to Dry Branch was to take the horse and wagon back to the livery stable. It was good to see Star again, but for the time being, he left her in the care of the livery man. It was just past noon, so he walked up the street to Baxter's to fill his stomach, and with any luck, see Polly. As soon as he walked through the door he noticed how busy the place was. It took almost a five minute wait before he could get service. He ordered a steak, potatoes, beans, and a beer. The bartender told him to take a table if he could find one and his order would be sent over.

James sat down at the only table he could find and waited in anticipation, hoping the meal would be delivered by Polly. While he waited, he could not help but hear the conversation going on among the three men at the next table. The man doing most of the talking sat with his back to James. He was obviously very angry and extremely profane with his language. James thought the angry man seemed familiar and he understood why when he heard the man say, "It's been almost a month since them goddamn niggers ran off. Every day since, I been expectin somebody to bring them sons a bitches back. Now I don't think I'm ever gonna see them sons a bitches again. Beats me how they got away especially draggin their black wenches with em. I'd druther they was dead than to get away."

It was gratifying to James to hear old Silas Turner complain so. As he listened to more of the conversation, it was apparent that Turner didn't even suspect that the slaves had been aided in any way. For his first effort at least, he had gotten away clean.

The eavesdropping was interrupted by a middle aged woman bearing a tray that held his order. When she sat it on the table James asked, "Is Polly here today?"

"Do you know Polly?"

"Actually I met her when I was here once before."

"Oh," said the woman. "She will be back in a couple of days. Her mother passed away night before last. The poor thing's takin it pretty hard." James was about to say how sorry he was, but the woman didn't wait for his reply. She picked up the empty tray and was gone. James considered going to Polly's house but it didn't seem like the right thing to do under the circumstances, especially because of the way their first meeting ended. He would just have to wait for her to return to work to see her.

After he finished his meal, he went to the house to see if all was well. It was much on his mind to go home for a visit; he missed his family a great deal. But he really hadn't been gone long enough to warrant a leave of absence and he didn't want to arouse suspicion. He decided to rest for a day or two and plan his next move. This time, rather than continuing to hire a horse and wagon, James would buy them instead.

Once again he focused on Live Oak Plantation as the place to affect an escape. This time it would take something more elaborate to accomplish his purpose. Live Oak was a much larger place than Silas Turner's farm and it would not be as easy getting in and out.

Forty-eight hours later, James was ready to strike again. He waited until midnight and then he moved in as close as he dared to the slave quarters at Live Oak. After examining the situation, his thoughts gave way to an idea.

73

He made a wide circle around the crude little dwellings and came up behind a ginning shed. He opened a small window, lit a match, and tossed it inside. In a matter of minutes, the building was engulfed in flames. His idea produced the desired results, quickly spreading an alarm and drawing the attention of every hired hand on the plantation. Like a fox to an unguarded henhouse, James moved in to make contact with the occupants of the nearest slave cabin. Following the same procedure as before, he explained his presence to a wide eyed young black man and told him to bring his family, if he had one, and to hurry down to the road where the wagon was waiting. Then he withdrew quickly. But halfway back to the road, James heard a desperate scream; something had gone terribly wrong.

Filled with the irresistible notion of escape, one of the slaves split the overseer's head open with a shovel. For James, chaos hit when they started showing up at the wagon. Thinking that only a few would follow, in no time there was a crowd of twenty-five or thirty black men, all trying to get aboard. James began to panic, believing that he had incited madness. He started to lose his composure, shouting, "I cannot take all of you! We're going to be caught!"

By now, the situation had reached riotous proportions. Some of the men were pulling others out of the wagon to make room for themselves and fights were breaking out. Finally, James did the only thing he could do. He climbed into the wagon and lashed the horse until they were flying down the road at breakneck speed. The wagon bed was packed full of bodies; others chased after, pleading for him to stop, while a few more clung to the back and were dragged until they could not hold on any longer. His mind was racing like a rat trapped in a box. Any second he expected to hear the sound of gunshots behind him.

How completely different this was compared to the first time. Everything had gone smoothly and quietly. This time it had blown up in his face. It was difficult to think straight enough to decide what to do. But he did understand that he could not stay on the road for long and he could not continue on in the wagon. And although just four sets of manacles would have been of little use to him with a wagon load of slaves, it still added to his anxiety when he realized he'd left the house without them. Now, it would turn into a version of the classic escape attempt: hiding in the woods, crossing and re-crossing streams to throw off pursuit, and walking every step of the way.

With every mile he drove, James believed that he was pressing his luck. He did not know, with the pandemonium he'd left in his wake, how soon a pursuit could be organized. What with the fire, the slain overseer, and the slaves left behind who had scattered into the countryside, James hoped he had created enough of a diversion and that the upheaval had taken everyone at Live Oak by complete surprise.

Eventually he had no choice but to find some cover and stop to rest the horse. When he finally counted heads, he saw that there were twenty-three black men of varying ages crammed into the small wagon. What a daunting task it would be to get them all to safety. Having calmed his nerves a little, James began to wonder if he could make it to the closest station on the list that Reverend Pyle had given him. It was a farm located near Chattanooga, Tennessee. If that goal could be reached it would give him a safe place to leave his rig; then he could lead from there on foot, keeping mostly to the mountains for cover.

Before leaving the rest stop, which was close to a trickle of a creek, he advised his passengers to quench their thirst and then quickly return to the wagon. While James waited, he searched his mind to retrieve the information concerning the exact location of the farm, the farmer's name, and the proper way to approach him. There was a sign to be given, a question that had to be asked word for word. The proper response was the counter sign.

He checked his pocket watch for the time. It was almost four in the morning and he was getting impatient. He was just about to climb down and hurry the slaves along when he heard a shout and one of the men ran up to the wagon shouting, "Boss, boss, Joe's done been bit by a snake! He's bit by a snake down by the creek!" James jumped down from the wagon and ran towards the commotion, met halfway by two men carrying a third by the arms and legs.

The injured Negro was not much more than James's age, maybe eighteen or so, and he appeared to be in shock. There was a nasty bite wound on his right arm, and it was beginning to swell. James's father had taught him how to care for a snakebite but he had never actually performed the procedure.

With very little light to work by, he took his knife and made a shallow cut across the fang marks. The young man twitched convulsively as the blade opened his skin. As best he could, James sucked out the poison then instructed one of the men to find some tree moss and dampen it from the creek. He applied the moss to the wound and tied it in place with a handkerchief. The wagon was so crowded that it was necessary to lay the man across the legs of several others.

He headed back to the road, slapped the reins down on the horse's back and prayed that he could find Mr. Gilmore's farm. He did not know, however, if finding the farm would guarantee that he would find help.

Just after sunup, they came to a turnoff that separated a field of corn on one side, tobacco on the other. Perhaps a mile or so in the distance, James could see a barn roof sticking just above the horizon. He knew that he was close to his objective but he couldn't be sure it was the place up ahead. But there were no other houses or buildings anywhere in sight, and the young man with the snakebite was moaning in agony. With no other alternative, he kept driving towards the only visible landmark.

It was a beautifully maintained farm with a little white house featuring a wraparound porch and flower boxes at the windows. The barn appeared to be freshly painted and the cattle grazing in the pasture were a product of good breeding. As they made their approach, two boys about ten or twelve years old stepped out through the open barn doors. When they saw James and the wagonload of slaves; they raced to the house, ignored the steps by jumping up on the porch, and then disappeared inside. The front door opened a moment later and a short, heavyset man in bib overalls came out on the porch with a double barrel shotgun cradled in his arms. He did not appear to be menacing, just cautious. When James pulled the horse to a stop, the man with the shotgun walked right up to the wagon.

"Can I help you, stranger?" he asked.

"Is there a railroad somewhere near here?" James asked him.

"Yes. It runs south to north," was the reply.

"Mr. Gilmore?"

"That's right. I'm Sam Gilmore." Then he smiled, raising the shotgun a little, and said, "Don't worry about old Betsey here, she ain't even loaded." Then he broke open the breech to show that he was telling the truth. James extended his hand and said, "I'm happy to meet you, sir. I'm William Mason. I was warned that your station may not be operating any longer but to try anyway if I ran into trouble."

"Well, it has been a while since we've had passengers, but I'm certainly not going to turn you away. What can I do to help, Mr. Mason?"

"We need food, rest, and something more. I have a young man who was bitten by a snake about three hours ago. I've done what I can, but he needs a doctor in a hurry."

Concern covered Mr. Gilmore's face and he said, "Pull your wagon over to the barn. I'll see what I can do to make him comfortable." The injured man was carried into the barn and laid on a pile of straw covered by a blanket. The rest of the men spread out, finding places to sit and relax. James removed the handkerchief and Mr. Gilmore inspected the arm. "I think you probably saved his life for now, William, but he does need a doctor sure enough. And if that arm gets infected he could lose that much for sure. I'll go to the house and tell my wife to make you all something to eat. I'll send my oldest son to Chattanooga for a doctor."

"Can the doctor be trusted?"

"The one that I'm sending for can. Don't worry."

He hurried off to the house. When he returned, James told him all about the escape from Live Oak the night before. "That is why," said James, "I want to leave my horse and wagon here and travel by foot. We'll never make it any other way. We have to stay off the roads."

"I guess you're right about that. Of course the sick man will have to stay behind. Ordinarily, we don't keep runaways here too long. It's always risky having them here at all. But I reckon we can hide one man for a while. When he can travel I'll see to it that he gets up north somehow."

"I do appreciate everything."

"Don't mention it."

By five o'clock that afternoon, James decided that it was time to begin the long, arduous journey to Pennsylvania. Mr. Gilmore's son had returned from Chattanooga with the doctor and it looked as though Joe would keep his arm. The farmer was more than a generous man, providing so much food and water that each man had a load to carry. James thanked Sam Gilmore profusely and promised to return for his rig as soon as possible. Then, the little band of fugitives moved out in the direction of the Appalachian Mountains.

On the second night after leaving the Gilmore farm, while resting in the foothills, James could hear barking dogs in the distance. They broke camp and moved out quickly, and the chase was on. Using every devious maneuver he'd ever been taught to stay out ahead of the posse, it took five grueling weeks before James stumbled across the Pennsylvania line, leading twenty-two runaways to Reverend Pyle's Church.

After a two-day rest, he purchased a roan pony in Mapletown, thinking he may be able to sell it to Mr. Gilmore when he stopped to pick up his horse and wagon.

When he was halfway back the turnoff to the farm, he suddenly realized that he couldn't see the barn roof. Pushing the pony to a full gallop, he continued back the lane until he could see farther ahead. Then he pulled hard on the reins and sat in the saddle, staring in horror. The pretty white house and the big red barn had been burned to the ground. The pasture fence was wrecked and there wasn't a single head of livestock to be seen. James was sure that it was no accident. What had happened? Had his anti-slavery activities somehow been discovered? Or maybe the trustworthy doctor who had tended to the snakebite was no longer trustworthy. James was devastated. With tears welling up in his eyes, he prayed for the goodhearted Mr. Gilmore and his family. And James understood one thing as he had never understood it before: the South was serious about their slaves. He turned the pony around and got away from the place as fast as he could.

NINE

Serious Suspicion

James arrived in Dry Branch at about five o'clock in the afternoon. Fortunately, the man at the livery stable was interested in buying the pony that he'd purchased in Mapletown. He actually sold the pony and the saddle for fifty dollars more than he had paid. The extra fifty was at least some compensation for the loss suffered on the rig he'd left at the Gilmore farm.

As always, the livery man was of few words, but James thought that his manner had changed a little. It was something in his expression when he looked at James that was different.

After looking in on Star, he walked up the street towards the house. As he passed by others who were out and about, he couldn't help feeling that he was drawing odd looks from some of them as well. His curiosity was satisfied about two minutes after he'd gone into the house; a very heavy knock was laid upon the front door. When he opened it, he was face to face with the town sheriff, who was pointing a pistol at his stomach. Before the sheriff said a word, he reached out and grabbed James's revolver from his waistband. Then he took three steps forward, forcing James to move back to the table. "Sit down," he ordered. James complied without objection. The sheriff was evidently in a very ugly mood and James sensed that he was in a difficult situation.

"What's your name, mister?"

"My name is William Mason."

"William Mason, is it? You're a stranger in town, aren't you?"

"Not entirely. I've been living here for over two months now."

"That doesn't exactly make you well known. Where are you from?"

Then James made a bad move by offering a bit of resistance. "What's this all about sheriff?" But the sheriff's irritation was growing roots. He leaned a little closer to James and began yelling, spraying spittle all over his face.

"I'll ask the goddamn questions and you'd better be ready to answer them! Now where in the hell are you from?"

"I come from Atlanta."

"You got family there?"

"No. I was raised in an orphanage."

"If you grew up in Atlanta, what are you doing in Dry Branch?"

"I don't care for city life. I wanted a quieter place to live."

"And how do you make your living?"

"I hunt down runaway slaves and return them for the reward."

"Is that so? Have you caught any lately?"

"It's been a while," said James. "But the rewards are pretty good, and if you're careful with your money you can make a living from moderate success."

"Well from everything I've heard about you, I'd say that your activities seem mighty suspicious. The way it seems to work out is that since you showed up in this town, there has been a lot more slaves escapin than there is bein caught. About three months ago four niggers ran off from Silas Turner's farm about five miles north of here. Just over a month ago there was a hell raisin escape from Live Oak plantation. A fire was deliberately set and about fifty slaves ran off. All of them were caught except twenty-three. Owing to all this, a white man was killed; the overseer's head was split open with a shovel."

The sheriff hesitated for a moment after his last statement, apparently hoping that the serious nature of it would get a reaction from James. It did, but not the kind the lawman was probably expecting. James was supposed to crumble under the pressure and expose a guilty conscience. Fortunately for James, he had not known about the murder and his reaction was the shock and surprise of the innocent. He was genuinely upset about the killing. He wanted to help free slaves; he did not want to be even indirectly responsible for the loss of a life.

The sheriff did not seem as sure of himself, but he wasn't through yet. "After questioning the niggers that were caught, I understand that a white man with a horse and wagon was involved. You rented a rig from the livery about the time those niggers ran off from Turner's farm. You were gone a couple weeks and then came back. Then, just before the trouble at Live Oak, you *bought* a horse and wagon from the livery, you're gone about a month and a half or so and then you come back riding a saddle pony. How do you explain all that?"

"It is true, sheriff, that I often use a horse and wagon in my business. When I make a capture, it is often more than one slave. Sometimes a buck will run off and take his woman and kids with him. I can't very well haul them all on my horse. It doesn't bother me if they have to walk a couple hundred miles while I ride but the owners can become difficult about the reward if their property isn't in good shape. It can get costly, hiring out a rig, so I finally decided to make an investment and buy one. But as far as the time frame of those events you described, and my coming and going, it is purely coincidental."

"And what happened to the wagon you bought?"

"It was stolen one night when I was camped out in the mountains. I was taking a bath in a stream about a hundred feet away and I didn't even hear the thief over the noise of the running water. I had to walk for quite a way until I found a farmer who was willing to sell me that pony."

"Where did all this happen?"

"In Virginia."

"So your wagon was stolen. Another coincidence I suppose."

"I guess so," said James. Then he had a thought. When he returned the rented wagon to the livery, he naturally removed all of his belongings from it including the manacles he'd purchased. "Can I show you something, sheriff?"

"What is it?"

Slowly, James got up from his chair and walked over to the bed while the muzzle of the sheriff's pistol followed him. He reached under the bed and pulled out the small wooden box he'd used to carry his things. Then he walked back and sat the box on the table. Extracting the manacles, he dropped them on the table making a loud and purposeful clatter. "If I'm not what I say I am, what use would I have for these?"

The sheriff looked at the manacles for a minute, and then he grew an expression like that of a gambler in a card game who has just been shown a better hand. James was sure that the sheriff was not convinced, but he also knew that he had planted the seed of doubt. "I'm gonna tell you something, boy. I'm lookin at a total of twenty-seven runaway niggers and I'm lookin at a white man whose been murdered in the middle of it all. If I had the smallest piece of hard evidence against you, I'd throw you in my jail and sell tickets to your hangin. But you'd better be careful about what you do. I mean you better be as still as a heavy man hangin on a weak branch over a snake pit cause I'll be watchin every move you make from now on. I'll be watchin."

Then he got up, tossed James's revolver on the table and walked out, slamming the door on the way. James took a deep breath and exhaled slowly. The success he had achieved to that point seemed heavily outweighed by the trouble he'd caused for himself and his operation. It would now be nearly impossible to operate anywhere near Dry Branch. In spite of everything James remained unafraid, but he had no death wish either. He would have to adjust in some way in order to continue. It was funny sometimes, he thought, how misfortune can actually be beneficial. He was glad now for the loss of the horse and wagon. If he had brought it back it may have somehow produced evidence against him. But now he was being watched and he would never know for sure, when, or by whom. The sheriff only had two eyes and other duties as well; he couldn't be everywhere at once, but James didn't know who else might have been instructed to cast a glance his way. He needed to unwind and maybe get an evening meal.

Out on the boardwalk everything was quiet. He headed towards Baxter's wondering if at that moment he was under surveillance. Just as he reached the tavern, the door opened, and who should emerge but Polly. Forgetting his hunger, he removed his hat and said, "Good evening, Polly." When she looked up she was smiling. When she recognized him, the smile ran away from her face. "Oh, Mr. Mason," she said dryly.

"I would consider it a privilege if I could walk you home," he said politely.

"I hardly think that would be appropriate or possible," she said.

"I just wanted to say that I heard about your mother and I am deeply sorry."

She seemed to soften a little at his kindness and she replied, "I do thank you for your condolences, Mr. Mason, but I must be going now."

By then they were walking slowly down the boardwalk, and in spite of herself, Polly didn't seem to object to the fact that he was still by her side.

"At the risk of further damaging your opinion of me," said James, "I must ask you about the day we met. What did I do to make you angry?"

Now she looked annoyed, as if the answer to his question was extremely obvious. She stopped and faced him, then after looking to see that no one else was around she said, "It might interest you to know, Mr. Mason, that not everyone who lives in the South is in favor of slavery. It might also be of interest to know that some of us are decidedly against it. Now maybe you can understand why I find complete distaste in someone who would chase down those unfortunate souls and return them to captivity for money."

As surprised as James was by her remarks, Polly would be equally surprised when he said, "So do I."

"I must say that I am confused."

"I know . . . I know you probably are. But I don't feel comfortable talking about it here. Can we . . ."

"Yes. Walk me home."

As glad as he was for the chance to clear things up with Polly, he was also aware of how vulnerable he would render himself by confiding in her. One more mistake on his part and he could be finished.

Polly unlocked the front door and they stepped into a very well appointed little parlor. The furniture was a little outdated, but very neat and in good condition. There were paintings on the walls and pillows placed about; all in all, the décor was very pretty. It rather reminded him of home. "You have a very nice place here," said James.

"Thank you. My mother was a wonderful homemaker. She liked everything to be just so."

"That sounds like *my* mother."

Polly gave him a strange look. Then he remembered he told her that he had grown up in an orphanage. No matter; he was ready to explain everything anyway. "May I sit?"

"Yes of course," said Polly, waving to a chair. When they were seated comfortably, James began to unveil the true nature of his presence in Dry Branch. He told her everything, including his real identity, and where he came from. When he was finished, she wore an unexpected look of shock. James might have expected surprise but not panic. "I am so sorry, Mr. Mason, I mean James. I'm afraid that I might have done something to endanger you." Now it was James who didn't understand. "I have to warn you," she continued, "that Sheriff Wilkes will be paying you a visit. He has been in a crazed state these past few months, like a lot of other people around here. Your activities have put a real scare into them. He came into Baxter's a few weeks ago and was asking everyone if they've noticed any strangers in town lately. I'm afraid that I told him about you."

"What did you tell him?"

"Just what you told me; your name, or what I thought your name was, and I told him you grew up in an orphanage in Atlanta. I don't remember mentioning that you hunt runaway slaves for a living. Maybe I should have. Maybe he would be less suspicious of you."

"I think you did just fine," said James. "The fact is I have already been called upon by the good sheriff."

Polly caught her breath.

"It's all right, Polly. I told him the same thing that you did. Our stories matched and that is what's important. And if either of us has put the other in danger, I fear that I am the bad guy. The sheriff has assured me that I will be watched very closely from now on. I am sure that he will continue trying to tie me to those two escapes. He is probably aware of my presence here in your house and he will certainly wonder about it."

"What are you going to do?" she asked.

"I don't know yet. I need time to think and I need a way to get the heat off me if I can. I guess I should have had a better plan before I started all of this. You might say that I am making it up as I go along. I guess if I was going to live in this town I should have gone elsewhere to free slaves. Maybe South Carolina. After all, a smart thief wouldn't rob the bank in the town where he lives. I could move, but that would only make me look guilty. If I stay and there are no more escapes that might also look suspicious."

In the midst of a demoralizing situation, Polly said one little thing that reinforced James's spirit like nothing else could have.

"I wouldn't want you to leave town."

"I'm very happy to hear that," James said with a smile. "It has troubled me greatly, not knowing why our first meeting went awry. I'll stay and try to find a way to outwit Sheriff Wilkes. In the meantime, we should keep our distance from each other. I don't want you to get any deeper into this. We can talk a little when I come into Baxter's. We can keep in touch that way without attracting any attention."

Then he got up to leave and Polly walked him to the door. "I am so glad that I was wrong about you, James. I am sorry for the things I was thinking. You are a noble gentleman." Then she raised herself on her toes and kissed his cheek.

It was nearly nine o'clock when James started back up the boardwalk from Polly's house. He looked around in an attempt to see if he might be receiving any attention; he didn't seem to be. He suddenly remembered that he still hadn't eaten and was amused, somehow, that he no longer felt hungry. Baxter's was right in front of him but he knew that the kitchen closed at eight. The bar was still open though, and James decided that a beer might help him to sleep.

Only two other patrons sat at a table talking, and for no particular reason he took his beer to the table next to them and sat down. He nursed his beer, thinking about Polly and the chance to get to know her better. There was no doubt that he was smitten and it started James to thinking about home. He discovered that when a young man is teetering on the brink of romance, it is something that he wants to share with his family. He decided that he would visit very soon. It was also time he found out how his letter explaining the change of plans had been received.

The beer in his glass was beginning to get warm; something that James usually couldn't tolerate. But he was far too preoccupied to be bothered. Even bits and pieces of conversation coming from the next table barely dented his concentration. However, as he basked in the glow of Polly's change of heart toward him, he also worried that he may have put her in danger by association and he knew it was his responsibility to keep her out of harm's way.

Two days later, James was startled once again by a heavy pounding on the front door. The sound was familiar and he wasn't surprised when he opened it and there stood Sheriff Wilkes. He was not pointing a pistol this time but he was still wearing the same menacing expression as before. James stepped back so the sheriff could enter, then he offered his unwelcome guest a chair. "After you," said Wilkes. James took a seat at the table and the sheriff sat down across from him.

"I sent a wire to the City Marshal's Office about you, Mr. Mason, and I just received a reply. There are three orphanages in Atlanta and after a short investigation it turns out that none of them have any record of a William Mason ever living there." The sheriff seemed poised as if he expected James to make a dash for the door. Instead, he received a very calm reply.

"There was a fourth, sheriff. St. Mark's Church on Greenbrier Street used a small building behind the church as a home for orphans but it was destroyed along with the church by fire a couple of years ago. That was where I grew up."

James could see Sheriff Wilkes relax his posture. "OK," he said. "I'm a reasonable man. Your answer is verified by the information sent to me, so maybe you are who and what you say you are. I would much rather believe you were huntin runaways than helpin them." The sheriff got up to leave. "By the way," said Wilkes. "Those rewards are still offered for Turner's slaves and for the ones from Live Oak. Could be money in your pocket if they ain't in Canada by now."

"I'll keep it in mind," James replied, chuckling inside.

When the sheriff was gone, James said a silent prayer thanking God for watching over him. Luckily he'd heard more of that conversation at Baxter's after the evening at Polly's house than he had originally realized. The two men had been talking about the time St. Mark's Church and orphanage in Atlanta burned down. So it was a near miracle that turned the trick and got him off the hook. Now it was up to James to keep his activities away from Dry Branch and trouble away from his door.

He could not wait to see Polly again and tell her about his triumph over the sheriff, and to let her know that he would be out of town for a few days. James was going home for a visit.

TEN

Unexpected Duty

James rode out of Dry Branch and headed for Macon. He had some business to attend to before going home.

Upon arrival, he could see immediately that the city was buzzing with excitement. Everywhere along the main street there were small groups of people laughing and talking; men were slapping each other on the back, women were hugging their men folk. It was July 22ⁿᵈ but it seemed more like July 4ᵗʰ—except that now it was the Confederate flag flying from every home and place of business.

When he had tied his horse to the hitching rail and entered the bank he found out the reason for the celebration. As soon as he got in line, the man in front of him turned around and said, "Quite a day, hey, friend?

"What's all the excitement about?" James asked. The man looked astonished. "Haven't you heard? Our army trounced the Yankee invaders at Manassas Junction in Virginia yesterday. They drove those blue bellies the whole way back to Washington along with a flock of their high and mighty citizens."

"Is that so," said James in a phony tone of enthusiasm.

"Yes, sir. The elite of Washington society, including politicians and other highly placed men and women, came out in their carriages with their picnic baskets like they were going to a cotillion. They came out to see their army thrash the Rebels and we sent them running for their lives. The way I hear it, the hero was General Thomas Jackson. The Yankees were pushing us back but Jackson and his Virginians refused to retreat. The rest of the army rallied behind him and they routed the Yankees good and proper. People are calling him Stonewall Jackson now. Why, I heard they even took a congressman prisoner and locked him up in Richmond."

"My God," said James. "I should say we do have reason to celebrate. I just rode in from Dry Branch. The news hasn't reached there yet."

"Well, it will soon. It may be the first and last celebration of the war, except for when we hear the Yankees are calling it quits."

When James left the bank, he bought a newspaper and read the story for himself. It was just as the man in the bank had said. The Yankees and the civilians from Washington must have thought the world was coming to an end. One thing the excited man hadn't told him though was the extent of the casualties. The Yankee army lost almost three thousand men and the Confederates lost close to two thousand. James was shocked at the thought of it. He would have imagined that it would take a lengthy war to produce five thousand casualties. He couldn't believe that even the victorious Southern army would be experiencing the same elation as the folks at home. And what of the families that had lost a husband, father, or brother in the conflict? James wondered if *they* were celebrating. He folded the paper, put it in his saddlebag, and mounted his horse. He was more anxious than ever to get home.

It was mid-afternoon when he rode up to the barn and dismounted. At first glance, everything appeared to be as he'd left it over three months ago. The carriage that his family always used for worship and for social functions was sitting in front of the barn; George Lynch was on the far side working on the rear wheel. When he heard James ride up, he stopped what he was doing. His look of curiosity changed to a broad smile upon recognizing the visitor. "Well I declare. It's good to see you, James. Where did you come from?"

"Richmond," said James. "All the way from Richmond."

"Yes. Your father told us all about how you're workin for the Signal Service. That must be real interestin."

"It *is* interesting, George, but there is a lot to learn about that business. How are things here?"

"Everything is pretty good except that your father got his left leg broken a few weeks ago. He got kicked by that stallion he bought up in Kentucky. He's doing all right but it's hard to keep him off his feet so that leg heals proper. You know how your father hates to sit still."

"Yes, I know how he is. I'd better go see him."

"Sure, James. It's good to see you. I'll take care of your horse."

James hurried to the house and took the front steps two at a time to the veranda. The first person he saw inside was Millie White, busy as usual, cleaning in the hallway. Seeing James, she put down her feather duster and greeted him with a motherly hug. "Welcome home, James. This is an unexpected pleasure, how are you?"

"I'm fine, Millie. I talked to George when I rode in. How are mother and father?"

"They're doing fine, James. Your mother is upstairs resting. It's taking a lot out of her, worrying about your father. I guess George told you about his broken leg."

"Yes, he did."

"If he would just take it easy and stay off his feet until he heals . . . but they're both doing all right."

"Where is Father?"

"He's in his office. I believe he's in there working but at least he's sitting down."

"I'll go see him. Thank you, Millie."

He walked down the hallway and knocked on the office door but didn't wait for a reply. His father was sitting at his desk, left leg propped up on a footstool. Seeing his son walk through the door, he made a move to get up but James raised a hand to stop him. "Please, keep your seat, Father. I heard what happened."

The two men exchanged a firm handshake. "This is a wonderful surprise, son. I'm real glad to see you. Sit, sit and tell me what you've been doing."

"I will, Father, but tell me first about yourself and Mother. Millie said she is upstairs resting."

"Yes, she is. She's fine, James, just a little tired. It's my fault really. I've been hard to get along with ever since I broke my leg. Dr. Mead comes out every couple of days and he raises the devil every time but I can't just sit still with a plantation to look after. Things are especially difficult right now. It's that damn Union blockade at Hampton Roads. It's part of the Yankee plan to cut us off from the rest of the world. It makes it very hard to get anything shipped in or out. I have to rely on blockade runners to ship my cotton and so many of them are being caught. I've already lost quite a few tons to the Yankee fleet. You cannot wage a war without the proper tools and there is no Confederate Navy to speak of. Of course, the government is working on it; fortunately we were able to drive the Yankees out of Gosport Naval yard. Much of it was destroyed, but the dry dock was still intact. But how far behind will we be until we can effectively fight on the water, protect our ports, and break up the blockade? I guess we do have reason to be optimistic after the battle in Virginia yesterday. Of course I'm going on about things you already know about. The Signal Service is the first to get information."

"That's true, Father. I receive my orders from and report directly to the government in Richmond."

"Be assured, son, we were all very proud when we read your letter. The work you do is vital to our cause. I understand that General Beauregard was well informed about the movements of the Yankee army before the battle at Manassas. He had plenty of time to prepare."

"That is also true, Father, and still there were plenty of mistakes made. We were victorious, but we were lucky. It will take time before our army can benefit from more effective planning."

"I agree, son. Mistakes will need to be corrected. But I believe that we have better generals than the Yankees. I think we proved that yesterday. The news is both good and bad. The good news is that we did win the day and we drove the Union army completely out of Virginia. We stunned Washington with the measure of our resolve. They expected to put down the rebellion with one bold stroke. The bad news is that we were wrong to think it was going to be a short war. I believe now that there will be many battles before our future is decided. It may be a while before the North is ready for another fight, but the day will come."

"That is the feeling in Richmond, Father. I was fortunate to be able to make this trip home. It seems like orders are changing every day and security is getting tighter and tighter. It may be quite a while before I get home again. I'll be here for a couple of days and I want to make the most of it."

His father seemed a bit dejected by his last remark. "I'm sorry to tell you this, James, but Ashton and Kate went to stay with Uncle Joseph and Aunt Sarah for a couple of weeks. They wanted to spend some time with Jenny and Bret. Mother thought it was a good idea to pick up their spirits. They have been a bit melancholy since you left. I think they might be afraid that your leaving is a sign of things to come. Uncle Stanley's boys are gone, too. They left for the army the day after you did. Stanley hasn't heard from them yet."

James was sad to learn that he wouldn't get a chance to see his sisters.

And his cousins, Clark and Jessie, were off somewhere with their artillery regiment. James thought about his eighteenth birthday and how they had all been together in that very house. Now the war was heating up. Would all of them ever be together again?

Then, as if on cue, a wave of guilt crashed over him. It did not come as a surprise. He knew that it would be his most formidable enemy. No matter how much he believed in his own cause, it was not always easy to find solace in it. He wondered if it would be easier to join the Southern army, kill Yankees, and defend that peculiar institution. But if he believed that he was going to be plagued by guilt either way, then he might as well choose the persecution he would receive for doing the right thing. James was very familiar with the bible passage that says those who are abused for the sake of God are blessed. He was hoping that God would bless him.

Early that evening, his mother came down from her room. She was overjoyed to see her son and slightly disappointed that no one came to wake her. James eyed his mother cautiously, noting her unusual lack of color. His father said that she was just tired, but James was concerned that it might be something more. The cheerful radiance that had always appeared in her face was not there. She was showing her age; that was something he had never noticed before. It worried him that the events of the past few months had taken such a toll. How would she look if the war and the changes it brought should go on for years?

James told her about Polly—what little there was to tell. Of course he had to lie about where and how he met her. His mother seemed happy about the news although she cautioned him about beginning a relationship during such uncertain times. That in itself was strange, James thought. His mother simply never saw anything in a negative way.

The three of them talked until ten o'clock, then it was decided that everyone was ready for bed. Ignoring weak protest, James helped his father up the stairs to his bedroom. They said their goodnights and James went to his own bedroom, anticipating the best night's sleep he'd had in a while. He could not wait to stretch out on the big, comfortable bed. But after lying there for over an hour he was still awake. He was worried about his father and the broken leg he'd suffered. Would he be able to run the business without James's help? How long could the business tolerate the losses at the hands of the Union blockade?

As much as he objected to his father owning slaves, slavery was the only thing he wanted to see destroyed. He wanted the war to end, slavery to be abolished, and the plantation to flourish again with a newly structured labor force. The workers could be white or black as long as they were free men earning a fair wage for their effort. As ideal as it sounded, James knew he was asking for the impossible.

Eventually he drifted off to sleep, but it proved to be a restless one. Bad dreams consumed the night. He was awake by six a.m. and got out of bed without hesitation. Olivia was in the kitchen when he got there, but the coffee wasn't ready yet. The family cook greeted him with her usual cheerful disposition. The two of them talked while they waited for the coffee and she told him a bit more precisely how things were going. By her account, they were a little different than everyone else had led him to believe. He found out that his mother had been feeling poorly for weeks and that Dr. Mead had been coming to see her as well as his father. And as for his broken leg, the doctor had concerns about how it was healing. According to Olivia, his parents had been sleeping later than usual, and when they did rise they never seemed to feel like eating. What's more, they were having trouble getting through their day without frequent periods of rest. James did not like this new report. He didn't understand why they had allowed Ashton and Kate to go to Uncle Joseph's. They should have been home helping their mother and father.

When the coffee was ready he sipped his cup, nibbled a muffin, and considered staying a little longer than he had intended. As he gazed out through the kitchen window he saw two riders come down the main road and turn in towards the house. Sitting his cup on the table, he went out to the veranda to check on the visitors. He was happy to see that it was his Uncle Stanley and another man James recognized as one of his uncle's hired men. "Well bless my soul if it isn't my nephew, the government servant. When did you get home, boy?"

"Yesterday. How are you, Uncle Stanley?"

"I'm doing fine, James, considering."

"Father said you haven't heard from Clark and Jessie since they left for the army."

"No," he said in a disappointed tone. "But I know I will soon. I figure they're pretty busy with their training and they have to be ready now that the real fightin has started. War doesn't allow much time for writing letters."

"Would you come in for some coffee?"

"I'd sure like to, James, but the fact is we're trackin a runaway that took off sometime last night. He's a buck named Israel and he has an eight year old boy with him. We tracked him with one of my dogs as far as Johnson's Creek then the dog stepped in a beaver trap that somebody left behind. It snapped his leg off above the knee. I had to shoot the damn dog and that buck is still runnin. They were headin this way so we stopped to have a look around."

"I'm surprised to see that you've taken up the chase personally," said James.

"Times are changin. Seems like they change more every day. It's this damn war, you know. It's creating a manpower shortage. You can't depend on the local law for help anymore because they have to keep a close watch on what's going on in town. It's hard to tell what we might have to do until this war is over. It could be that things will never get back to normal. Anyhow, we better be on our way if we're going to find those two. That buck can't be that far ahead, not with a small boy. If you don't mind we'll just look around a bit, maybe search the barn before we leave."

"Help yourself," James told him. "George should be back there. Ask him if he's seen anything."

"Much obliged. Will you be home long?"

"Couple of days."

"I see. Listen, James, maybe it's not my place, but your father told Joseph and me about your conversation after you saw the whipping Bo Sampson took. I mean no disrespect to your father—he does what he thinks is right. It's just that Joseph and I always told him that he shouldn't be keeping the truth from you. You're a Langdon and we're all proud of you. We knew you'd do the right thing. You proved that when you joined the Signal Service."

James was glad that his uncle couldn't read his mind. There was nothing in it that would have pleased him. It didn't matter anymore. It didn't matter at all. His only reply was, "Thank you, Uncle Stanley."

"Well, you take care of yourself. Tell your parents hello for me."

"I will. Give my love to your family." His uncle waved a hand in reply and the two men rode back to the barn.

Breakfast was ready when James went into the house and his parents had finally come downstairs. He noticed that, as Olivia had said, they did not eat much. Afterwards, he went to the office with his father, and James told him about Uncle Stanley's visit.

"It's another problem that is getting out of hand, James. Since the war began, escape attempts are becoming more common. It is difficult to keep news like that from getting to everybody's ears. The blacks seem to think it's a sign that slavery might come to an end and it's making them restless."

He said no more as if he suddenly remembered that it was not a comfortable subject to discuss with his son. For a while they talked about business, and at length his father told him that there was some paperwork he needed at the field office. He asked James to ride along. With the bad leg, his father had resorted to driving a buggy for transportation. James insisted that his father stay off his feet; he would ride to the compound and bring back the paperwork.

On the way to the barn, James passed George and discovered that he was just about to leave for Macon to pick up some horseshoes and other supplies. James told him to go ahead; he did not mind saddling Star himself.

As he worked at the task, he felt something fall into his hair from overhead. He reached up to brush the top of his head and discovered some small bits of wheat chaff. He wiped it away and continued with his chore. A moment later he felt the same thing. Taking a step back, he noticed more chaff and dust dropping through a gap in the mow floor. As slowly and quietly as possible, he climbed up the ladder until he could see above it. There were several large piles of straw, side by side, across the width of the mow floor. He watched and listened, and after a couple minutes of nothing, he decided it could be mice. Then, as he started back down the ladder, he saw some straw shift on the side of the pile right in front of him. Cautiously, he stepped out onto the floor and walked over to the pile. Bending down to move some straw aside, he heard a creaking floorboard behind him. When he turned around, he was confronted by a tall, lean black man dressed in slave rags, terror in his face and a pitchfork in his hand. In spite of the potential weapon, the man did not appear to be threatening. It was as if he was waiting to see what James was going to do. Remembering the earlier conversation with Uncle Stanley, James said, "You must be Israel." He did not answer, but his expression clearly showed that he was surprised to hear James call him by name. "Where is the boy?"

This time he spoke, but not to James. "Boy, get outta dare," he said.

Again James heard a noise behind him and a small, dark-skinned boy came out of the straw pile, walked passed him keeping plenty of distance, and stood next to Israel. It was a touchy situation to be sure, but James was not afraid. What worried him most was trying to get Israel to trust him before someone happened by or his Uncle

Stanley decided to come back. All he could do was to try talking to the frightened man. "I am not armed, Israel, and even if I were you would have nothing to fear from me. In fact, if you'll let me, I'll help you and the boy. My uncle was here searching for you, but he's gone now. Were you here in the barn when it was searched?"

"We wuz under da straw, but da man, he don't look round real good. He jes walks up and down a little. I wuz sho we wuz gonna be caught, but da man don't look round too much."

"That's good," said James. "At least for now you're safe." He took a step toward Israel, but the man raised the pitchfork as a warning. "If I'm going to help you you'll have to put that thing down."

"Why you wanna help us? No white man helps no slave. We run off from Massa Stanley and he your uncle."

"That's right, he is. My father owns slaves, too, but they don't see how wrong it is . . . I do. I have helped others escape and I'll help you, too. Look at it this way. If you think I'm lying to you and you take off running I can call for help and we'll catch you in no time. If you manage to kill me with that pitchfork you'll have a head start, but if they catch you then you'll hang immediately. No matter what you do, just getting caught will guarantee you punishment. I'm offering to help you if you'll let me. I think your best choice is to trust me, but you have to decide right now. I have things to attend to and in about two minutes I'm going down that ladder."

"What den?" said Israel.

"Then you can run and take your chances, but you'll never make it . . . not with the boy."

Israel lowered the pitchfork and looked at James with appeal in his eyes. "I don't know why I gonna trus you, mister. I guess cause like you says, I guess I can't get away wit da boy. Massa Stanley sold off da boy's mamma when he's jes little and I promise da boy we gonna find his mamma someday. All da time he ax me when is we gonna find his mamma. I know we dasn't run away, but I can't look da boy in da eye no more."

"So you ran off to try to find the boy's mother?"

"Yeah, mister, dats it."

The guilt James had been feeling since coming home was gone. In fact, at that moment, he was sure that all of his deceit would never bother him again. All he felt was sympathy for Israel and the boy. He had promised himself that he would not attempt to free slaves that belonged to his father or his uncles. However, he was caught off guard by this unexpected duty and he was not going to turn his back on it. Fate wills out, he thought. "When did you and the boy eat last?"

"We et nothin since yesterday."

"I'll take care of that as soon as I can. I have to do something for my father, and when I get back I will bring you food and water. For now, let me show you where I want you to hide."

James led them to the far corner of the mow to the last pile of straw.

"Hide yourselves between the wall and the straw pile. There is no reason for anyone to come up here anymore today. Even if the man who takes care of the barn needs straw he'll get it from the pile nearest the ladder. I'm just home for a visit. I'll be leaving in a day or two. I'll hide you here and feed you and when I leave I'll find a way to take you and the boy with me."

James made sure they were well hidden, and then he hurried down the ladder and mounted his horse.

About halfway to the compound he saw two men on horseback coming towards him. When they got closer he could see that it was Uncle Stanley and the hired man who was helping with the search for the runaways. Then James saw something else that made him feel uneasy. Just ahead of the two men, a hound dog trotted along with its nose to the ground. James pulled up as did the other two men. Uncle Stanley got down and took the dog by the collar. "Hello again, James," said his uncle.

"Any luck?" James asked.

"No, not much. We've covered this area for about ten or fifteen square miles and not a sign of that buck or his boy. I borrowed one of your father's hounds. It's the only way we're gonna find them."

"Did you talk to George?"

"Yes I did, and my man Jack here looked through the barn."

"I searched it myself before I left," said James. "But I didn't find anything."

"Thank you kindly, James. I guess that buck's headin for Virginia."

"Virginia?"

"I'm just foolin about," said his uncle with a chuckle. "I sold his woman about two years ago to a man named Zachary Stark. He's a banker from Petersburg, Virginia. I met him when he was in Macon on business. He was looking for a housemaid so I sold him Israel's woman. But that buck has no idea where she is. Well, we better get moving. We're gonna cut through the woods up here and head back to Johnson's Creek where I lost my dog. We have to stop by my place for a while but should be back at the creek by around midnight to see if we can pick up their trail. We'll run them down." Then to his hired man, Jack, he said, "Climb down and hand this hound up to me when I get in the saddle. Might as well save his feet a little wear."

Jack did as he was told then he got back on his horse and the two men headed up the road. James breathed a sigh of relief. Considering the direction his uncle and the hired man took when they left the road, there would be little chance that they would get anywhere near James's house. With his uncle hauling the dog he was even more assured that for the time being Israel and the boy would be safe. But he knew that would change come nightfall. If the hound dog was able to pick up the trail he would lead Uncle Stanley straight to the barn. James would have to get the runaways out of the barn soon after it got dark.

George had gotten back from his trip to Macon and gone home for the day by the time James got back from the compound. After he delivered the paperwork his father wanted, he secretly filled a brown paper bag with food and sneaked it out to the barn as promised. He told Israel to be ready because they would be leaving sometime that evening. The difficult part was breaking the news to his parents that he would have to shorten his stay. James told them that because of the recent battle at Manassas, he should be getting back to Richmond. He knew that his explanation was rather vague but in spite of their disappointment, they said they understood.

By nine o'clock, the Langdons were ready to retire and James was ready to leave. He assured his parents he would write to them soon and they quickly concluded their goodbyes. As he got to the barn, he looked back at the house in time to see the light go out in the upstairs hallway. It was very difficult to leave after such a short visit; especially since he had no idea when he might get home again. He saddled Star, then with a lantern in one hand, he climbed the ladder to the mow. James called to Israel in a low voice and the slave and the boy came out from their hiding place. They all climbed to the ground and James went outside to take another look towards the house. It was completely dark. He mounted his horse, sitting back in the saddle as far as possible. "Hand the boy up," he told Israel. He sat the boy halfway on his lap then he helped Israel to climb up behind him. He was glad that it was a cloudy night. Shrouded in darkness, they headed down to the main road and turned in the direction of Dry Branch.

ELEVEN

Showdown in Dry Branch

A light rain was falling by the time James reached the edge of town with Israel and the boy. It was very early in the morning, but no time day or night would be safe in the company of the two slaves. He swung to the right of town, rode down behind the buildings and stopped about a hundred yards out from the back of his house. He was bending the rules again by not keeping his activity completely away from Dry Branch. It didn't matter that he had not taken Israel and the boy away from his uncle's plantation, that he had merely intercepted them. It didn't matter that his uncle had reported nothing and was, in fact, conducting his own search. He was still pushing his luck, which he would be out of if Sheriff Wilkes caught him.

His idea was to sneak them into the house, hide them in the cellar, then devise a plan to move them north the following night. James dismounted and told Israel to stay put until he could make sure that all was quiet. It took several minutes to cross the distance to the house as he carefully checked his footing in near complete darkness. Fumbling with the key at the back door, he was about to insert it into the lock when he reached for the knob and realized that the door was already ajar. His first instinct was to clear out fast, but instead he pushed the door open slowly and stepped into the pitch black room. Holding his revolver in one hand, he struck a match with the other. Even in the dim light James could see that someone had been there, and whoever it was had not been polite about it. Cupboard doors were hanging open; furniture had been overturned and tossed about. Whatever had happened, he knew for certain that it was not safe for him to be there.

As quickly as possible, he groped his way down to the cellar and retrieved the leather money pouch that was hidden in the stone wall. Then he gathered the few belongings he kept there and left. "Something is wrong," James told Israel when he returned to where he'd left him and the boy. "Stay on the horse." He grabbed the reins and led Star through the darkness until they were behind the livery stable. Again he told the two of them to wait and to stay quiet no matter what. Fearing that his next move might be a very regrettable one, he went to the back of Polly's house and tapped gently on the door. He kept it up until finally he saw light through the window. From inside, a nervous voice whispered, "Who's there?"

"Polly, it's James."

"James, my God," she said as she opened the door. "What's wrong? What are you doing here at this hour?"

"I just got back to town. Something is terribly wrong. Someone ransacked my house. I have to get away from here, but I just had to say goodbye. I can't come back here again."

"Oh, James," she said sadly. "Won't I ever see you again?"

"If the world ever becomes normal again you will. I promise you, Polly. When all of this is over I'll be back."

"Wait just a minute," she said. "Don't leave yet. There is something I want to give you."

She walked into the parlor and a few seconds later James heard a loud crash as someone kicked in the front door. Then Polly screamed and a loud voice shouted, "Where the hell is he?"

James wanted to leap out the back door but Polly was in trouble. He hurried into the parlor with his revolver at the ready but it would do him no good. Who else would the intruder be but Sheriff Wilkes? His gun was also drawn and pointed at Polly's head and he held her tightly around the waist.

"Drop that shooter or this young lady's gonna have a bad accident." James immediately dropped his weapon and the sheriff shoved Polly towards a chair. "Sit down and be still," he told her. Then he ordered James to sit in the chair next to her. He sat down feeling like the biggest fool in the world for believing that he had gotten the sheriff off his trail. Either Wilkes was the smarter one or something had happened to point a finger back at James. In any case, he was kicking himself for not moving away from Dry Branch. Far too much had happened and he should have known that the ice was too thin.

Suddenly, the sheriff's mood changed from bad to an imitated version of pleasant. Apparently he had James right where he wanted him and he was enjoying the moment.

"Well now, young people," he said. "I hope you all are in a lively mood because we're gonna have a party. But we can't start yet because not all of the guests have arrived. It will only be a minute or two." James looked over at Polly. She was white knuckled and terrified. He felt a paralyzing sense of regret inside for getting her mixed up in such a mess. The sound of a horse's whinny came from out back, and then footsteps entered through the door. Into the parlor walked Israel, the boy, and another man behind them carrying a shotgun. "Here we are at last," said the sheriff. "Now the party can commence. Just a couple small details. Roscoe," he said to the man with the shotgun. "Tie that nigger up and sit him on the floor then tie that nigger lover, too, and tie em tight. Sit that boy down, but no need to tie him. He ain't goin nowhere."

When everything was to the sheriff's satisfaction, he holstered his pistol and stuck James's revolver in his belt. Roscoe took a seat and laid his shotgun across his lap. "I must say, Mr. Mason, if that's your real name, that you had me fairly convinced for a while there and you are a man of considerable luck. But your luck has run out for good. You ever hear of the Carlton brothers?"

"No, I never have," James answered.

"Well, that ain't important. But what is important is that there are only two of them and there used to be three. The third brother was the overseer at Live Oak Plantation, you know, the one that was killed the night of the escape? All three of em worked over there. After they rounded up all the niggers that didn't get away, the remaining two Carltons couldn't wait to go after the wagonload that did. So the following morning they took two extra men and picked up the trail. What you didn't know was that your horse had a loose shoe on his right front hoof and it left a real funny print. Now these two boys are pretty damn good trackers and it wasn't any trouble at all to follow that wagon right to the farm owned by a man name Sam Gilmore. I know you heard of him." James didn't answer and the sheriff continued. "After a search of the place, do you know what they found? That's right. They found the wagon and they found the nigger you had to leave behind. I'll tell you that those Carlton boys were real upset with Gilmore what with him helpin niggers escape, especially since their brother was killed. So they gave his wife five minutes to get what she could from the house before they set fire to it. Then they scattered the livestock and set the barn on fire, too. Those boys sure do have a good sense of justice. It was their intention to take Gilmore to Chattanooga to stand trial for treason, but don't you know he tried to run and the boys just had to shoot him down. But that's not the end of the story, not by a damn sight. The brothers sent one man back to Live Oak in the wagon that hauled them runaways along with the nigger they found in the barn. Then they took up the chase again. By the way, that nigger that went back to the plantation is dead. It turned out that he was the scum that did in the overseer. They hanged him and threw his body in the hog pen. And now we come to the part of the story that will interest you the most, Mr. Mason. Our livery man here in town, Merle Fitch, goes out to Live Oak now and then to do some blacksmithin chores. As it happens, he was out there yesterday, and when he saw the wagon that the Carlton boys sent back he recognized it as the one he sold to you. When I found out you were out of town I had Roscoe here, do some sentry duty, and when he saw you sneakin around out back tonight he came and got me. But, I promised you all a party, and I always keep my word. We're gonna have a necktie party."

Up until that moment, Wilkes had been smiling and having a very good time. James despised the man and his matter of fact way of describing the destruction of a good family like the Gilmores. Then the sheriff's demeanor changed, the smile turned ugly, and he said, "After all you did and you still have the guts to come back to this town with two more runaway niggers. I warned you before about what I'd do if I could prove that you were up to no good. Well, I won't waste time or expense on you now my friend. I don't even need to know if your name is really Mason. I reckon I can put Nigger Lover on your marker and it will serve you just as good. As for you, Miss Polly, I think I'll let you sit in my jail for a few days so you can think twice about getting mixed up with a lowlife traitor like this again. Roscoe, go over to my office and fetch that hangin rope that's on my desk and hurry up about it. I wanna get this thing done."

Roscoe stood his shotgun up against the wall and hurried out the front door. James was frantic in his mind trying desperately to think of a way out of his predicament. He knew if he failed he was going to be dead in a very short time.

The minutes ticked by. It wouldn't take Roscoe long to get back with the rope. James wondered where the sheriff intended to take him. There were trees close by that would be large enough. He looked at Polly as if to say that he was doomed.

"Sheriff Wilkes," said Polly. "Since you mean to put me in jail, may I please get a few things from the trunk over there to take with me?" At first, the sheriff did not seem inclined to be at all agreeable, but then he relented.

"You can take a change of clothes if you want to." He did not pay much attention to the seemingly harmless girl as she went to the trunk and opened the lid. He just sat there holding a steady stare at James. Polly bent over, took a dress from the trunk and while maintaining her posture, she folded it. But when she straightened up and turned toward the sheriff, she was holding a six shot pepper box in her hand. James had never seen a man so taken by surprise. "What in the hell do you think you're doing?" he asked.

"I'm keeping you from committing murder," she answered.

"Murder! Have you lost your mind?"

"Don't try to stall, Sheriff. Roscoe will be here any time now. With your left thumb and finger, pull those guns out one at a time and toss them across the floor. If you don't, I'll shoot you."

James had no idea whether or not Polly would actually pull the trigger, and apparently the sheriff wasn't too sure either. But he was not willing to find out. He did as he was told, and when he was unarmed, she backed over to James and produced a straight razor, which she had also removed from the trunk. Polly cut the ropes from James's wrists and he quickly gathered the guns from the floor. Then he removed the shells from Roscoe's shotgun and put it back against the wall. He took his seat again, holding his revolver behind his back. "Now, Wilkes, you be still and don't be tempted to call out to Roscoe. We'll just let him walk in like the obedient little fellow he is."

Just a single breath later, Roscoe walked through the door carrying a coil of rope with a noose on one end. He picked up the shotgun then turned to Wilkes and said, "Are we all set, Sheriff?"

"Not quite," said James, as he stood up aiming his revolver in their direction. To give credit where it is due, Roscoe showed more nerve than the sheriff as he raised the shotgun and pulled back the hammers. To James he said, "You better be a good shot because if we both pull the trigger, there ain't no way I'm gonna miss." James didn't answer. He just reached into his pocket, pulled out the shotgun shells and held them up for Roscoe to see. "Now lay it down and push the door shut. OK, Wilkes. You and your partner go sit on the floor with your backs to the wall. Polly, cut Israel loose."

James reloaded the shotgun and handed it to Israel. "Do you know how to use this?"

"Yes, sir, I knows."

"All right, then you stay over here far out of reach but you keep that thing pointed right at them. If they move a muscle, shoot."

James knew he had nothing to worry about. Nothing in the world would keep those two bigots still like a black man pointing a gun at them. Then he took Polly out behind the house so they could talk without being heard.

"Are you all right, Polly?"

"Yes. I'm just a little shaken, I guess. I'm so thankful that the sheriff didn't challenge me. I'm not sure what would have happened."

"I owe you my life. I'm very grateful."

"I had to do something. I wouldn't have been able to live with myself if they'd hanged you."

"You'll have to go with me now, you know that."

"Yes, I know."

"I'm sorry, Polly. This is your home."

"It's all right, James. It was different when mother was alive. There is nothing here for me anymore. I *want* to go with you. Where did Israel and the boy come from?"

"I'll explain that on the way," said James.

"Will we go to Pennsylvania?"

"Eventually we will. First we'll head to Petersburg, Virginia. I'll explain that, too. Right now we have to decide what to do with Wilkes and Roscoe. We have to keep them quiet for as long as possible. Once they spread the word we will all be fugitives. We won't be safe until we are up north. We also have a transportation problem. We need a horse and wagon, or at the very least, one more horse."

"There is a wagon down in the shed. It belonged to mother but it hasn't been used since our old horse died three years ago."

"That will help except that the only horse we have is Star. She's a saddle horse and I don't know how she will like pulling a wagon. But, I guess we have to try it. First I'd better get our two friends inside taken care of."

"What are you going to do?" she asked.

"I'll tie them up and gag them. Hopefully they won't be found until sometime tomorrow. That's the best we can hope for. We'll try to hide Israel and the boy in the wagon. Maybe we can pass for two harmless travelers. You should pack whatever you need to take along. We have to get moving."

James went inside and secured the hands and feet of Sheriff Wilkes and Roscoe with Israel standing guard. All the while, the sheriff spewed threats about what he'd do when he caught up with them. Irritation finally gave way to anger and James told him, "You know something, Wilkes, if I had it in me, I'd take you out someplace and shoot you. Then he shoved a gag into Wilkes's mouth to shut off further comment. James hitched Star to the wagon and led her up to the back door. Everyone helped to load what they could take from Polly's house, Israel and the boy hid under blankets, and they headed north leaving a lot of trouble tied and gagged in Dry Branch.

TWELVE

Deception in Petersburg

It was obvious from the start that Star was not happy with her new job, but James managed to keep her moving along. This trip north would be much different than the others because now he had Polly to worry about. More and more he was concerned that what he was trying to do was affecting the lives of so many people. He was already indirectly responsible for the deaths of the overseer and one of the slaves from Live Oak. What happened to the Gilmores could have happened at any time but it still preyed upon his mind. James realized the unfortunate truth that nothing in theory is ever the same in reality. But his situation seemed to resemble the war itself in as much as now that it had started there was nothing to do but fight until the end.

As they rode through the night, James told Polly how he had come to be in the company of Israel and the boy. She was very touched when he told her about his Uncle Stanley, how he sold the boy's mother, and how the boy yearned to see her again. "That is why we are heading to Petersburg. Uncle Stanley sold her to a banker named Stark two years ago. If I can locate him, maybe I can free the boy's mother and we can reunite this family."

"This is a wonderful idea, James. Have you told Israel?"

"No, not yet. I want to see if I can find her first. I don't want to get their hopes up in case I fail. Two years is a long time. Maybe the banker doesn't even own her anymore."

All night long they traveled in a northeasterly direction and by seven o'clock in the morning they had reached Jackson, South Carolina. Before entering town they stopped to allow Israel and the boy a chance to eat as much as they could because, until they moved on, the two of them would have to remain concealed in the wagon.

Jackson was a small town and had no telegraph office; therefore, James was not terribly concerned for their safety. He put Polly in a hotel room so that she could rest and freshen up; James slept in the livery barn next to the wagon. Early that evening, they had supper at the town's only eatery. They also had a basket of food fixed up to take along for the slaves; something better than what they had stored in the wagon.

The trip had gone well to that point, and as James expected, Polly was very pleasant company. It began to take on the feeling of a courtship, and even in the short time they had spent together he began to feel very comfortable with her.

After dark that evening, as they rolled through the countryside, off in the distance to the west they could see the glow of a large number of campfires.

"Must be an army camp," said James.

"Is it anything to worry about?" asked Polly.

"If they found out we have runaway slaves it would be. They would arrest us as quick as the civilian authorities. We just have to hope no one has a reason to search the wagon; better yet, we have to hope we don't even get stopped." Over the course of the following few days, they passed by a number of Confederate infantry and artillery units, but managed to travel around them inconspicuously.

Petersburg was a thriving rail center with all but one rail line running to the Confederate capital of Richmond. It was a large city with plenty of danger for anyone trying to smuggle runaway slaves. The important thing was to keep them out of sight. If the four of them were not seen together it would help to foul any description that might be sent out. Surely Sheriff Wilkes and Roscoe had been freed by now, James thought.

However, getting to Petersburg was not the primary objective, but merely the temporary. James needed to locate the boy's mother, if possible, and steal her away from her owner. He had casually asked Israel about his woman, ostensibly out of curiosity. Her name was Emaline; she was light skinned and approximately five feet tall. She had a noticeable scar on her right cheek put there by an overseer's riding crop. James hoped this would be sufficient enough to find her.

They drove down Main Street until they came to a tavern with a sign out front boasting about their roast beef sandwiches. It was mid-morning and the establishment was packed with either late breakfast customers or an early crowd looking for lunch. James ordered four of the large, overstuffed sandwiches, a jug of coffee, and a sarsaparilla for the boy. He paid for the food and asked the man behind the counter if there was a place outside town where he might camp for the night.

"Just passin through, stranger?"

"That's right," said James.

"If you head north out of town you'll come to a bridge that crosses the Appomattox River. Just before the bridge there are wooded areas on both sides of the road. Just pick a spot and go to campin."

"Thank you kindly." On the way out of the tavern he picked up a newspaper, climbed into the wagon, and headed north.

They found a likely spot down by the river, far enough from the road to afford them some privacy. James devoured his sandwich while reading the local paper and when he started reading the back page, an advertisement caught his eye. "Listen to this, Polly," he said. "For Sale. Four hundred acre farm with large house and out buildings. Perfect for raising crops and livestock. Interested parties should contact Zachary Stark, at Merchant's Bank, 450 Canal Street, Petersburg, Virginia. That's my man. That's my opportunity to talk with him."

"That's wonderful, James. I just know you'll find a way to get some information."

"I'll see him this afternoon. First I need a change of clothing. I have to look like someone who can afford to buy that farm. I'll probably be gone for a few hours. Will you be all right?"

"I'll be fine. I have my pepperbox and I'm not alone."

"No, you're not. Israel says he knows how to use the shotgun. I think you'll be safe enough in daylight. I'll hurry back."

James saddled Star and rode back into town. First he bought a fine looking suit in a secondhand shop. It may have been used, but it was in impeccable condition. Next he went to a bathhouse to clean up. When he walked out he could have passed for a rich Virginia planter.

He had no trouble finding the Merchant's Bank. Sporting a look of importance, he strolled in and asked to speak to Mr. Stark. The banker was also very well dressed and was about sixty years old, completely bald, with a full gray beard. He may have been a banker by trade, but he was a bootlicker by nature and no doubt a man who slept with his money. For the masquerade, James had to change his name for a second time. He felt he had worn out the name William Mason, not to mention all the trouble attached to it. This time he introduced himself as Sterling Hargraves.

Stark ushered James into his office, offering brandy and a cigar, both of which James declined. He proved to be a consummate actor, and after half an hour Stark was begging him to take a ride out to the farm. "We can be there in ten minutes, Mr. Hargraves." James agreed to have a look and the banker quickly opened his office door and said, "Miss Trumbull, have Jerome hitch up my carriage and bring it around front immediately." Then he escorted James to the door, and when the black servant, Jerome, pulled up in the handsome carriage, they got into the backseat.

The farm was a beautiful place with fenced in pastures, two large ponds, and flat open fields just perfect for cultivation. The house reminded James of his home in Georgia with the same Greek revival architectural influence. It was surrounded by flowers, lots of mature trees, and a manicured lawn adorned with marble statues. Inside, the house was fully furnished with fine oak and mahogany furniture; gold frame paintings, and a huge tapestry hanging in the foyer depicting Monticello—the home of the great Virginian and former president, Thomas Jefferson.

As they walked about the place, James began to wish that things were different; that he really was a prospective buyer. He thought the farm would make a wonderful place for him and Polly to live and raise a family. What a strange time, James thought, to realize that he was in love.

"What do you think?" Stark asked when the tour was over.

"I think it's just perfect," said James. "Of course I will have to talk it over with my wife and she will want to see it for herself. We're staying in town at a hotel. We'll be here for a few days."

"I have an idea," said Stark, with a gleam in his eye. "Why not spend your stay right here? You'll save the price of your hotel room and you and your wife can really get the feel of living here. I'll even throw in your meals. I can send a wagon over this evening with enough food to last your stay and I'll leave a Negress here to cook and serve you. What do you say?"

What could he say? It was all made to order. They would all have lovely accommodations, complete with food, and James could question the slave woman that Stark would send to find out if Emaline was still the banker's property.

"I must say, you do make an offer that is difficult to refuse, Mr. Stark."

"Splendid, splendid. Just bring your wife out as soon as you've checked out of your hotel. Let's see now, today is Tuesday . . . I'll stop out say, Friday morning and maybe you'll be ready with a decision?"

"I think you can count on it," James replied.

He wasted no time getting back to the campsite. He told Polly all about the meeting with the banker and the invitation to stay at the farm. He also told her that he had introduced himself as Sterling Hargraves. Polly agreed with James about how well things were working out.

Driving back through Petersburg, Polly sat very close to James, holding his hand. Again he tried to imagine away reality, almost pretending they were simply going home after having spent a wonderful day together.

Near the center of town, however, he noticed the pressure of Polly's grip increase until her fingernails were digging into his skin. When he looked at her, the fear was unmistakable in her expression. She turned her head slightly toward the left side of the street. "Look over there," she whispered. His eyes searched along the boardwalk and his heart skipped a beat when he discovered what had caught her attention. Tying his horse in front of the sheriff's office was their arch enemy, Sheriff Wilkes. There were two other men with him, neither of which was Roscoe. Wilkes had his back to the street and did not look in their direction. All James could say was, "Thank God he didn't see us."

Not another word was uttered until they reached the farm and climbed out of the wagon. "Let's get what we need and get it inside. I want to get this rig in the barn, out of sight." To Israel he said, "You and the boy go in the house. Take him upstairs and find a bedroom in front. From now on until we leave here, I want you to spend as much time as possible looking out that window. You'll be able to see for quite a distance so if you spot anyone coming shout out a warning."

"Yes, sir," he replied, picking up the boy and hurrying into the house.

After putting the wagon away and tending to Star, James went in and found Polly absorbed in the beautiful décor. "Isn't it grand, James?"

"Yes, it is." Then he blurted, "I wish things were different and we were here because this is our home." Polly looked at him with a smile that said she was thinking the same thing. On impulse, he took her in his arms and kissed her deeply and meaningfully. Then he held her at arm's length and said, "Can you imagine anyone with a poorer sense of timing than me?"

"Poor timing notwithstanding, I'll take it." Then a tear escaped her eye. "Will we ever reach Pennsylvania?" she asked.

"We'll get there, Polly. I promise you we'll get there. We just have to be vigilant. We'll all take turns sleeping and watching. Hopefully Wilkes will move on soon and he'll be out ahead of us. There is really no reason why we wouldn't be safe here for a couple of days. No one knows we're here except Stark and he poses no threat. We'll find out this evening if he still has Emaline, then we can plan our next move."

About an hour later, Israel called to James from the top of the stairs. "Someone's comin, sir. Looks like a horse and wagon wit two peoples in it."

"All right, Israel. You and the boy stay in your room." James stood by the window, revolver in hand until he clearly made out who the visitors were. He could see that the driver was a black man and a black woman sat next to him. It had to be the food and the cook Stark had promised. The wagon stopped in front of the house; the man kept his seat, but the woman got down and came up to the door. James laid his revolver on a table in the foyer and waited for her to knock. When it came, he opened the door and there stood the most beautiful black woman he had ever seen. She was about twenty-five years old; light skinned, maybe five feet tall, and even the scar on her cheek did not spoil her exceptionally good looks.

"Mr. Hargraves?" she asked.

"Yes, that's right."

"I was sent by Mr. Stark to take care of you and your wife."

"We've been expecting you."

"I'll have Jonas unload the wagon, and then I'll fix supper."

James was amazed. Not only did she lack the worn, neglected appearance of a slave woman, but unlike Israel's field hand dialect, she spoke as one who had been educated. He waited until the food was unloaded and Jonas was gone before asking, "What is your name?"

"My name is Emaline, sir."

"How long have you worked for Mr. Stark?"

"I have worked for him for a little over two years, sir. Before that I lived in Georgia."

Indeed, she spoke intelligently but still maintained the demeanor of a slave, which was to say, she assumed her place. "Would roasted chicken with all the trimmings be satisfactory, sir?" she asked.

"It would, indeed," said James. "But, Emaline, I want you to set five places for supper." She gave him a queer look and repeated the request as if she'd misunderstood. "You want me to set five places, sir?"

"That is correct."

"Very well, sir," she replied. James took Polly into the parlor; he could see the excitement in her face. "I cannot wait to witness the reunion," she said. "This is simply wonderful, James," and she kissed him most enthusiastically.

"Excuse me, Polly, dear, I'd better go upstairs and speak to Israel."

Being most accomplished at her work, Emaline laid a beautiful table. Again, it reminded James of the grace and civility he'd grown up with. When the food was ready, he seated Polly then he pulled out a chair for Emaline. For the slave woman, seeing must have been disbelieving and she began to protest. "But sir, I cannot—"

James interrupted her.

"Please, Emaline, sit. We are just people sharing a meal together as it should be." Staring up at him, she slowly slid down into her chair.

"Everything looks wonderful, Emaline," said Polly.

"Thank you, ma'am."

"Please, call me Polly."

James stood at the back of his chair and said, "And now, I shall go and get our other two guests."

Poor Emaline looked so bewildered that James wondered if she would be able to stand the biggest surprise of all. He went upstairs and returned a minute later, leading Israel and the boy into the room. Israel and Emaline locked eyes and remained motionless as if frozen. Then Emaline began to shift her gaze from Israel to the boy and back again. When she was able to control her faculties, she pushed back her chair, rose very slowly, and walked around the table to face them. "Israel," she said. "My God, Israel how . . ." Her voice failed her; she opened her arms as the tears fell in a downpour. They embraced each other so hard they nearly restricted their abilities to breathe. Together, they cried out many years' worth of tears as Israel pulled her down with him to their knees. Then, grabbing the boy, they encircled him in their arms. "And my boy," sobbed Emaline.

James and Polly were unable to allow them all of the emotion as they became caught up in their own hugging and crying. It took some time before they could all separate themselves and regain a modicum of composure. Finally James said, "If we can manage it, let us enjoy this wonderful meal, then we can sit and talk." Emaline and Israel sat on one side of the table with the boy between them; James and Polly sat on the other side as they broke bread as equals.

Afterwards, Polly helped Emaline clear the table and wash the dishes, and then they all settled into the parlor. James sat by a window to keep a watchful eye while telling the entire story, beginning by describing the encounter with Israel in his father's barn. After the conclusion of the tale he said, "We'll leave tonight, and it will be days before Mr. Stark discovers that Emaline is missing. We will have a great advantage."

As James surveyed his audience, he saw all smiling faces except for Emaline. She wore a very somber expression; it was obvious that something was troubling her deeply. "Emaline, is something wrong?"

She looked at James, then at Israel, then she put her head down and started crying again; but this time they were not tears of joy. Israel attempted to comfort her while begging for an explanation. She looked around the room, took a very deep breath and said, "I cannot go with you."

In an instant, Israel dropped to his knees before her, pleading with her to tell him why.

"I am so ashamed," she said. "I cannot leave because I have a child by Mr. Stark." Jaws dropped and eyes grew large; Israel sat back on his heels in disbelief.

"Mr. Stark took a liking to me from the moment he saw me. When he brought me here, he treated me much better than the other slaves. He even allowed me to learn to read and write in spite of the fact that it is against the law. I was granted many extra privileges, sometimes right under his wife's nose. As time went by he became more and more friendly; I knew what he was leading up to, but I was always able to escape his advances. Then one night when his wife was in New Orleans he got very drunk. He promised that if I would sleep with him, he would free me and send me north. I didn't believe him and it wouldn't have matter if I had. He forced me to have relations with him and he has been doing it on occasion ever since. The same thing happened to my mother. That is why my skin is so light. After a few months I became pregnant. I have an eighteen-month-old daughter. Her name is Jasmine. Mr. Stark does not admit to being her father, mostly because of his wife. But I think she knows anyway. Ever since Jasmine was born he has threatened me, saying that if I ever resist him he will sell her away from me. I had already lost Israel and a son. Please do not misunderstand me: I despise the man, but I can't leave my daughter behind."

James could see the rage that had come over Israel. He jumped up and shouted, "I is gwine ta kill dat man Stark!" Then he headed for the door, not even knowing where to find the banker. James stood in his way. "Hold on Israel— you've got to hear me out."

"You is a good man, sir. I owes you a powerful lot but I gots to kill dat man for what he done to Emaline. It's jes too much what the massa do to da slaves. Emaline and me never even jumped de broom cuz your uncle done sold her off afore we gots da chance. Now this man done had a baby wit her. It jes ain't right, sir. It jes ain't right."

"No, Israel, it isn't right at all, and believe me—I can understand how you must feel. But if you lose your head and go after Stark, you risk losing all you have gained, not to mention putting everyone here in danger. Please do this my way."

"What way is dat, sir?"

"No one can change what has happened. Some things you just have to live with. Having lived as a slave I know that you can understand what I'm saying. But I'm making you a promise. We have Emaline. We will get Jasmine. We'll get Jasmine and then we'll all go north. You will have your family, Israel, and that's what counts. What do you say?"

It took several minutes for the distraught man to calm down and think things through. Then Emaline said, "Please, Israel." He looked over at her, and then he looked at James. "Yes, sir," he said. "We do it your way."

It was small relief to James. He had been so grateful that everything seemed to be going so smoothly. They could have just slipped away and by the time Stark found out he had been fooled they would have been well on their way to Pennsylvania. Now they would not only have to risk trying to rescue Emaline's daughter, but there was a good possibility that Sheriff Wilkes was lurking somewhere in the shadows.

"All right, Emaline, how should we go about getting Jasmine out of there?"

"I can get her out, sir. If we wait until it's late enough, I can get in and out without any trouble. Jasmine lives in a small cottage out behind the main house with me and Mammy Watkins. Mr. Stark probably wouldn't notice her missing right away. He doesn't pay any attention to her and Mammy won't say anything."

Wonderful, James thought. If Emaline could get her daughter out quietly, they may still get away with the element of surprise intact.

While they waited for a later hour, James sat in the parlor and wrote a letter to his parents. He kept it simple, basically letting them know that he was busy but otherwise doing fine. He hoped that they were fine as well. Not a day went by that he did not worry about them.

By eleven p.m., Emaline assured James that everyone in the Stark household would be asleep. He had gone out earlier to hitch up the wagon so that it would be ready. It was decided that only James and Emaline would go. He did not trust taking Israel due to his animosity toward Mr. Stark. He would stay behind with Polly and the boy and they would be ready to load the wagon and leave the minute that James returned with Emaline and Jasmine.

It was a clear night with a sky heavily speckled with stars and a moon that was nearly full. The banker's house was only five miles away, sitting about a quarter mile off the main road. The lane leading back was lined with trees on both sides and a split rail fence covered in places with rose bushes. They drove within fifty yards of the house then James pulled off to the side and stopped. "I'll go in closer to the house with you in case of trouble," he told Emaline. "I'll find a spot where I can keep out of sight." At the edge of the driveway James ducked into a clump of bushes. Emaline hurried across toward the house and was swallowed up by the darkness.

James watched from his place of concealment as the minutes ticked by. The night was calm and quiet, which should have bolstered his confidence, but somehow it worked on his nerves instead. Maybe he thought it was too quiet or maybe he felt that it was doom disguised as silence and would at any second make its presence known. He consulted his pocket watch. Only five minutes had passed since Emaline disappeared. Prodded by his impatience, James crossed the driveway and melted into the darkness by the side of the house.

From his new vantage point he could see a small cottage like the one Emaline had described. Having gone that far, he decided he might as well continue on to the cottage when something caught his attention. Thirty feet from the little dwelling was a privy, and through a knothole in the door glowed a dim light. James felt a chill go down his spine. Before he could react, Emaline appeared in the light of the moon with her daughter in tow. He took the woman by the hand and the three of them hastened toward the driveway.

Just when it looked like they might make good their getaway, there was a creaking sound behind them followed by the slamming of the privy door. James turned around and instinctively stepped in front of Emaline and her daughter to offer protection. There, in front of the privy, stood the banker; the moonlight reflecting off of the pocket pistol in his hand.

"Stop right there!" he shouted. Then, holding the pistol steady, he hurried over until he was close enough to recognize James. "Mr. Hargraves what is the meaning of this?" James tried desperately to think of a logical story but it was useless. The banker would have already put two and two together; it was easy to deduce that Emaline was trying to run off with her daughter and that James had not come to him to buy any farm.

Stark grew very angry very fast and his disposition had absolutely no resemblance to the pandering lackey James had met the day before. "Put your hands high in the air, Hargraves. We'll walk over to the house nice and easy so I can summon my man, Jonas. Then I'll send him to town for the sheriff." James raised his hands and Stark grabbed his revolver. "I'll take that. Now all of you walk to the house." As they got to the front lawn, the door opened and a woman dressed in a flannel nightgown came out to the veranda. She surveyed the scene, then walked boldly down the steps and confronted her husband.

"What is going on here, Zachary?"

"Go and wake Jonas, Ruth. I want him to go into town and get the sheriff. It seems that Mr. Hargraves here is not interested in the Danville farm after all. I've caught him trying to help Emaline and her child escape."

James expected her to hurry off and do as she was told, but to his surprise she said, "Let them go, Zachary." Clearly the banker was shocked as well and he said, "Have you lost your mind? This man tried to steal some very valuable property. Now go and get Jonas at once."

"I understand all too well her value to you, Zachary. I am quite aware of your indiscretions . . . I've known for years. You, sir, are the father of her child."

Stark let out a moan of protest and started to dispute his wife's accusations but she cut him off. "Don't bother to deny it. I will only hate you all the more; you and all of your kind—you Southern gentlemen strutting about with an aristocratic air, thinking you set a fine example. And all the while impregnating your slave women and selling your own children into bondage. I want that slave woman and her bastard child off of this place. You will let them go or you will deal with the truth as I will spread it all over this state."

"Perhaps," said Stark. "I shall just get rid of you instead. Emaline's value far exceeds your own," he said in a mocking tone. But Ruth was not intimated; instead, she held out her hand and said, "Give me that weapon."

Then she grabbed his wrist. Her adulterous husband pulled his hand back sharply to break her grasp and the gun went off, sending the bullet into his chest. Instantly, he dropped to the ground and James did not need to check his pulse to know that he was dead. For a moment, everyone stood still. Then Mrs. Stark said, "Take the woman and go. I will take care of my husband."

"It's true that it was an accident," said James. "But you'll have no witnesses."

"How chivalrous of you under the circumstances to worry about me, Mr. Hargraves. But the sheriff is my brother. Now leave and consider how fortunate you've been this night."

James did not hesitate further. He picked up his revolver, hurried Emaline and Jasmine out to the wagon, helped them in, and they were gone. Polly and Israel and the boy were waiting; within half an hour they were packed up and set to continue their journey. Deep inside, James was grateful to God for helping thwart an injustice and reunite a torn family. But he could not shake the guilt concerning what had happened to Mr. Stark. Some people might say he had it coming; James believed it was not his place to judge. He drove through the moonlit night in a solemn mood that even Polly could not change. If only they could reach Mapletown without any further trouble. But even if nothing in the form of a new threat confronted them . . . there was still Sheriff Wilkes.

123

THIRTEEN

Sheriff Wilkes's Last Stand

Mrs. Stark waited until the sound of James's wagon had faded away, and then she woke Jonas, told him to bring another man, and come out to the driveway. When they got there she told them that Mr. Stark had had an accident. "Go to the barn and hitch up the carriage. I'll get dressed and then we'll take the body in to town." Jonas brought the carriage up to the house and the two men loaded the banker's body into the backseat. His stoic wife was helped into the front, and Jonas climbed up beside her. "Drive me to the sheriff's office," she said.

Sheriff Braxton was awakened by a loud pounding on the door. He rolled out of bed and fumbled around for a match to light the lamp. Then he got into his trousers, pulled the suspenders over his shoulders and went to the door. He was surprised to see his sister, Ruth, on the other side.

"Zachary has been murdered," she said. The sheriff looked past her and saw a body lying on the backseat of the carriage. "Come in, Ruth. Come in and sit down. What in the world happened?" As Ruth began her explanation, another man came out of the back room. "This is Sheriff Raymond Wilkes, Ruth," he told his sister. "He's up here from Georgia huntin a man and a woman accused of assault and helpin two slaves escape."

"Go on with your story, ma' am," said Wilkes. So Mrs. Stark told the story except that when she got to the part about the shooting she said, "Mr. Hargraves suddenly seized Zachary's arm; they struggled, then Hargraves wrested the gun away and shot Zachary in cold blood." She managed a few tears to lend credence to her story and Sheriff Wilkes said, "Can you describe this Mr. Hargraves?"

124

She complied with the request and when she was finished Wilkes said, "Did you see his wife?"

"No. I only saw Mr. Hargraves but he told Zachary that his wife was with him."

"Any idea where they went when they left your place?" asked her brother.

"I guess they went back to the Danville farm."

"All right, Ruth," her brother replied. "You'll have to get Zachary to the undertaker. I am sorry this happened. I'll gather some men and we'll go after this Hargraves and his wife. Will you be OK?"

"Yes. Jonas will help me with Zachary and then I'll go home. I will anticipate the capture of his killer. I won't rest until he is hanged along with that slave woman, Emaline."

Sheriff Braxton helped his sister to her feet and walked her to the door. Then he kissed her cheek and said, "Don't worry, Ruth. I will find Zachary's killer." When she'd gone, he turned to Sheriff Wilkes and said, "Are you going with me?"

"I sure as hell am. I'd bet a steamship load of cotton that this man calling himself Hargraves is the same man I'm looking for."

"Then we'll go over to the Danville farm first. I think it's a small chance that they are still there, but if not it will be a good place to pick up their trail."

"I'll go over to the hotel and get my men," said Wilkes.

"I'll round up a few of my own and meet you back here," Braxton replied.

Ordinarily, James avoided heavily traveled roads and populated areas like cities and towns as much as possible. It was simply a fact that fewer people meant fewer problems. But Richmond was only forty miles from Petersburg. If they could get there it would be easier to elude pursuit than if they were out in the open. Also, James considered that the railroad was the way to make good their escape. He remembered a time years ago when his father decided to raise some beef cattle. When they were ready for market, they were driven to the railhead in Macon and shipped to the packing house. It was only a matter of paying for the space in the cars needed to transport the cattle. James thought that he could do the same with the horse and wagon.

About five miles from the city, they could see lights flickering against the night sky. As they reached the outskirts, they could see soldiers guarding the approach. "We're going to have to pass through a guard post," James told Polly. "I'm sure that all of the roads to Richmond are guarded. Just remain calm."

The roadblock was lit up brightly with many torches on both sides of the thoroughfare. James slowed the horse to a walk. A man in a gray uniform held his rifle on an angle at arm's length and said, "Halt." James stopped the wagon and the young soldier walked over and said, "Where you headin, sir?"

James decided to give him the same story he'd used on Captain Blackwell of the 1st Virginia Cavalry down in Tennessee months earlier. "We came from Georgia; that is where I am from, but my wife is from Lynchburg. I've decided it's time I join the Confederate Army so I'm taking her to live with her parents until we whip the damn Yankees."

"I reckon you decided right, sir. If the war lasts a while I expect you'd get drafted sooner or later anyhow. Sit still a minute while I write you a pass."

They waited as ordered and in a short time the soldier returned, handed James a piece of paper and said, "This will get you through the other guard posts. You'll run into another one at the edge of the city and two more on your way out no matter which way you go. But all you'll need to do is show your pass. Good luck to you, sir, and be mighty careful on your trip. There are skirmishes breaking out all over Virginia now and you just might run into them Yankees sooner than you think."

"Thank you for your courtesy," said James. The soldier stood aside and they drove past a dozen other sentries and a couple of cannons. At the next stop, as instructed, he presented the pass and the old corporal on duty merely glanced at it and waved his hand forward. He stopped long enough to ask the corporal for directions to the train station.

They had no trouble finding the station and it was not a problem buying passage for the horse, wagon, and six passengers. "You and your lady friend can ride in the passenger car but the niggers will have to ride in the boxcar with the horse and wagon," said the station master.

"That's all right," James told him. "We'll all ride in the boxcar."

"Suit yourself," he said with a sour expression. A half hour later, the train that would take them as far as Morgantown in western Virginia, pulled out of the station.

They were an hour gone by the time sheriffs Braxton and Wilkes reached the first guard post with their posse. When they described James and Polly and explained why they were after them, the same guard who had spoken to James was outraged to learn that the story he'd been given was a pack of lies. In addition, he said that he did not know the slaves were in the wagon, thus admitting that he did not conduct a search.

When the lawmen got to the second stop, the old corporal informed them that James had asked directions to the train station. The station master was also irate when he found out that he had allowed an abolitionist murderer to escape.

"How long have they been gone?" Wilkes asked.

"A little over an hour. They're going to the end of the line, Morgantown."

"Does the train make any stops along the way?"

"Twice for wood and water, but they will be short stops. Damn it all! I shoulda known something wasn't right when that son of a bitch and his woman insisted on riding in the boxcar with their niggers. Respectable white folks would have ridden in the passenger car."

"Well, don't worry about it," said Wilkes. "We'll ride hell bent for leather straight to Morgantown, and when they pull in, we'll be waitin."

At one end of the boxcar was a clean pile of straw. James helped Polly put down blankets and make beds for everybody. A sense of security settled over them. It seemed like they were on a nonstop ride to freedom. When they reached Morgantown, they would only be about twelve miles from Reverend Pyle's church. James was looking forward to seeing the reverend again, but this time he had more than one purpose for the visit. It was his intention to ask Polly to marry him. If they got married in Mapletown James would rent a house there, and then he would have a safe place to leave her when he went south again. These thoughts filled his head as exhaustion won him over.

The train slowed as it approached the station and the clanging of the bell brought him fully awake. The others were responding to the sound as he got up and went over to the side of the car. Peering through a large knothole, he could see the station about a hundred feet ahead. He could also see Confederate soldiers milling around on the platform.

The train was barely moving now, but their car eased closer and closer to the station. As it drifted by the building, James saw his seemingly perfect escape plan completely collapse. Standing on the platform was a group of men dressed in civilian clothing and they were armed to the teeth. It was Sheriff Wilkes, and at least a six man posse. James knew that this time they were trapped. There was no place to go and no possibility for a group made up of two men, two women, and two children to defend itself. Maybe, thought James, if he surrendered, the most severe punishment would be unleashed upon him. Maybe the others would at least survive. He turned away from the knothole feeling weak in the knees. He had come to failure after all, to his purpose and to his responsibilities. For a moment he was sure he knew exactly how John Brown felt when he was trapped in the firehouse at Harper's Ferry.

The train jerked to a stop. It would only be a matter of seconds before the door would slide open and he would be staring into the sinister smile of Sheriff Raymond Wilkes. He went over to Polly and took her by the hand, but before he could speak a shrill blare sliced through the morning air followed by a screeching cry from a hundred throats. Suddenly, gunfire exploded from everywhere. Someone on the platform started yelling, "Yankees! Yankees!" Then

James yelled, "On the floor! Everybody get down on the floor!"

For the next half an hour, the occupants of the boxcar pressed themselves against the wooden floor while hell swirled around them. For all, it was the first time listening to the sounds of battle. The terrorized screaming of men and horses went on and on amidst the thundering din of thousands of discharges. Bullets cut through one side of the boxcar and out the other raining splinters of wood down on those inside. Finally, the shooting subsided and a voice just outside shouted, "Sergeant! Take some men and start searching the cars." Having gone to school in New York, James could clearly detect the soldier's Brooklyn accent.

He got up from the floor of the boxcar and looked to the others to see if anyone was hurt. Fortunately, no one had been hit by anything but a serious grip of fear. Then he hid his revolver in the wagon so the Yankees would find him unarmed.

"Now I want us all to stand by the door with the children in back of the adults," James told them. "When the door opens I want everyone to raise their hands high in the air."

They stood at the door as he instructed and when the door slid open, all hands went up. Two soldiers in blue stood there holding rifles. The ranking man said, "All right, climb down." James and Israel jumped to the ground then helped the women and children out. They were herded, with the rest of the civilians, to an open grassy area near the station and ordered to sit down. A half dozen soldiers stood guard. Fifty yards away, a handful of Confederate prisoners were also surrounded by Yankees.

While James and his companions sat and waited to see what would happen next, the dead were being gathered and separated. The Union casualties were laid out in one area while the Confederates were carried past the group of civilians and placed in another. James had mixed feelings when he saw the bodies of Sheriff Wilkes and the other members of the posse carried past. Regardless of what Wilkes had tried to do to James and in spite of his sense of relief; he was still sorry about the end result. And he did not know what to expect from the Yankees, but he had to admit that for the time being, the enemies of his native South had saved his life. Sheriff Wilkes would threaten them no more.

There were approximately fifteen men, women, and children who had been passengers on the train, not counting James and his companions. They, too, had been very fortunate to survive the attack on the train station with no more than a few cuts from flying glass. Most of the people were trying to get to their homes or the homes of friends or relatives in Morgantown. Of all the men in the group, James was the only white man young enough for military service.

After almost an hour of waiting, a major came out to inspect the civilians, apparently to determine whether or not any of them appeared suspicious, warranting an interrogation. He looked the crowd over very carefully, then turned to one of the guards and said, "Send these people on their way." Then he looked at James and said, "Not you. You follow me."

When James stood up, so did everyone else. "Just you," said the major, pointing a finger at James.

"These people are traveling with me, sir."

"Then have them sit back down and wait."

James motioned for the others to sit, and then he followed the officer into the station. The major took a seat behind a desk and James stood facing him.

"Who are you and what is your reason for being in Morgantown?"

For the first time in quite a while, James introduced himself using his real name. Then, in elaborate detail, he told his story, all to the fascination of the Yankee major. When he was finished, the officer said, "If you're telling the truth, it sounds like we saved your ass."

"Yes, sir, you did. Before I heard that bugle blow, I was convinced that I was as good as hanged."

"So you and your lady friend helped those slaves escape from way down in Georgia?"

"Just the man and the boy, sir. The woman and her daughter were picked up in Virginia. They are all one family but they were separated a few years ago when the woman was sold to a man in Petersburg."

James had already explained everything and he suspected that the major was trying to catch him in a lie.

"Well that is quite a story, Mr. Langdon, and one that might be worthy of praise. But you understand why I would have reason to doubt it. After all, your people *are* fighting a war to preserve slavery. What makes you see things differently?"

"Who can say, Major? I just don't believe in it. I've turned my back on practically my whole life. I have my family believing that I work for the Confederate government. If they knew the truth it would break their hearts. It isn't easy to live with."

"Indeed," the major replied. "But that is what I am a just a little concerned about . . . that you work for the Confederate government."

"No, sir," said James. "I am not a spy. I can prove that my story is true."

"How?"

"Do you know where Mapletown is?"

"I do. We came through Mapletown on our way here."

"Then get in touch with Reverend Percy Pyle at the Mapletown Community Church. That is where we are headed. The reverend can vouch for me."

The major studied James for a moment then he said, "Very well. When our business is finished here I will be moving my cavalry detachment back across the state line. But I won't make you wait around while we destroy the contraband here. I will release you in the custody of three of my men. They will escort you to Mapletown and question the reverend. But I warn you, if you're lying, my men will place you under arrest and you will likely face a military tribunal."

"I am in your debt, Major. You have not misplaced your trust."

"Tell me something, Mr. Langdon. Once you've reached Mapletown, do you plan on going south again?"

"Yes, sir, I do. I intend to do what I can until slavery is gone from existence."

The major smiled and said, "You were born with more than your share of courage, I'll give you that. I guess we all fight in our own way for what we believe in. Good luck to you."

"Thank you, Major." The three men picked for the escort helped James and Israel unload the horse and wagon. Although none of the soldiers did or said anything out of line, James had the distinct feeling that to them, his Georgia accent made him a Rebel in spite of his worthy intentions. They were helpful but not exactly cordial.

James never felt better than he did when the Mapletown Community Church came into view.

FOURTEEN

A Tale of Two Weddings

Reverend Pyle happily verified James's story for the three soldiers and they were on their way. "It's wonderful to see you again, James. I see that you have a young lady with you this time. Will she be going back to Georgia when you leave?"

"No, Reverend. There is nothing left for her in Georgia and it might not be safe for her to go there. I intend to find a place for her to live here in Mapletown, and I also intend to ask her to be my wife."

"I think that's wonderful, James. Does this mean that you will be settling down?"

"If you mean am I finished going south, the answer is not yet. I will stay for a while, but eventually I will be leaving again."

"Far be it from me to stand in the way of such a noble cause, James, but you know this war may eradicate slavery in time."

"I pray that it does, Reverend. But for now, there are still many people suffering. My only other concern right now is Polly. I have enough money for her to live on for quite a while. When my work is finished there will be time for us."

Until Reverend Pyle could make the arrangements to send Israel, Emaline, and the children on to Canada, they were all made comfortable in the room beneath the church. James asked the reverend if Polly could spend a day or two at the parsonage until a house could be rented. He was told that it would be no problem finding room for both of them.

It was a Friday evening in early August and the weather was very hot, but the humidity was very low. When supper was finished, James asked Polly to go for a stroll. As they walked hand in hand along Main Street, he reflected on the past four months and found it difficult to believe all that had happened. He thought about the trips he'd made, the close calls he'd had, and how easily the world could now be without him. But on that peaceful evening, in the middle of all that was going on, it was as if he'd found a place that was protected from any kind of threat. It would be so easy for him to marry Polly, go to Canada with Israel and Emaline, and let the devil take the rest of the world. But he discovered in the beginning that he had a purpose in life, a pledge to fulfill and he couldn't just walk away no matter how much he wanted to. James felt that God had guided him so far, and he would continue on, regardless of the end result. That was the measure of his faith and trust. In the meantime, he would secure for himself a true personal reason for facing up to the challenges that life had earmarked for him.

When they reached a quiet spot on the edge of town beneath a spreading chestnut tree, James guided Polly to a public bench and asked her to sit.

"My father once told me that for some men, the instant they meet the right woman, their destiny becomes something over which they have no control. I guess he knew this because it is exactly what happened when he met my mother. Now I understand what he meant because it happened to me the first day I saw you at Baxter's. I believe that telling you that I love you is now a formality. It is something that you already know. So I will set aside the formality and ask you if you will marry me so that destiny may have its way."

At first Polly seemed to be overcome with emotion. Then she locked her fingers around his neck, kissed him and said, "Never let it be said that I stood in the way of destiny. This moment is like a dream come true."

They sat for a while longer, immersed in that most pleasant of conversations, that of young people in love; conversation about the future, children, and a home.

After a while they returned to the parsonage to speak to the reverend about their intentions. "I would be delighted to marry you," said the reverend. "There is something else that I want to ask the two of you. What would you say to a double wedding?"

"Double wedding?" James asked him.

"Yes. I am sending Israel, Emaline, and the children on their way Sunday night. They asked me to marry them before they leave. You know that they have never had the chance before. They'll need witnesses and so will you. Why not stand up for each other?" James and Polly looked at each other and nodded in unison. "Splendid," said the reverend. "Then it is all settled. On Sunday evening we'll have a quiet ceremony at the church."

That night James could not sleep as a child cannot sleep on Christmas Eve. He simply could not quell the excitement he felt inside. There was, however, one undeniable damper. The wedding would not be entirely as he wished. He would never have believed that such a special day in his life would not include his family. He imagined how hurt his parents and his sisters would be if they knew they were missing such an event. James missed them all very much and the feeling seemed to be magnified by the circumstances. He worried about his parents' health, especially since his last visit. It hadn't been since the day he first left home that he'd seen Ashton and Kate. He found himself cursing the war that he believed to be a punishment for slavery. And slavery, besides being the most evil practice ever conceived by the mind of man, had put him at odds with his father. Then, he remembered, if not for both of those things, he probably never would have met Polly. He remembered the saying: when God closes a door he opens a window.

On Saturday morning he found a lovely furnished house for rent not far from the church. It was small but in very good condition; just perfect for a newlywed couple. If not for certain circumstances, James felt that he could live there happily ever after. Except for his family he did not miss Georgia, which surprised him greatly. He was beginning to grow quite fond of the quaint little town, already thinking of it as the place where he was married. Only one more day and it would become reality.

On Sunday morning, James became obsessed with time. The clock became his enemy as the more he coaxed it the slower it seemed to move. But everyone involved had to be careful and quiet because, aside from the reverend and his wife, only James and Polly knew that the slaves were hiding in the church. Maybe there was no slavery in the North, but still most whites did not see blacks as equals and thus they had no sympathy or tolerance for them. If word got out that a white couple and a black couple were to be married at the same ceremony, it could cause trouble.

At eight o'clock that evening, they were all assembled in the church. The intended couples took their places, Mrs. Pyle kept a vigil at the window, and the children watched from the front pew.

Reverend Pyle performed a lovely service, and by eight-thirty everyone was helping the slaves, who were at last a real family, prepare for the trip to Canada. It was a difficult parting, for all they'd been through had forged a friendship. Emaline promised to write so that everyone would know how they were doing.

At half past nine, Reverend Pyle's friend was behind the church with his covered wagon and the happy couples exchanged their final farewells. To Israel and Emaline, James said, "There is something that has bothered me for the longest time and I must dispose of it before you leave. Ever since I met Israel, the only reference to your son that I have ever heard is, 'boy.' It's gotten to the point that I have accepted it as his name. So let me ask you now, what do you call your son?"

The couple looked at each other for a minute and then Israel said, "When dat boy got born we never did give him no name. If you is born a slave you is nuthin and all you ever gonna be is nuthin. It don't matter if you jes call something what it be so maybe you jes call a dog a dog. So we jes call him boy cause dats what he be." James immediately understood the full meaning of Israel's explanation and he felt ashamed. He realized how sad it was that a race of human beings could be put so far down that it didn't even seem important to them to name their children.

"I am sorry," said James. "I didn't mean to cause you any pain today of all days."

"It's all right, James," said Emaline. "We know without doubt that it is through no fault of a wonderful man like you. Hopefully it will ease your mind to know that Israel and I talked about this very thing last night. From this day on our son has a name that he can be proud of. We called him James."

An uncomfortable moment had been turned into joy and James was deeply moved by the honor. He extended his hand to the young man and said, "I am pleased to meet you, James."

The boy offered his small hand in return and he replied, "Thank you for my mama, my sister, and my name."

The wagon rolled away; James and Polly watched until it was out of sight. Then they said goodnight to Mr. and Mrs. Pyle and strolled arm in arm up the street to their little house.

FIFTEEN

A True Taste of War

For the next few months James settled into married life, and for a while he was so preoccupied that he nearly put all other things out of his mind. He even went so far as to take a part-time job at the bank in Mapletown. Nevertheless, he kept telling Polly that when spring came he would be going south again.

Christmas came and went for the first time without seeing his family in Georgia. James wrote a very long letter giving many false reasons why he couldn't be there and the gesture only made him feel worse. Polly was a wonderful wife and she understood his anxiety, especially since it was her first Christmas without her mother. But the love and happiness they shared was enough to keep them content.

In March 1862, the war was in its second year. The two dormant armies had come to life again and they were on the move. There was fighting in Strasburg, Kernstown, and many other places in Virginia. Then, in early April, a colossal battle at Shiloh, Tennessee cost the lives of almost twenty-four thousand soldiers. It was constantly becoming more dangerous to travel from North to South and back.

James knew that Polly had so much respect for him that she would never attempt to sway his judgment. He knew that she hid the deep fear she felt for his safety and secretly wished that he would decide to stay with her in Mapletown. It was not to be, however, and on April 25th, James quit his job at the bank and was preparing to leave.

He knew that leaving Polly would be extremely difficult and when the moment came he nearly caved in. "I know you understand why I must go," he told her. "There are matters that must be put right before this country can move forward. It is a huge undertaking and I cannot be at peace with myself until I know that I have done my part. I believe that you'll be safe here and that is the thought that enables me to go."

"I do understand, James, and I will keep your home and I will be here each time you return. Then one day, when all is right, you will never leave me again."

Then they held each other tightly, exchanged endearments, and James mounted Star and turned her south.

As Polly watched after him she wondered if she was making a mistake. Although she believed it wrong to say anything that might have caused James to abandon his principals, was she just as wrong for not telling him the real reason she wanted him to stay.

A few miles from Mapletown, James left the road, traveling over hill and hollow until he reached Virginia. Avoiding patrols from either army was essential because both sides were highly suspicious of anyone who wasn't in uniform. On this trip his first priority was to make his way back to Georgia and visit his family. The war had not yet seriously damaged the Deep South, if it ever would; the only real effect was from the Union blockade. And who could say how long it would take for that move to weaken the Confederacy's ability to wage war. All things considered, James was expecting to find everything in reasonable order at home.

For three days he traveled along the western border of Virginia encountering no opposition along the way. By the evening of April 28th he had crossed into Kentucky, and by nightfall he decided to make camp near Cumberland Gap. After a night's rest, his plan was to head into Tennessee toward Chattanooga, then continue south into Georgia.

The night was very peaceful and it was not at all difficult to imagine there was no war going on. As he waited for sleep to take over, he thought about his parents, his sisters, and how anxious he was to see them. Naturally, he thought about Polly. After having been with her for several months, the separation was already causing a serious longing in his heart. He wished she were with him . . . he wished she could meet his family.

By and by, sleep interrupted his thoughts and he drifted off with the fire burning brightly. By morning it had died out but for a spiral of smoke still rising from the ashes. James awoke with a start.

"Rise and shine, mister," said the man dressed in butternut. He sat up and looked around at the grim, bearded faces. There were eight of them in all and none of them were wearing shoes or hats; their uniforms were dirty and full of holes. The man who had awakened him seemed to be in charge. "Who the hell are you and what's your business here?" he demanded. If nothing else, James was getting used to that same old question and he immediately resumed the practice of withholding his real name. "My name is Sterling Hargraves and I'm just passing through on my way to Georgia."

"Georgia, huh? You a deserter?"

"No. I'm not in the army. I've been working as a slave catcher. It's big business these days."

"I reckon it is for sure, but there ain't no time to be worryin about them rich plantation owners now. Let em run down their niggers their own selves. We need to be worryin about killin Yankees right now. Ifen we run across a nigger we jus shoot him dead and leave him lay."

There was a noticeable tone of unfriendliness in the man's voice. James guessed that he was irritated by the fact that James wasn't in the army. He decided to try a little levity to ease the tension. "From what I've heard, our armies are given the Yanks all they can handle."

"What do ya mean our armies?" snapped the disgruntled soldier. "You ain't in the army, remember? You are runnin around fillin your pockets whilst we is getting shot at and figurin ourselves lucky if we can do it on a full belly. But I reckon you'll be gettin a taste of it now."

"Meaning what?"

"Meanin you'll be comin with us. Our camp is jus a short piece from here. We smelt your smoke and the major sent us over here to either shoot whoever we found or bring em back to camp. Lucky for you you're a Georgia boy. And since you ain't in the army you can bet you're gonna get your chance to join up."

Then the soldier pointed at Star and said, "Our captain had his horse shot out from under him two days ago. He's gonna be real happy when I tell him I found him another."

Once again, James was disarmed and forced to walk ahead of his captors about a quarter of a mile to the Confederate camp. It was indeed a dismal turn of events. For the time being, he decided the best thing he could do was to cooperate and see what developed. Maybe the commanding officer would be more reasonable and James could talk his way out of the situation. However, when he was taken before Major Samuel Rodgers, commanding the infantry detachment of the Army of the Mississippi under General P.G.T. Beauregard, James quickly realized that he wasn't going to talk his way out of anything.

The major was a middle aged man with cold blue eyes and a stern disposition. He was easily six feet tall with broad shoulders and the left sleeve of his uniform coat was empty from the elbow down. James sensed that losing the arm had a great deal to do with the major's demeanor as his frustration with the difficulty caused by the missing limb was obvious. When he spoke it was through gritted teeth as if speaking was an effort and he'd rather if others could simply read his mind. As a result, he spoke quickly using short sentences.

"How old are you, boy?"

"Almost twenty-one, sir."

"You heard of the new draft law?"

"No, sir, I haven't."

"Explain it to him, Sergeant," he said to the soldier who had escorted James to the tent.

"President Davis just approved a Congressional proposal that requires a military draft in the Confederate States. The law says that all persons livin in the Confederate States betwixt the ages of eighteen and thirty-five will be held to be in the military service and that means you, Georgia boy."

"What's your name, boy?" asked the major.

"Sterling Hargraves, sir."

"It's Private Hargraves now. Go with the sergeant. He'll see to your needs." James stood and stared at the major, completely dumbfounded.

"You've been given an order, Private! It is customary to render a salute."

James raised his right hand over his right eye then dropped it after the major executed the same. Then he turned and walked out ahead of the sergeant. Once outside, he was directed to a supply wagon and instructed to remove his shirt and trousers. "What for?" James asked.

"Cause you're one of us now, Georgia boy, and you gotta look like one of us." The sergeant climbed into the wagon and after a few minutes of rooting through a large trunk, he jumped down and handed James a gray flannel shirt, a butternut jacket, and trousers to match. "This was Shelby Jenkins's uniform. He was about your size. Poor Shelby took a ball through the heart a couple days ago. New uniforms is hard to come by so we been keepin some from our dead in case we pick up a new recruit like you. You already got a hat and what appears to be a mighty fine pair of boots. That makes you better dressed than most of us. But we all is lookin to get some new footwear tomorrow."

"Tomorrow?"

"Yep. Over yonder a mile or so is a Yankee camp. We is waitin for some reinforcements that be due in by tonight. In the morning we is gonna attack them Yankees. Then we be getting some Union leather for our feet. All we gotta do is shoot a Yank who be wearin our boot size. That is, them of us that don't catch some Union lead first. Now get that uniform on and I'll get you some grub. Then you can get acquainted with some a the boys."

The sergeant walked away and the first thought that rushed to James's mind was to hightail it into the woods. But he'd never get away on foot. Even on horseback his chances would be slim and it was broad daylight, which left no way of getting to Star. In addition to that, his revolver had been taken, leaving him no way of defending himself. In complete disgust he put on the uniform, which was filthy, stinking of old sweat, and ill fitting. Not only that, but the shirt and the jacket had large holes in the front surrounded by dried blood stains. It nearly made him sick to be wearing a uniform that had so recently clothed a dead man.

Now he was a Confederate conscript when just an hour before he was on his way home to Georgia. He tried to remain calm and think positively with the intention of wining the trust of his new comrades. Then perhaps an opportunity would present itself when night fell again.

To a certain extent, James found it interesting conversing with the other soldiers; listening to their stories about where they were from and why they were fighting. For most it seemed to be a territorial issue. They saw the Yankees as invaders who had to be stopped and forced to go back to where they came from. It was as if they were fighting a war over trespassing. Not one man that James talked to owned more than a few acres of land and none of them owned a single slave. James thought it sad that the average Rebel was drawn into the war because of the rich plantation owners. They were the people with the money, the power, the influence in government, and the people who owned the slaves—people like his father and his uncles. These soldiers were fighting and dying to protect the interests of the wealthy. In truth, the men who filled the rank and file had very little to gain or lose with union or disunion.

However, the wheels had been set in motion and they were all caught up in it now. Many had to admit that the war had started out as an adventure; an adventure they now realized they could have lived without, especially since the revelation that it would be no short war.

Shortly after dark, the expected reinforcements reached the camp. They were South Carolina troops all the way from Charleston. James guessed there must have been three or four thousand, bringing the Confederate force up to roughly nine thousand men. He wondered how many men the Yankees had.

After an evening meal of something that James could not exactly describe, except to say that it might have contained squirrel meat, the troops began to turn in. Most of the conversation had dried up and he suspected that everyone was thinking about what was to happen the following morning. He could not deny that his own thoughts were the same. It was difficult to imagine what it must be like. The closest he had come to the experience was the fight at the train station in Morgantown. He could vividly remember the horror of that morning and he had not even been directly involved. It would be much different to charge an enemy position on the field of combat. It was a given that many of the men in camp that night would die the following day. It was also very possible that he might be one of them.

In spite of the impending threat, James could see that escape from the camp would be impossible. About an hour before sunrise the men began to stir. James could smell coffee cooking; the sound of meat sizzling in a frying pan was mixed with the murmur of quiet conversation. Although he knew that the meal would not make one's mouth water, he was very hungry and hoped that someone would offer him breakfast. He needn't have worried because before long the sergeant who had supplied him with the uniform stopped by.

"How'd ya sleep, Georgia boy?" he asked. "I've heard a man's last night on earth he sleeps sound cause there ain't no worries left to keep him awake."

"Was last night my last sleep on earth?" James asked.

"Any man who ain't thinkin so the night before a battle is a fool. Anyhow, I got some grub cookin over yonder and after you've et I'll be takin you over to the major's tent."

"Any special reason?" The sergeant stopped and looked at him in a very strange way. It was rather, thought James, the way you might look at a man who is standing on a gallows. "You is bein assigned to the 5th South Carolina. They requested a man for a special job." James prodded the sergeant for a clearer answer but the man would say no more. When he had finished eating he was taken over to Major Rodgers's tent and told to wait outside. "Wait here for Lieutenant Trask. He'll explain things to you." Then the sergeant said, "So long, Georgia boy."

One thing that James was completely aware of was just how much his fellow soldiers resented him for being a conscript. They took it as a personal insult if a Southerner didn't volunteer to defend his country. It was for that reason he was standing outside the tent waiting for Lieutenant Trask. He was being forced to volunteer for the second time in twenty-four hours.

After waiting for about an hour, the lieutenant finally came out of the tent. James saluted without a prompt. The officer ignored the formalities and stepped up to stand so close that James could smell cigar smoke mixed with stale liquor on his breath. He was a large, burly creature with long greasy hair and an unkempt beard. The thing that bothered James most was that he was sure he'd met the man before. Then, when the lieutenant spoke, he was able to place him.

"I reckon you must be the new recruit. Tell me something, boy, do you think you're too good to join the army or are you jes plain yeller?" There was no mistaking the ogre's rough voice. It was Virgil, the slave catcher from Greenville, South Carolina; the man James had tied to a tree along with his partner, Henry; the man who swore he'd kill James if he ever saw him again. How terribly true, thought James, that it really was a small world. The only thing left to ponder was whether or not Virgil recognized him. If he did he dropped no hints, which bolstered James's confidence a little. He did not consider an oaf like Virgil to be intelligent enough to carry off a convincing deception. So James maintained his composure and pretended he had never seen the lieutenant before.

"I am not a coward, sir, and I do not think that I am too good to be in the army. I will prove to be a good soldier. But, my revolver was taken away. Could you have it returned to me, sir?"

The lieutenant smiled, showing the brown teeth James remembered having seen before. "You ain't gonna need a gun, boy. You are gonna be the new color bearer."

The realization struck like a bolt of lightning. Virgil might as well have handed him a shovel and told him to dig his own grave. The color bearer led the army into battle. He was right out front, waving the flag, the prefect, and the favorite target of the enemy. James had read accounts of battles where as many as a dozen color bearers were killed. What better way to teach a conscript a lesson? There was no way out. James was sure that he would die that morning.

"Move out, Private," said Virgil. "The regiment is forming up."

James was marched to the front of the long column of twos. A soldier ran up and handed him a wooden pole with a tattered battle flag attached to it. "Hold it high," he said.

When the order was given, James started off through the woods leading the column with Virgil on horseback right behind him. As he marched along, he thought of the same things he imagined all doomed men thought about. First was his lovely wife. He knew deep down that she had wished him to stay in Mapletown with her. He also knew that she would never have tried to change his mind. He could see now how selfish he had been and it was very painful to know that he would not have the chance to say he was sorry. Then he thought about his parents and his sisters. Perhaps if he ended up dead in a Confederate uniform they could at least be proud of him. They would never know what he'd been doing since first leaving home. That was some consolation, he thought.

In seemingly no time at all they reached the edge of the woods and Virgil shouted for the column to halt. James could see across a half mile of open ground—the whole way to the Union defenses. The Yankees were well dug in behind a wall of earth and felled trees. At least six cannons were visible as well as several Yankee flags planted atop the earthworks. Virgil shouted another command, dividing the column of twos with a single column going right and the other column going left.

When the men were spread out along the tree line, Virgil dismounted and walked up to James. "When I give the command you run at them Yankees like the devil hisself is right behind you cause he will be. And you can bet your ass if the Yankees don't get you the devil will you nigger lovin son of a bitch."

So there it was. Virgil *did* remember him after all and he was all set to carry out the threat he'd made a year before. James saw his chance of survival go from nothing to something less than that. Virgil got back on his horse; drew his sword, and James took a deep breath. Then Virgil yelled, "Charge!"

The peaceful morning was decimated by the famous Rebel yell; James took off running as fast as he possibly could. He held the flag high and screamed at the top of his lungs if only to live a moment longer by denying Virgil a reason to shoot him in the back. As he raced across the open field, he could see the blue clad soldiers getting into position. Thousands of rifle barrels were leveled along the top of the dirt wall, the head and shoulders of an officer raising his sword was visible as he rode his horse back and forth behind the line. James's only hope was to make it to the earthworks unscathed and be taken prisoner.

Halfway to the Yankee line, the cannon opened up, lobbing canister at the attacking rebels. Through the deafening noise, the screams of those hit by flying metal were horribly audible. As they got closer and closer to those hostile muzzles, James felt like every one of them was pointed directly at him. Then, suddenly enough to make it seem almost unexpected, the rifles belched a maelstrom of smoke and fire. James was slammed to the ground as a bullet struck his right shoulder and another hit his left side. He landed hard on his back just in time to see Virgil's head ripped from his body, throwing him backwards from the saddle. Someone tore the flagstaff from his grip as he ran by, stabbing James's hands with several large splinters. Although the battle continued on for some time after he was hit, the sights and sounds slowly faded away as he lost consciousness.

SIXTEEN

No More a Rebel Soldier

When James opened his eyes the sun was going down, which meant he had been lying on the field for many hours. It did not take a lot of time to collect his thoughts because there was not a lot to remember. He had charged a Yankee position that morning, and upon reaching a spot within a hundred yards of the line he was shot in the right shoulder and left side. The important thing now was to receive medical attention.

What had begun as a burning sensation was now a deep, aching throb. His throat was parched and he imagined that his agony would decrease greatly if he could just have some water. The battle was long since over but all was not quiet. Everywhere around him were the cries of other wounded begging for help. James could also hear muffled voices; probably stretcher bearers, but he couldn't tell where they were or if they were Yankee or Confederate. It did not matter to James who it was. He knew his wounds were serious and that he needed attention soon.

Mustering all of his strength he attempted to rise to a sitting position, but the pain in his side was too great. All he could do was lie still, wait, and be grateful that it was not winter lest he freeze to death.

For a time he dozed off, waking after dark when someone kicked the heels of his boots. James opened his eyes and was blinded by the lantern being held over him. "You alive, Reb?" said a voice. With a raspy reply, James confirmed the fact that he was indeed still alive. "Grab his arms, Joe."

The first man sat the lantern on the ground and took James by the ankles while the second man grabbed his wrists. He could not hold back the screams as the two men hoisted him a couple feet in the air and laid him on a stretcher. The painful ride ended about ten minutes later when he was carried into a dimly lit tent and placed on a makeshift operating table. The Yankee surgeon examined him carefully and said, "All things considered, you've gotten off pretty lucky, young man. One bullet cut a deep gash in your shoulder but it did not hit the bone. That bit of good fortune has saved your arm. The wound in your side is worse, but the bullet went straight through and I don't believe it hit any of your vitals. If I have any real concerns it would be with infection. A bullet has an unfortunate tendency to drive pieces of material from the uniform into the flesh, which can cause serious problems. Your uniform is grade A filthy and no doubt infested with all kinds of germs. I will clean the wounds as best I can and dress them. Then you will be taken by ambulance to the hospital at Jefferson Barracks in Missouri."

The surgeon administered laudanum then set to work, first removing the splinters from James's hands. During the procedure he lost consciousness again and when next he awoke, he was in an ambulance on his way to the hospital.

For many days and nights, the terrible journey continued until the train of ambulances reached their destination. By the time James was taken to the ward for enemy wounded he was delirious, suffering from chills and a very high fever. The ward was kept under guard, but very few of the patients had the strength to get out of bed let alone try to escape. The care that James received at the hospital was better than the care at the field hospital and still it posed a real challenge to the medical staff to bring his infection under control. Days became weeks and weeks turned into months. In the end, it was owing to James's youth and strong will that he was able to survive.

After six months in bed he was finally able to get up and walk around. His wounds had healed, but he was weak from so much inactivity and his freedom was limited to a small fenced in yard behind the ward. Sometimes he passed an entire day just walking the fence line around and around to get some exercise. As he walked he thought about Polly and how she was doing. He knew that she must be frantic with worry wondering what had happened to him. But he was a prisoner of war and not afforded the privilege of sending correspondence.

Then one afternoon, the doctor in charge of the hospital, Major Kendal, came into the ward to see James. After a brief examination the doctor told him that he was no longer in need of medical care. "In fact," said the major, "you will soon be leaving here for a prisoner of war camp. But that is not really as bad as it sounds."

"How is that, sir?"

"Last July, the two governments agreed to parole or exchange all prisoners within ten days of their capture. Unfortunately for you, you were wounded or you would have been released long ago. When you get to the prison I'm sure you won't have to wait long. For that, you will be very grateful. I hear that the conditions are nothing less than terrible." James thanked him for the care he'd been given as well as for the information.

In November 1862 he was transferred along with ten other men to the prison at Camp Douglas near Chicago. Upon arrival, the first thing James noticed was the near criminal lack of heat. One small stove in the middle of a room that measured roughly fifty feet by seventy-five feet did not stand a chance against the frigid air that passed constantly through numerous cracks in the walls. How thankful he was that before leaving Jefferson Barracks he was given a heavy overcoat, compliments of a man who had died from a head wound.

Looking past the cold, a man quickly realized that conditions went downhill from there. Rations were scarce and not fit to eat, usually consisting of a stale piece of hardtack and a rancid slice of beef or pork. Water was adequate for drinking but none for cleaning one's person, and even the icy weather could not stifle the human stench. But Major Kendal had been right about the exchange program; consequently, the prison was not overcrowded. In less than a week he was taken before Colonel James Mulligan, an Irishman and ex-Chicago politician who served as camp commandant.

When James entered the office, he stood at attention in front of the desk and waited for Colonel Mulligan to put down the folder he was reading.

"You are Private Sterling Hargraves of the 5ᵗʰ South Carolina, wounded and captured at Cumberland Gap, Kentucky?"

"Yes, sir."

"Well, Private, I am sure it will not upset you to learn that you will be exchanged and leaving here in about three days."

"If you please, sir," said James. "I do not wish to be exchanged, instead I wish to be paroled and sent home."

"I see. Am I to understand that you have had enough of the 5ᵗʰ South Carolina and perhaps the fighting as well?"

"Not exactly, sir. The fact is, I never joined the Southern army."

"I beg your pardon," said the Colonel.

Once again James found himself telling the story, in detail, of his adventures since leaving home in April 1861. In conclusion he said, "My real name is James Langdon and I wish to get to Pennsylvania to see my wife before resuming my mission. I do not consider you to be gullible, sir, and I am willing and able to provide you with names and locations of persons who can verify my story."

Like the Yankee major in Morgantown, Colonel Mulligan was more than a little surprised. "That is quite a story, young man. Such courage on the battlefield would be worthy of a medal. If your story *is* true, after all you've been through, do you really want to risk your life again?"

"Yes, sir, I do. The history of this country is about freedom and the sacrifices that were made to pay for it. What is the value of my life compared to an entire race of people in bondage? Yes, sir, I will risk my life again." For a moment, the colonel sat in silence. Then he said, "I will make the necessary inquiries, son, and if I find that what you are telling me is fact, I would offer to you this suggestion."

"Please, go on, sir."

"Why don't you consider joining the Union army?"

"That thought occurred to me at one time, Colonel, but I dismissed it. Mr. Lincoln is concerned with keeping the country together, North and South. While that is a worthwhile goal and one I wholeheartedly support, the president himself has stated that he will not interfere with slavery except, perhaps, to try to halt the expansion of it."

"How long has it been since you've seen a newspaper, James?"

"Months," James replied. The colonel opened a desk drawer and extracted a copy of the *Chicago Tribune* dated September 23rd, 1862. He handed the paper to James and said, "Read the story on the left hand column of page one."

James unfolded the paper and the headline he saw nearly jumped from the page. "PRESIDENT LINCOLN ANNOUNCES EMANCIPATION PROCLAMATION," he read aloud. He continued to read the story of the new proclamation that Lincoln had presented to his cabinet. When he finished, he looked at Colonel Mulligan and said, "This is wonderful."

"I thought you would be pleased," said the colonel. "Now you can see why I suggested that you join our army. Once this goes into effect, the war will not only be about union but about liberation as well. As our armies sweep through the South, freed Negroes will be left in their wake. You can fight alongside thousands of men whose mission is the same as your own. There is strength in numbers. It would be safer for you in the army than going south alone. We need men with your kind of dedication because the sooner we win this war, the sooner we can bury slavery in an unmarked grave."

James could find no way to dispute the colonel's argument. If the North was underwriting freedom for the slaves, then that is where he felt he should be.

"You've convinced me, Colonel. I would like to join the Union Cavalry under one condition."

"Name it."

"I must first return to Pennsylvania to see my wife."

"If your story is verified, the condition shall be granted. I can guarantee you a thirty day furlough before you report for active duty. You say that you grew up on a large plantation in Georgia?"

"Yes, Colonel, I did."

"I imagine that you have some fine horses on this plantation?"

"Yes, sir. We have some of the finest thoroughbred horses in the world."

"Then you must be a pretty good horseman; I assume you ride well."

"Proficiently, sir."

"Yes, that is what I was hoping you'd say. I am having a thought, Mr. Langdon. I am going on the premise that your desire to join the cavalry stems from your lifelong capabilities with horses. From the outset of this war, when you stacked our advantages up against the Confederacy's, we came out first in most categories, but to this point, there is one area where the South beats us every time: a cavalry battle. We have many farm boys who are familiar with horses, but they are mostly draft animals. They can ride well enough to stay in the saddle, but when it comes to maneuvering, when it comes to expertise as a mounted soldier, they simply cannot compete with Southern boys like you. I have some political connections in Chicago and a modicum of pull in the War Department; I would like to send a few telegrams and see if I can secure a commission for you based on your much needed ability."

"I would appreciate that very much, sir," said James.

"Splendid. I will see what I can do. I think you would be a real asset. I'll have my orderly find a spot for you in the guards' barracks. Maybe the next few days here can be passed more pleasantly than it's been to this point."

"I appreciate all that you're doing, Colonel. I will try to repay your kindness with more than adequate service." James assumed the position of attention, saluted Colonel Mulligan, but the colonel extended his hand and said, "I will let you know the minute I receive some information from your references and from the War Department."

With that, he was taken to the guards' barracks, afforded the opportunity to take a long, hot bath, given clean clothing, and favored with a decent meal.

Two days later he was called into Colonel Mulligan's office again. James could tell from the colonel's lively mood that his telegrams had garnered the desired replies.

"I now have the privilege of addressing you as Lieutenant James Langdon," he said. "Everything is in order for your furlough as well. One more thing,

Lieutenant; I am sure that you would prefer to be assigned to a Cavalry Corp in the east and not here in the west."

"Yes, sir, that would be my preference."

"Understandable. For that reason, when your furlough is over, you will need to report to the War Department in Washington for your assignment. However, I will send you into Chicago to the quartermaster for your uniform and weapon issue. They will also fit you out with a mount. Then you may leave for home. The very best of luck to you." This time the colonel returned James's salute; an hour later he was on his way to Chicago.

After the trip to the quartermaster, James was adequately supplied with a complete issue of everything needed for his position and rank. Finally, he was directed to the corral behind the warehouse to pick a mount. It was not until that moment that he truly felt the stinging loss of his beautiful horse, Star. He wondered where she might be. Nothing in the corral could compare with Star, but he settled for a coal black gelding that was only about two years old. His second disappointment was with the stiffness of the military saddle after having had the pleasure of the custom saddle he'd received on his eighteenth birthday.

Once he was packed and ready to leave, however, all disappointments were gone and forgotten; pushed from his mind by the thought of heading to Mapletown to see Polly. His only concern was the uncertainty of how she would react to his joining the army. For that reason, he packed his uniform inside his bedroll so that he might choose the right time to tell her.

James believed he had done the right thing, but like most young men in wartime, innocence is the first personality trait to go. He was glad that the president himself was now behind the eradication of slavery, but he was not naïve enough to think that suddenly all Northerners cared about the slaves. So he decided to pretend that *he* was using the Union army to accomplish *his* purpose instead of the other way around.

As for his family in Georgia, he now realized that he may not see them until the war was over; maybe it was for the best. James had come to believe that nothing can so radically change the course of people's lives like war, and few things demand a higher personal price. He had already been so deeply separated from his father because of his beliefs, and now, even if his father didn't know it, he had committed the ultimate sin by joining the Union. He couldn't possibly know if there would be anything left of the relationship with his family when the war was over. For now he was stuck in the moment like so many others; putting his future on hold, waiting to see the outcome. All he could do was focus on his priorities: his wife and a Union victory.

SEVENTEEN

New Born Perspective

Heavy snow was falling and the wind was blowing hard as James headed southeast out of Chicago. His intention was to push hard, spending as little time possible making the trip. Thirty days would go by quickly and leaving home continued to be more difficult each time. In spite of his best effort, contending with the weather, it took three days for him to reach the western border of Pennsylvania. The spunky little gelding he had chosen, which he decided to call Tar because of his color, held up well over the long trip.

James dismounted to give the animal one last breather before covering the remaining thirty miles to Mapletown. It was hard to believe that he was so close. His long ordeal had been exceedingly more difficult without any communication with Polly.

It was seven p.m. and pitch dark when he reached the edge of town. Snow was falling when he left Chicago and it was falling again as he made his way up Main Street. It was very cold and the light in the windows of the houses he passed increased the yearning for his own fireside. As he approached the little house he shared with Polly, he could see a familiar horse and buggy parked out front. Upon closer inspection he could see that it was Reverend Pyle's rig. It was a comforting sight. James was grateful that they had such good friends in Mapletown, friends that would keep Polly from becoming too lonely.

Weary of the saddle, James climbed down and led Tar to the stable behind the house. He gave the gelding a hasty rubdown and an ample helping of grain. Then he hurried to the front porch, and feeling almost like a stranger, knocked on the door. It was opened by the good reverend who was so surprised to see James that for an instant, he seemed not to recognize him. Then he reached out, took him by the hand and fairly pulled him inside. With his eyes tearing up he said, "My Lord, James! Where have you been? We've all been so worried and no matter how hard we tried, we could find nothing concerning your whereabouts."

The reverend's deep concern touched a nerve; James ignored his questions and said, "How is Polly, Reverend? How is my wife?"

"She is doing fine, James, just anxiety because of receiving no word from you. Mrs. Pyle is upstairs with her." James turned away and started for the stairs but Reverend Pyle grabbed his arm.

"Wait a minute, James. There is something you don't know, something Polly never told you."

"What is it, Reverend? Has something happened?" The reverend hesitated as if he were unsure of how to put his thoughts into words. Tension from sudden fear gripped James's whole body.

"There is someone else upstairs with Mrs. Pyle and Polly."

"Who?"

"Your son."

James stared at the reverend in disbelief. He was hit harder than when he'd been struck by bullets at the battle of Cumberland Gap. He sat down in the nearest chair and the reverend pulled another up beside him.

"My son? Polly was with child when I left?"

"Yes, James, she was."

"My God, why didn't she tell me?"

"Because she loves you, son, and she has so much respect for what you're doing. She was afraid that if she told you, you might have stayed home. For as much as she wanted you to, she didn't want to be the reason that you abandoned your cause. She knows how important it is and she believes in it as much as you do."

James felt a lump in his throat that was too large to swallow. The love he felt for Polly burst through every pore. "I guess she knows me pretty well. If I had known she was pregnant, I *would* have stayed. I still wish she'd told me. Polly is my whole life now. I still have other goals, other purposes; but I put nothing ahead of my wife . . . and my son. When did she give birth?"

"Two weeks ago. Everything went perfectly. She was in the capable hands of Dr. Pierce. You remember Dr. Pierce."

"Yes. He saved my life the first time I came to this town."

"Indeed. He stops by every few days to make sure everything is all right. Mrs. Pyle and I visit often. That is why we are here tonight."

"Bless you, Reverend. I am very grateful for your friendship."

"And you, James, you haven't told me what kept you."

"When I left, I intended to visit my family in Georgia. I was fallen upon by Confederate soldiers in Kentucky and forced to join their army. I was wounded in battle, once in the shoulder and again in the side. The Confederates were driven from the field and I was left behind. After months of fighting off an infection in a hospital in Missouri, I was sent to a prison camp near Chicago. I was paroled three days ago and I made my way here as fast as I could."

"Good heavens. You've had a difficult time of it. I knew something had gone wrong, but I wouldn't let Polly know what I was thinking, and I tried not to think the worst. But we all prayed very hard and the good Lord brought you home."

"That He did, Reverend. I am reluctant to tell Polly the story. I don't want to upset her, especially now."

"You're home, James. That alone will restore her spirits in no time. And now that the president is making war on slavery, there is no need to continue going south. The slaves will be freed—God and Mr. Lincoln will see to it."

"God, Mr. Lincoln, and me, Reverend."

"How is that, son?"

"I've joined the Union army."

"I see. How long will you be home?"

"I have to report before the end of December."

James got to his feet and began pacing the floor. "I'm so confused, Reverend. I just wish I'd known Polly was pregnant, maybe I wouldn't have acted so hastily. Does this make me irresponsible? Am I a terrible husband and father?"

The clergyman looked at James with a bewildered expression. "Of course not, son," he said. "This country is involved in a serious conflict but behind it are some very good reasons. Thousands of good men have left their families and marched off to make things right. You are one of those good men. You want a better world for your wife and son. No one can call you irresponsible."

"But will Polly understand? How much should she have to bear? And my family in Georgia; when this is over, if they should find out the truth, will they understand that I did what I felt was right?"

The reverend was pensive for a time. Then he said, "I have to be honest with you, James. I have to tell you that under the circumstances, this war may have driven a permanent wedge between you and your family in Georgia. You've tried to keep your true loyalty a secret . . . maybe for now you have. I doubt that you can do it forever and I don't believe that you should try. It is deceitful and I do not believe that you have the conscience for it. If they do find out, I think they may reject you. This war is more than just a difference in ideas. It is a matter of heritage, respect, and unconditional devotion. You, my friend, have had the misfortune of being caught flatfooted. You were born into a way of life that you do not agree with. This would have caused friction in any case. But now that it has come to bloodshed, it becomes a line you cannot cross and ever return."

"I understand," said James. "I have made my choice."

"I'm afraid so. Now you must take comfort in the fact that you made the *right* choice. And God has provided a failsafe: your wife and son. They must be your first concern now, and they *will* understand what you are doing and why."

"I think you're right, Reverend. Somehow I feel that everything will work out. Thank you."

"That is the peace of the Lord, James. That is the peace of the Lord."

At that moment, footsteps descended the stairs and Mrs. Pyle came into view. Her excitement rose quickly when she saw James. She rushed over and wrapped him in a motherly hug.

159

"Praise the Lord, James; we've all been so worried. Where have you been?"

The reverend interrupted her saying, "I will answer your questions later, dear. It's time we were getting home. James has had a long trip and he is anxious to go up and see his family."

"Polly is asleep," said Mrs. Pyle. "But I don't believe that she would be upset if you wake her."

"I can't thank you both enough."

"It was our pleasure, James," said the reverend. "It was good to see you, son. Take care of yourself and your little family."

When the Pyles were gone, James went over to the fireplace and knelt down by the crackling fire. It was wonderful to be home. In just a moment he would be going upstairs to see Polly and his new son. He could not believe how much his life had changed in two years; he could not believe how much he'd been through. He wondered what the next two years would bring. Hopefully the end of the war and perhaps a reunion with his parents and his sisters. In spite of the good reverend's words of warning, James decided to make a point of thinking positively. Maybe one day, all of his family would get a chance to know one another. Maybe out of the ashes of this fiery struggle would come a new and brighter tomorrow for all. Filled to the brim with anticipation, James stood up and headed for the stairs.

A coal oil lamp sitting on a table by the headboard cast a dim light over the room. After his eyesight had adjusted, he could see Polly lying on her side near the edge of the bed. In the back corner sat a cradle with a tiny, blanket-covered bundle inside. Quietly, he picked up the lamp, went over to the cradle and knelt down beside it. Holding the lamp aloft, he stared down at the sleeping baby. Between the blanket and the bonnet, he could see very little but he was looking at his son and the feeling was indescribable. James fell in love with him instantly. He began to think about all the time they would spend together and about all of the things he would teach him. He hoped that they would be close, the way James and his father had always been. Then his happiness was checked when he thought about what he might have done to that relationship. What if one day, for some reason, he found himself in a similar situation with his own son? How would he handle it?

James took one more prolonged gaze at the sleeping infant, and then he put the lamp back on the table and knelt down beside the bed. He kissed Polly gently on the forehead and she stirred a little. Then he stroked her cheek ever so lightly and she opened her eyes. A loving smile spread across her face and she said, "Am I dreaming?"

"No, dear, you're not dreaming."

"I was hoping I wasn't." She encircled his neck with her arms and kissed him long and passionately.

Then James whispered," My darling, why didn't you tell me? I wouldn't have gone away."

"I know, James, and that's what gave me the strength and the security I needed to let you go. I knew that I would be all right. We have some wonderful friends here. And what you are doing is so important."

"But not as important as you and our son."

"For now, knowing you feel that way is what really matters, James. You must carry that feeling with you and continue to do what you have to do. I cannot deny that it tears at me almost constantly when you're away. But I keep telling myself that it will not be forever, and it won't be. I tell myself that it is no more terrible for me than it is for you. There is a power inside all good men that just naturally takes over in time of crisis. The proper name for that power is duty. There is a horrible injustice living in this country that has existed for far too long. Now, our generation has the chance to put an end to it. In fact, we have the best chance because the struggle has already begun. We cannot let it slip away. It may have happened before we were born or it may have happened to our son's generation, but it didn't. It has come about now and we must and we will live through it."

James was so proud of his wife; he marveled at her courage. He had given much thought to finding a way to tell her he had joined the Union army. Now he was confident that she would accept the announcement and give him her complete support. Still, he thought, it could wait until tomorrow.

"It is getting late, Polly. Tomorrow I will tell you everything about my absence. For now, I am going to wash up, come to bed, and hold you until morning."

"Nothing in this world would be more pleasing."

Then James laughed and said, "Just one more thing, what is our son's name?"

"Oh," said Polly, laughing in turn, "I named him after his father."

James was overjoyed. He would not have chosen to do otherwise. After a thorough washing, he put on a comfortable cotton nightshirt and lay down next to his wife. In a few weeks he might be face to face with hell once again; but at that moment, he was in heaven.

The days that followed took James through a very pleasant life changing experience. He was learning to be a father, which simultaneously forged an even stronger bond with Polly. They talked about plans for the future. They also talked about the past. He told her that he never made it back to Georgia. He told her everything that had happened. In spite of her strong constitution, she was visibly upset when she learned that he had been wounded in battle. To that point he had gone to great lengths to keep his scars covered; now he revealed them. He did his best to assure her that the wounds were the result of being forced into an unusually dangerous situation. She actually seemed relieved about his joining the army because she knew that he would no longer be alone; the same sentiment, he told her, as Colonel James Mulligan's. Unlike the past, when he could not always be sure who his enemies were, now they would be more easily recognizable.

When the day came for James to leave, however, their courage was severely tested. Secretly, James cursed himself for his military commitment, and he could imagine Polly weeping uncontrollably the minute he was gone. He rode out of town with enough determination for an army; telling himself that if necessary, he would single handedly defeat the Rebels so that he could return to his beloved wife and son.

EIGHTEEN

The Bill of Goods

On December 30th, 1862, after a cold, lonely journey, James arrived in Washington D.C. He had heard a great deal about the Capital city but he had never been there before. Obtaining directions did not pose a problem because it seemed that half the men on the street were dressed in uniform. The first soldier he hailed was able to direct him to the location he sought, which was in President's Park on Pennsylvania Avenue. As he rode up the avenue, heading for the War Department, his fascination with the city courted his attention. He passed by the Capitol building with its unfinished dome. Scaffolding surrounded the structure but there were no workmen present on that cold winter day. He seemed to be walled in by huge government buildings with tall granite columns and facades like architectural marvels. The War Department itself, imposing in size, spoke of trepidation to all those who posed a threat to the nation it guarded.

Dressed in his new uniform and overcoat, he climbed the steps, excited at the prospect of his first assignment. Perhaps he might even catch a glimpse of President Lincoln.

Inside, the scene resembled bees around a hive. Long hallways were brightly lit illuminating the doorways to many offices. Wooden benches like church pews lined the walls, seating men waiting their turn to dispose of their business. Some were military personnel, officers of all ranks, and others were gentlemen dressed in fine suits of clothing. Everywhere, clerks with rolled up sleeves and hands filled with paperwork darted in and out of office doors. As James was unsure of where to go, he stopped a bookish little man with wire rimmed glasses and a receding hair line to ask for help. "Excuse me sir, my name is Lieutenant James Langdon and I'm here on orders to

163

receive my assignment. Could you direct me to the correct office?" The little man looked him up and down with a curious expression on his face. "What did you say your name was?"

"Lieutenant James Langdon." Again the man hesitated and James said, "Is anything wrong?"

"No, I mean, no. I'm sorry, Lieutenant. You caught me slightly off guard is all. I mean, your accent doesn't fit your uniform."

"I'm from Georgia if that helps you," James said.

"Again, I apologize, Lieutenant. It's just that the war is between the North and the South. You understand."

"Yes," said James, trying to control his anger. "Now can you assist me or should I come back when I've lost my accent?"

"No, Lieutenant, I can help you. You will have report to Mr. Scott's office. It's the last one on the left down this hallway," he said, pointing his finger. "Mr. Scott is the assistant secretary."

"Thank you," James replied.

"Good luck, Lieutenant." James didn't answer. Of course he understood how out of place his southern drawl must sound. Still, he hoped the conversation with the clerk was not an indication of how things were going to be. He was sure there were others whose loyalties demanded they chose against their homeland in the conflict. No doubt they, too, had some difficulty being accepted. He would have to give it some time. After he settled in with his unit, everything would be fine.

James walked down the hallway; Mr. Scott's name was on the last door on the left. He went inside and found, to his surprise, that it was not as crowded as he had expected. There were several desks arranged in two rows from front to back and behind them was a door to another office marked, private. He stood for just a minute before the man at the first desk on the right waved him back. "Can I help you, Lieutenant?" James handed him his orders along with his identification and said, "Lieutenant James Langdon reporting."

This time the man, younger, with a full head of red hair and a pleasant smile, did not seem to notice his southern accent. "Yes, Lieutenant Langdon," he said after reading the orders. "You are to be assigned to a cavalry unit. I will have to take this to Mr. Scott. Unfortunately, he is in a meeting and will be for most of the day. Where are you staying?"

"I have no accommodations at the moment. I arrived in the city about an hour ago."

"I see. I'm afraid that billeting for personnel in transit is very limited at present but I can suggest a place where you can find lodging."

"Very well," said James.

"Just a few blocks down the street you will find Willard's Hotel. It is very popular with military men and it is convenient to the War Department. I will record the fact that you have reported and are accounted for. Secure a room at Willard's and I will send a messenger when I have your assignment. In the meantime, enjoy the hospitality of our Capital city."

"Thank you for your assistance."

James walked out feeling disappointed by the delay, but the congeniality of the clerk in Mr. Scott's office made up for the claptrap he encountered from the first man he had spoken to. He hurried outside to his horse and headed back down Pennsylvania Avenue to the hotel. It was just past noon and James was ready for something to eat.

Willard's was a large seven story establishment on the corner of Pennsylvania Avenue and Fourteenth Street. As James would soon learn, Willard's was so prominent a place as to be looked upon as the center of Washington. Everyone could be seen there.

He tied Tar to a hitching post, went into the crowded lobby, located the registration desk, and asked for a room. The desk clerk explained that he only had a few available rooms and they were on the top floor. James told him anything would be fine and signed the register. Before going up to his room, he walked Tar over to a stable run by James W. Pumphrey on C Street.

After washing up in his room which, as it turned out, appraised at less than acceptable, James went downstairs to the sprawling dining room. At that hour there were many patrons, still he had no trouble finding an empty table. It did, however, take a short while before he could hail a waiter. While he waited, he surveyed the room and the other diners as well. This group, he thought, could have been chosen by eclecticism. There were well dressed gentlemen—some with ladies, some with other gentlemen—soldiers, and rough looking types both male and female. Some appeared to be involved in lively chatter; others had their heads close together as if their conversation was of a very serious and very private nature. The immediate area surrounding James was fairly quiet until two men dressed in patched, dirty work clothes sat down at an adjacent table. From the looks of their scruffy beards and long hair, neither had seen a bathtub or a barber in quite some time. And if their unkempt appearance was not proof of the serious lack of hygiene, their odor was. With all of that to their discredit, it was still their loud voices and vulgar language that James found most offensive. From the moment they sat down they were cursing everything from the weather, to the Rebels, to the dirty hussy from New York Avenue who had apparently given both a case of the crawling crotch. But mostly they cursed President Lincoln and the Emancipation Proclamation.

"I told ya a hundred times, Bill, if that hick son of a bitch got elected he'd pull a low down stunt like this. I can go along with savin the Union, any good man can. But why does he give a shit about the goddamn niggers? Did you ever take a good hard look at a nigger?" Without waiting for his chum to reply he continued. "They ain't human. I tell you they just ain't no way human beings."

"Yeah, I looked real hard afore, Charlie." Then he laughed in a repulsive sort of way, displaying half a set of decaying teeth. "Did I ever tell ya, Charlie, that I railed one of them black bitches one time?"

"Is that a fact?"

"Hell yeah. I used to drive a freight wagon some years back. I was haulin this piece a farm machinry down through Virginia and I stopped along old Bull Run to water the team. I saw this black bitch down there fetchin a pail o water. There weren't no one else around so I chased her out to the middle a that crick and bent her over a tree trunk what fell into the water. I threw her long dress up over her head and gave her a hell of a reamin' while she yelled her head off."

"Hell," said his sympathetic partner. "When a man needs to relieve hisself that's different. I reckon there ain't nothing wrong with that. All they be good for is servicing white folks any way they can. I say why throw all that away by makin em free. No, sir. It's that goddamn Lincoln's fault all right. We maybe wouldn't even be in this war if it weren't for him. Shoulda elected Douglas or Bell or even Breckinridge. They woulda kept the Union together without startin a war. Now he's got the North all stirred up."

"He sure as hell has, Charlie. I was talkin to some soldiers from a Vermont regiment t'other day. They were tellin me that a lot of our boys ain't happy at all to be fightin for the niggers. Why they said there was one outfit that claimed they'd lie in the woods til moss growed on their backs afore they'd die to free niggers."

"Nothin can be done about it now, Bill, I reckon."

James was doing a slow simmer as he listened to the talk between the two thugs. It was all he could do to keep from expressing a few audible thoughts of his own. But he knew where it would lead and he couldn't afford to be arrested for assault. He would not put himself in a bad position for men of their ilk.

He was just about to get up and leave when a waiter appeared at his table. The anger he felt seemed to increase his desire for food. He ordered a meal but left quickly once he had finished.

It had been his intention to take a stroll around the city after eating but decided he was in no mood. Instead, he went up to his room and stretched out on the well worn bed. His mood did not improve as he looked around the room at the dingy, torn wallpaper and the stains on the ceiling indicating a leaky roof. The smell of stale cigar smoke had permeated everything. He had expected better from a place like Willard's, as close to the White House as it was.

To take his mind off the boredom, he decided to write a letter to Polly. He rummaged through his things for paper and pencil, settled himself back on the bed, but fell asleep before he could finish. By the time he awoke, night had fallen and no word had come from the War Department. Perhaps it would take a couple of days. Considering the volume of work heaped on such a concern and during wartime as it was, one soldier's assignment was probably not high priority. He had followed orders, they knew where he was, and all he could do was wait it out.

Feeling refreshed from his nap, he decided to put aside the letter to Polly and go out for a beer. He could have gotten his drink at Willard's but chose to take the walk he had passed on earlier. In spite of the January temperature, there were quite a few people on the street. It was soon obvious that, for the most part, they were night people. James knew that darkness usually brought out the more unscrupulous of humanity; in the city there were just more of them. He knew as he walked along, that many he passed were not trustworthy, men who reminded him of the two in Willard's dining room. Every block he covered yielded at least a half dozen drunks and the type of women referred to as soiled doves were plentiful as well.

Before he realized it, he had walked as far as the National Hotel. The warmth of the lobby was inviting as he walked inside, seated himself in the dining room, and ordered a beer. Over near the far wall, James noticed a group of people crowded around one of the tables. They seemed highly excited as if someone of great importance was seated there. Quietly sipping his beer, he heard a lady at the next table ask her waiter, "What is going on back there?"

"Why, Mr. J. Wilkes Booth is in town, ma'am. He always stays at the National when he's in town and he never fails to draw a crowd."

"How wonderful," the lady replied. "I must try to get his autograph."

James was impressed. He had learned a great deal about the flamboyant, charismatic actor from newspapers and dime novels. The entire Booth family starred on the stage. James had never seen Booth perform but had always wanted to. In a short while, the crowd moved away and James saw the man himself cross the dining room and disappear up the stairway. He certainly understood why it was said that all the women loved him.

James ordered a second beer and sat a little further back in his chair. He was beginning to relax a bit and without intention, he tuned in to another conversation coming from a nearby table. This time the talk was not coming from a pair of crude, loose mouth tramps, instead it was two refined looking gentlemen and two well dressed ladies. The topic of conversation was the concern for proper security in Washington.

"I understand," said the first man, "that when civil war breaks out and a dividing line is drawn there will always be enemies inside your territory. Most will head for the side for which they sympathize. Others will remain and become a disruptive force. The government must rid this city of all the secesh. It must be the first and foremost priority."

"But I believe that they are, Richard," said the second man. "Didn't they arrest that Greenhow woman and put a stop to her spy ring? That was a year ago, and last May they sent her to the Confederacy."

"That is true, Randolph, but while she was in Old Capitol Prison, despite tightening security, she still managed to carry on with her activities. And what of Belle Boyd? She was also in Old Capitol but after a month she was exchanged. God only knows what she's up to now. No my friend, by no means has the Secret Service a firm handle on the situation. This city is full of damn secessionists."

"Well," said Randolph, "I cannot say that the president takes the issue seriously. He can be seen everyday walking from the White House to the War Department and other buildings in President's Park without so much as an escort. Apparently *he* is not concerned about security."

"Well, what can you expect from a man who is more concerned about the slaves than he is about putting down the rebellion?"

From there the conversation went on and on, condemning the people of the South for everything from their way of life to disloyalty to the United States flag. James began to squirm a bit in his chair. The irritation he dealt with in Willard's dining room that afternoon was climbing the back of his neck again. He was on his third beer now and it was beginning to have some effect since his experience with alcohol was extremely limited.

As the crowd in the dining room grew he became surrounded by people and the same words began to circulate through his head as if they were purposely taunting him. "Despicable Southerners . . . goddamn Rebels . . . nigger loving abolitionists . . ."

It was becoming impossible to listen without being provoked. James had thought he was doing the right thing. In so doing he had, in principal, turned against his family. He had joined an army of men who were the enemies of his family. His family members could end up being killed at their hands. Now he was in a place where everyone cursed his birthplace and all the Southern states. He was in a place where everyone cursed his parents, sisters, aunts, uncles, cousins, and for no reason other than the fact that they were from the South. What made these people of the North any better? James saw no respect or equality for the black race in the North. They could not vote. They could not hold positions in public office. They worked as servants and laborers. They were lashed just as hard with the tongue as the slaves were with the whip. James knew that not everyone supported President Lincoln and his proclamation, but he was hearing the same kind of garbage everywhere he went and not just from riff-raff and rabble rousers. He was beginning to feel like a fool. Had he made a huge mistake? Did he let Colonel Mulligan sell him a bill of goods?

The alcohol was making him lightheaded. He had to get outside and clear his mind; get away from people; get back to his hotel room. Carefully he got to his feet, trying not to stagger, and walked outside. The streetlights illuminated the sidewalk along the avenue. Just ahead, James saw a woman standing by a light post, appearing as though she were waiting for someone. As he approached, she took a few steps toward him.

She wore a dark green overcoat open down the front, revealing a crimson colored dress with a low neckline. Her hair was long and dark; a cigarette dangled from her red painted lips. An overabundance of rouge smeared her face and the smell of cheap perfume covered her like a mist.

"Where you headin, honey?" she said without removing the cigarette from her mouth.

"My hotel," said James. He was pretty sure of her game but hoped he was wrong, being in no mood for it.

"How about a little company this evening?"

Anticipating her ability to take a hint he said, "I'm afraid not. I happen to be a married man."

"Is your wife in town?"

"No, she isn't."

"Then what's the problem, honey?"

Something inside let loose and James responded in such a way as he never had before. "What's the problem? You ask me what the problem is? If there is a problem, it lies with you. I told you that I was married. Maybe that means nothing to you and maybe it wouldn't mean anything to every other married man in this city, but it does mean something to me. Furthermore, even if I were not married I would not debase myself by consorting with someone of your low moral character. Now would you please step away from me before I call a policeman, who in this city would probably do nothing more than to avail himself of your services." With that, James walked away leaving the woman who commenced weaving a web of obscenities that would cover every vulgar way of expressing oneself. Out in the cold night air, the affects of the alcohol began to weaken it but did nothing to dilute his vexation.

When he reached Willard's, he picked up his key at the desk and went straight up to his room. Never being one to brood, the past two days had, nevertheless, reduced him to a sullen mass of despair. He lay on the bed with a hundred conflicting thoughts doing battle inside his head. He was fast beginning to think he did not belong up north or down south. All communication with his family in Georgia was gone. By now they must think he had fallen from the face of the earth. He was married to a woman whom he adored, a loving creature who bore him a son; he had no idea when he would see her again. The walls were closing in. Suddenly, he thought of deserting. He would leave immediately for Mapletown. Once there, he would pack up his family and head to Canada. They would be safe there and could simply wait out the war. When it was over they could come back and re-establish their lives in Mapletown or Georgia or anywhere. But what would Polly think of his plan? Would she lose respect for him? Would it scar their relationship? James's soul was in torment. How could a beginning with such good intentions end up going so badly?

Looking for a way to ease the pressure, he took out the unfinished letter. When he had completed it, he saw that he had not included a single discouraging word. It was a good letter; simply expressing his love, telling her how much he missed her and little James. Then he sealed the envelope, addressed it, and fell into a deep sleep.

NINETEEN

The Assignment

The following morning James awoke, surprised to find that most of his anxiety was gone. If only he could receive his assignment and be on his way.

After a quiet breakfast, he walked up Pennsylvania Avenue toward the White House. When he reached President's Park he sat down on a bench with very little purpose other than to kill some time. Only a few minutes passed before his attention was taken by the sight of a solitary figure walking across the White House lawn in his direction. As the man drew near, James began to wonder if his eyes might be deceiving him. The tall, lanky gentleman dressed in a dark suit and stovepipe hat changed direction to a course that would have bypassed the bench upon which he was sitting. Then, noticing the young soldier, the man turned and walked directly toward him. From a distance of about fifty feet, James knew that there was nothing wrong with his eyesight. Jumping to his feet, he found himself in the presence of President Abraham Lincoln.

"Good morning, Lieutenant," said the president.

"Good morning, Mr. President. It is both an honor and a pleasure to meet you, sir. I must say that I am rather surprised to see you out here alone."

"Yes," said Lincoln. "I hear that quite a lot. I am forever being chastised for my indifference to personal safety, especially by Mrs. Lincoln and my good friend, Ward Hill Lamon."

"Forgive me, Mr. President, I meant no offense."

"Not at all, Lieutenant. I believe that a president must be accessible to the people he serves. And I do not believe that any measure of security can keep a man safe if there are those who are determined to do him harm."

173

"I suppose that is sad but true, Mr. President. But perhaps a complete lack of protection might encourage an attack that might otherwise not be attempted."

"A deterrent?"

"Quite possibly, sir."

"I shall give it some thought. I do not mean to be forward, Lieutenant, but I cannot help noticing your accent. From where do you hail?"

"I was born and raised in Georgia, sir."

"That is very interesting. Could I be so bold as to ask why you joined the Union army?"

"I do not consider your question to be bold, sir. It is something that I hear quite a bit."

Having accepted the fact that he would find himself being asked to repeat his story, he explained it all again for the benefit of the president. And like the others before him, Mr. Lincoln was impressed by James's insight and equally impressed with his ardent compassion for the slaves.

"I can imagine how difficult it must have been to make such a decision. I daresay that not many would do as you have done. You say that you are waiting to be assigned?"

"Yes, sir."

"How long have you been in Washington?"

"I arrived yesterday, sir."

"I see. Well, in my opinion it is a serious misuse of a fine military resource, having you sit idly by. I was heading to the War Department this morning. Will you accompany me?"

"Of course, Mr. President, I would be pleased to."

At a leisurely pace, James walked side by side with President Lincoln, indulging in pleasant conversation. He felt like someone special in the company of the man whom everyone greeted and made way for. He was very taken with the president's warm, unpretentious personality.

Instead of going to Mr. Scott's office, James soon found himself being introduced by the president to Mr. Edwin M. Stanton, the Secretary of War. It was like being invited to dine with royalty. "Mr. Stanton, we have a very good man here who has been waiting since yesterday for his assignment. I would like to have him taken care of right away."

"Of course, Mr. President." Stanton took paper and pen; wrote a few lines, folded the paper, and handed it to James. "Take this to Louis Weichmann's office, Lieutenant. It is just up the hall on the left. You will be on your way by this afternoon."

"Thank you, Mr. Secretary," said James. President Lincoln held out a sinewy hand with long bony fingers. "I wish you God's speed and good luck, Lieutenant."

"And the very best of luck to you, Mr. President," James replied, grasping the bony fingers.

Amazed at the results of presidential power, an hour later, James had his orders and was on his way to Willard's to pack and check out. He had been assigned as a staff officer to 1st Brigade, 3rd Division, Cavalry Corps, Army of the Potomac, and ordered to report to the winter quarters at Falmouth, Virginia. It also pleased him to learn that he did not have to make the trip alone. A Corporal Thomas Milroy, assigned to the same unit, would be riding to Virginia with him.

Corporal Milroy was an affable man with a terrific sense of humor and James liked him immediately. He was tall and broad shouldered; a build that said he was no stranger to hard work. His red hair and green eyes were evidence of his Irish descent. But the corporal was about ten years older than James and somehow it didn't feel right having Milroy call him sir; especially since James had just joined the army and his subordinate had been in since the war began. However, it did not seem to bother his jovial companion. In fact, he seemed rather impressed when James told him the story of being a Confederate conscript at the battle of Cumberland Gap.

"If you ask me, you've already earned those shoulder straps, Lieutenant. It's a hell of a thing, a man getting all shot up. I haven't seen the elephant yet myself. I've been stuck in the Quartermaster Corp in Washington since I joined up. And I know it sounds crazy, cause I sure don't wanna get shot, but I got so tired of issuing supplies after almost two years that I just up and put in for a transfer. I'm good with horses so they put me in the cavalry. But I hope I don't wish I hadn't done it cause I sure don't wanna get shot."

"Well," said James almost laughing. "I will do my best to look out for you and I give you permission to ride directly behind me when we go into battle."

Milroy knew that James was teasing him and he mockingly replied, "I appreciate that, sir. Now I know I don't have anything to worry about."

"Are you married, Corporal?"

"Yes, sir. I have a wife back in Ohio and two young boys to help keep the farm going. How about you, sir?"

"I have a wife in Pennsylvania and a newborn son."

"I heard that you come from Georgia, sir. I guess that makes this war harder on you than most."

"I guess I'll soon be finding out."

"I'm sorry, sir. Sometimes my brain stops before my mouth does."

"It's all right, Corporal. I understand the curiosity that I arouse."

The two rode in silence from that point until they reached Virginia. "Reb country, Lieutenant," said Milroy.

"Yes. It will be dark soon. We'll stop in those woods up ahead and make camp. I figure we have another forty miles to ride. I'd rather do it in the daylight."

"I'm with you, sir."

After a suitable site had been found, the two picketed their horses, made a small fire, and dined on salt pork, beans, and coffee. Then they smothered the fire and made themselves as comfortable as possible. The moon came up almost full, and once their eyes adjusted they could see around the campsite pretty well. There were Yankee armies in Virginia as well as other states further south but the Confederates were nowhere near being run to ground. The enemy could be anywhere; consequently, they would have to take turns sleeping and standing guard. Neither man seemed ready to turn in so they sipped the last of their coffee and talked.

"God, how I hate the cold," said Milroy. "You would think I'd be used to it, coming from Ohio. We get some real hard winters sometimes. But I hate it just the same. What's Georgia like?"

"Not much snow as a rule. The average temperature in the winter is about forty-five degrees. It's mighty hot in the summer though. I'd imagine it's a little cooler in Ohio."

"I guess it probably is. No matter though. I don't care how hot it gets—I can take it. I just hate the cold."

"At least the wind isn't blowing," said James.

"Yeah, that is a point. Nothing makes the cold worse than a hard wind." There was a lull in the conversation then the corporal said, "You ever shoot anybody, Lieutenant?"

"No, I never have. I have been in a few scrapes when I had to threaten someone with a gun, but I never had to shoot."

"But *you've* been shot."

"Yes. I was hit twice in the battle I told you about and I still have to consider myself lucky. It could have been much worse."

"What's it feel like . . . getting shot?"

"I guess I would say that it burns considerable."

"Yeah, I'll bet. They don't call it hot lead for nothin."

"It's an ugly feeling and it's scary, too," said James. "It doesn't take a lot of bleeding to make you think you've lost it all."

"Terrible thing, men shootin each other."

"I couldn't agree more," James replied. "It's even more terrible realizing that so many men are more than willing to do it."

"I wonder if I can," said the corporal. "Maybe it's one of those things that when the time comes your mind just tells you to do what you gotta do. Something like a natural defense mechanism."

"I guess that's what it is," James agreed.

"Still," said Milroy. "A God fearin man is bound to have trouble with it. My farm is near a small town and my wife and I know everyone who lives there. They are all neighbors and friends; we all get along so well. When the war broke out, all the able bodied men in the community stepped right up and joined the army. We believed that we were doing it to protect one another. That's how much we care. To tell the truth, I'd have given anything to stay home on the farm with my wife and boys. But how could I have done that? How could I let people that I care about risk their lives while I stayed safe at home in Ohio?"

James knew that it was purely unintentional; still, Milroy had pushed a dagger into his heart. In the eyes of his Southern countrymen, *he* would be judged as guilty of abandonment. Even though they could not say that he hadn't risked his life; it certainly wouldn't have been for the right cause in their eyes. But like the corporal, James had his reasons for what he was doing. He hoped that in the eyes of God they were the right reasons. Beyond that, all he could do was to pray that the war would bring about the destruction of slavery. If it didn't, he was sure that he would never be able to live with himself.

Milroy took the first watch and then woke James around one a.m. The early morning was very still and covered with frost. The only thing that really bothered James was his feet. The high leather cavalry boots did little to keep them warm. As quietly as possible, he stamped them up and down and forced himself to think of something else.

Before long he was pondering the question Milroy had raised about whether or not he could shoot another man. James thought it strange that he had never considered that problem himself. He just assumed that men at war would shoot at each other when they had to. Thinking about it now, however, he realized that he had no desire to do it. In the past year or so, the possibility had presented itself more than once. But would he really have shot Sheriff Wilkes that time in Dry Branch, or the brute, Virgil Trask in Greenville, South Carolina? He didn't know. He *did* remember telling Sheriff Wilkes that if he *had* the nerve, he would take Wilkes out and shoot him.

James carried a gun now and he had carried one then. James considered: If a man carries a gun, he must think he has it within himself to use it. A man carrying a gun who is unwilling to use it is just asking to get himself killed. Maybe Milroy had it pegged; when the time comes, you do what you have to do. Surely, thought James, it was a bit late to worry about it.

At seven o'clock, the sun was up and it was time to wake his companion. They broke out some hardtack, boiled some coffee to dip it in, and then saddled their horses. James led the way through the woods out to the road. They had no sooner reached it when a shot rang out, then a second, then a handful. At about two hundred yards distance James could see four horsemen coming straight at them, firing pistols as they came. They had been spotted by a Reb patrol. "Back into the woods!" James shouted, wheeling his horse around. Milroy followed him into the trees to a spot where a couple large rocks and some decaying tree tops offered protection. Grabbing their carbines as they dismounted, each man found a vantage point from which he could fire at the charging Rebels. When the riders were within fifty yards, James yelled, "Fire!" and the Yankee rifles spit lead. Two of the attackers hit the ground and lay still. So much for wondering if they could shoot the enemy, James thought. The remaining two soldiers dismounted and kept up the attack while trying to use their frightened horses as shields. James was afforded a clear shot and downed his second man. The last Rebel, realizing that he was all alone, climbed into the saddle and lingered long enough to fire a few more shots. But he stayed too long as James, firing his six shot revolver now, hit him in the chest and he fell dead. During the final fury, James hadn't realized that Milroy had stopped shooting.

He called out to the corporal but there was no reply. Dreading what he might find, he hurried over to the spot where his new friend from Ohio had taken cover. That good man and good neighbor lay on his back, empty eyes staring at heaven. He had been shot through the neck and most likely died without time for one last thought of his wife and boys. For several minutes James was completely undone by what had happened. He felt as though his insides were frozen and it was difficult to breathe. Then he forced himself to kneel down by the body; not caring that someone might be close enough to hear him he screamed, "Damn it all, Corporal! Why the hell didn't you stay on your farm?" Then he wept without shame until the pain and the shock subsided, and in a whisper he said, "I'm sorry, Thomas . . . you were an honorable man." Then he put Milroy's body on his horse, mounted Tar, and headed towards the road once again.

TWENTY

A Demoralized Army

It was late afternoon before James finally rode into the sprawling winter camp of the Army of the Potomac. He was hardly aware of the soldiers who stopped and stared as he passed by leading a horse that carried a dead body. Not that it would have had a lasting effect since most of the men in camp were fresh from the terrible slaughter just across the Rappahannock at Fredericksburg. The army was in a somber mood and James would have no trouble fitting in.

Locating the commanding officer's hut, he tied up the horses and went inside. The man in charge was General Edwin Sumner, whose Right Grand Division had suffered the heaviest losses before the impregnable stone wall on Marye's Heights. Sumner, however, who was mistrusted for his rashness, had consequently been left out of the fight and kept behind at Falmouth.

James stepped in front of the general's desk and stood at attention. He raised a salute and said, "Lieutenant James Langdon reporting for duty, sir."

Bull Head Sumner, as he was known, returned the salute and said, "Yes, Lieutenant, I received a communication from Washington. You are my southern officer, I believe."

"Yes, sir," James replied through gritted teeth.

"Relax, Lieutenant. I have nothing against southerners, as long as they are on our side. I am told that you can be of some help as a scout."

"Yes, sir, I believe I can."

"Good. Scouts can be worth their weight in gold to an army. It may be a few weeks before you see action. In the meantime I think you will be quite useful for interrogating prisoners."

"Prisoners, sir?"

"Yes. Every week at least a dozen or so Confederates come through our lines to surrender. Most of them are sick of the war, most do not get enough to eat, and most are driven by desperate letters from home. They are looking to get paroled so they can return to their families. We get all the information we can before we ship them north to prison camp. Maybe you can make more out of the things they tell us since you are from the south."

"Or maybe they will resent me so much that they won't tell me anything, sir."

"Maybe, but you might be surprised at how eager some of them are to talk. The South was so much less prepared to fight this war than we were. Poor conditions concerning food, clothing, medical care, and so on can change a man's way of thinking pretty quick."

"I'll do my very best, sir."

"Thank you, Lieutenant. I was expecting a Corporal Thomas Milroy to be with you. Do you know where he is?" James's gaze fell to the floor.

"Yes, sir. He is outside."

"Very well. I will assign you your quarters, and then you can send him in."

"I'm afraid that I can't, sir. Corporal Milroy is dead." The general's face took on a stoic expression. James made no judgment about the man's demeanor. He understood that after more than two years of war, death simply becomes matter of fact.

"I will expect a written report, Lieutenant, but briefly tell me what happened."

"We camped about forty miles from here last night. This morning we were attacked by four Confederate cavalrymen. We managed to kill all four, but Corporal Milroy died in the fight."

"I am sorry, Lieutenant. It sounds like he died a hero."

"I hope that is enough for his wife and sons, sir."

"I will form a burial detail in the morning," said the general. "For now you can take his body down to the hospital tent and—"

"No, sir." The general looked at James, his face contorted with surprise.

"How is that, Lieutenant?"

"His body must be sent back to Ohio, sir. It is the very least we can do for his family."

"I'm afraid you don't know what you're asking. If we sent every one of our dead boys home we wouldn't get anything else done."

"I do understand that, sir. But I knew Corporal Milroy. He was a very good man. He joined the army because he took responsibility to heart. Just last night he told me that he would have given anything to stay on his farm with his wife and his two boys. He could not bring himself to shirk his duty. He also told me that he'd never shot a man and didn't know if he could. But when those Confederates attacked, he fought bravely and I think a man like that deserves better than to be buried nowhere other than his farm in Ohio."

General Sumner sat quietly for a moment. "Very well, Lieutenant. I will make arrangements to get the corporal's body sent home."

"I thank you very kindly, General. I should like to write a letter to his widow and send it along."

"Certainly." Handing James a piece of paper the general said, "The hospital tent is in the rear of the camp. This is your quarters assignment. Don't forget to write your report."

"You will have it in the morning, General."

That night James wrote a heartfelt letter to Mrs. Thomas Milroy, then he wrote a letter to Polly, and of course, he wrote out the report for the general.

Over the next few months, the command of the army passed from General Ambrose Burnside to General Joseph Hooker. Once again, the feeling among the men was that the new general would move the army forward, take the initiative, and whip the Rebels. There had been little or no success under McDowell, McClellan, Pope, or Burnside. Surely Fighting Joe Hooker had the confidence and the wherewithal to get the job done. For the most part, only minor engagements were fought in both the eastern and western theaters during the winter of 1862-1863 and it appeared as though nothing major would be attempted until spring.

As the winter days dragged on, James did his best with the job he'd been given. Just as the general told him, a steady trickle of Rebel deserters came through the lines looking for something to eat and an opportunity to leave the war behind. Almost all of them were willing to answer questions, but most were enlisted men who could contribute little except for troop numbers and locations that varied from man to man.

On March 17th, James was given the chance to break his daily routine. He was sent with a cavalry corps under the command of General William Averell to Culpepper, Virginia. With three thousand troopers and six pieces of artillery, they attacked General Fitz Lee and his eight hundred men at Kelly's Ford. The battle raged all day and even though the Rebels were outnumbered more than three to one, it was the Yankees who ended up pulling back. The corps sustained seventy-eight casualties, some killed, some wounded. It came as a surprise to James that he felt nothing when he looked upon the bleeding bodies and listened to their mournful cries. His emotions were so overshadowed by the death of Corporal Milroy that even *he* did not realize the change it had made in him. His whole nature was different somehow, and although he was well enough liked by the other officers and his subordinates, he made very sure that the bonds of friendship never took root.

Near Drainesville, Virginia on March 31st, James's cavalry corps clashed with Confederate troopers under the command of the Gray Ghost himself, Colonel John Singleton Mosby. Mosby was fast becoming a legend in his own time, equaling if not surpassing the reputations of such men as Jeb Stuart and Nathan Forrest. The corps lost sixty men in another defeat, and like so many of his fellow soldiers, James began to doubt their chances of restoring the Union. It was inconceivable that the North, with more of everything necessary to wage war, could be beaten by an underdog army of secessionists.

By the spring of 1863, it seemed that the Union was close to squandering all it had. More and more, James could see Colonel Mulligan's point about the superiority of the Confederate Cavalry. The only Union instrument that was clearly having any affect was the blockade.

Rumors of economic depression in the South came from every credible source available. But factions in the North, such as the Democratic wing known as the Copperheads, were anti-war. As they became more active and exceedingly vocal, the pressure on President Lincoln to squash the rebellion was becoming insurmountable. Besieging the entire South would never end the war in time. Lincoln needed the right general who could crush the Rebels on the battlefield.

On his return to camp, James went back to his mindless task of interrogating prisoners. In mechanical fashion, he asked questions and wrote reports with the monotonous repetition of a paddle wheel on a steamboat.

Then one day in early April, two things happened that restored a bit of life to his lackluster existence. The first was a letter in the morning mail from Polly. The re-assurance in her words that all was well worked wonders on his spirit. Little James was four months old now, and according to Polly, would someday be tall and handsome like his father. When he finished reading he held the letter to his cheek and tried to imagine, having come from her hand, that he could feel her touch.

The second bit of restoration came that afternoon when a Confederate prisoner from Georgia was brought to his quarters. Private Gerald Upson was not only from Georgia, he was, in fact, from Macon. When James heard this, he almost felt as if he'd run into a good friend he hadn't seen in years. Macon was home and he wanted to sit the man down, pour him a drink, and reminisce. But he realized that he could not approach the situation like a welcoming committee, especially when he saw that Private Upson was by no means in a congenial mood.

"Have a seat, Private."

Upson flopped onto the camp stool like a half empty sack of grain, propped his elbows on his knees and buried his face in his hands.

"Private Upson, why did you surrender?"

The soldier raised his head and gave James a scornful look.

"Who you been jawin with, Yank? I got ketched las night tryin to steal a hoss offen your picket line. They trussed me up like a runaway nigger and threw me in a tent. Been there til near a hour ago. I ain't et in two days and I ain't surrendered neither."

"Why were you trying to steal a horse?"

"Well, my first notion was to eat the damn thing but mostly I was gonna skedaddle back to Georgia."

"Yes, I understand that you are from Macon."

"No military secret, I reckon."

"Are you from the city?"

"Got a scrap a land jus outside."

"Have you been home recently?"

"Was there for a week las Christmas."

Only four months ago, thought James. Surely the private would know the condition of things. "How are the folks back home getting along?"

Upson was growing irritable. "What the hell do ya wanna know for? Ain't ya spose to be askin how we plan to whip the damn Yankees?"

James took a deep breath and said, "I'm from Georgia, too."

"Well I will jus be damned," said Upson. "I reckon I thought ya might be from down south but ya talk like ya is high educated and that there blue suit don't look like down home to me. Is ya a spy or jus a goddamn traitor?"

"Neither one," said James. "I'm just fighting for what I believe is right."

"And what might that there be?"

"Freedom."

"Freedom for who?'

"Freedom for all."

"Now I gets it. You is a nigger lover. Mus make your mamma mighty proud."

In an instant, James lost his self control. He jerked Upson to his feet and belted him as hard as he could, knocking him to the ground. Almost just as quickly, he felt remorse for his actions. He was ashamed to have attacked a hungry man whose hands were tied together. He wanted to apologize but decided it would do no good. Instead, he helped the man back to his stool and cut the rope that bound his wrists. There was no way he could escape in broad daylight in view of thousands of enemy soldiers.

To James's surprise, it was Upson who apologized. "Beggin your pardon, Lieutenant. Ought not to have said nothing bout yer mamma."

"Never mind. You said you were going back to Georgia. Was it your intention to desert?"

"Sho enough it was. Like I said, I was back at Christmas. My wife and younguns needs me at home. That there scrap a land barely feeds us. I was a fool to join the army. We was told that we was fightin for the rights of all Southerners, but it ain't so. We is only fightin for the rich man. You boys is fightin to free the niggers and our boys is fightin to keep em. That don't mean nothing to me no how. My family is all I got and the bes way I can help them is at home."

"Well I'm sorry to say that you may be delayed for a while. I'm told that the exchange and parole process is moving slower all the time."

"I heared that, too. That's why I tried to grab me a hoss. I sho wisht I could get a letter to my wife."

"Maybe we can make a trade."

"What do ya have in mind?"

"Can you write?"

"Not good, but good enough I reckon."

"Fine. I will supply you with pencil and paper. You sit here and write your letter. I'll see that it gets mailed and you can tell me what things are like at home in Georgia."

"You'll see the letter gets mailed?"

"You have my word."

"You mind if I take your word as a Georgian and not as a Yank?"

James smiled for the first time in quite a while and said, "I don't mind."

"It's a bargain," said Upson.

James set the private up with writing materials then stepped to the doorway and summoned a passing soldier. "Go to the mess tent and get me a plate full of whatever they have cooking; and bring something for this prisoner."

Then he sat patiently while Private Upson labored over his letter. When the food arrived, it consisted of a heaping plate of fresh hot beef stew with fresh bread, and a second plate with a few spoonfuls of the previous day's beans and a hardtack biscuit. Upson looked up from his letter and surveyed the two plates. The hunger reflected in his eyes. James sat the stew in front of him; took the other plate to the doorway, looked out, and seeing no one close by, threw the beans and hardtack on the ground.

When the letter and the stew were finished, Private Upson kept his end of the bargain. He told James all he could about how the people back home were fairing. All things considered, it was a favorable report. There had been some fighting in Georgia but nothing major. The biggest problem the plantation owners were facing was the difficulty in shipping their cotton. That meant a serious squeeze on his family's income. When the war was over, if the South was defeated, it would have to look to industrialization and mechanization as the North had done years before. When the conversation was over, James held out his hand and said, "Thank you, Private. Your letter is as good as mailed."

"I'm beholdin, Lieutenant. Take care a yourself . . . you got guts."

By early April, 1863, another morale boost came in the form of General Hooker's inspirational Grand Review. After taking command, Hooker redesigned all of the departments and made numerous useful and effective changes. Through the use of instructional periods and regular drilling, not to mention furloughs, he managed to ease the tedium of life in camp. By improving daily rations, which included supplying the men with fresh vegetables and fresh bread, the sick call list was quickly reduced. Daily changes of bedding, regulation latrines, and routine bathing, which had languished, now served to improve sanitary conditions. Aside from these improvements, steps were taken to control the problem of desertion. Best of all, the men received their back pay through arrangements finally made by Congress.

Hooker also separated the cavalry corps from the infantry divisions and a new cavalry corps was placed under the command of Major George Stoneman. James received an extra incentive when he was promoted to first lieutenant.

When all was ready, General Hooker staged his Grand Review on a huge open field on Falmouth Heights. James was among the fifteen thousand cavalrymen reviewed by President Lincoln.

But, as James discovered, band music and parades do not intimidate the enemy or bring about victories; desirable results are achieved by brilliant strategy and leaders who possess it. For all of General Hooker's bluster and loquaciousness, in the end, his only success was at failure.

In early May, the Army of the Potomac was soundly beaten by General Robert E. Lee and General Stonewall Jackson at Chancellorsville. Stoneman's cavalry had destroyed supply depots and cut some enemy rail lines. His horsemen had frightened the civilians of Richmond by riding within two miles of the city. But in spite of all this, the Chancellorsville Campaign had been little affected by the cavalry. As the Yankees would come to learn, their most significant gain had been the Confederacy's loss of General Stonewall Jackson, and even that damage had been inflicted by Jackson's own men.

Once again, James was finding it difficult to maintain a positive attitude. From the beginning of the war, the consensus was that the South had the more superior officers. By the summer of 1863, he could understand why. It was still a bit premature to say the South was winning the war, considering their losses of men and material. It *could* be said, however, that they were doing an outstanding job of not losing it. By day, James inwardly derided the Northern high command and all of the shortsighted fools who said that it would be a short war. By night, he thought of Polly and his son and longed to be with them almost to the point of desertion. He kept telling himself that God tries men most when they are mired in despair. He believed that God was, indeed, trying him. So, with renewed inspiration he accepted the challenge and at the same time requested a transfer.

By June 29th, all of the notable changes that had taken place were enough to temper James's depression. At the Union shooting gallery, the Confederates had succeeded in knocking down another duck: General Joe Hooker. The new commanding officer of the Army of the Potomac was General George Gordon Meade. Meanwhile, General Robert E. Lee and his Army of Northern Virginia were approaching a small farming community, called Gettysburg, in southern Pennsylvania. And First Lieutenant James Langdon, who had received his transfer, was with General John Buford's cavalry division near Emmitsburg, Maryland.

About eleven a.m. on June 30th, the division entered the town of Gettysburg. James listened as the terribly excited townspeople described a sudden approach and withdrawal, shortly before, of a Confederate infantry unit. If one had a keen sense of smell, he thought, a major confrontation could be detected in the wind.

That night, General Buford held a council of war and James was privy to it. After listening to one of his brigadier's predictions that the Confederates would not return and if they did they would be easily beaten, Buford said. "No they won't. They will attack you in the morning and they will come ready, three deep in rank. You will have to fight for your lives until reinforcements arrive."

Afterwards, the troopers made camp on Seminary Ridge on the west side of Gettysburg. James drove a picket pin into the ground and linked a rope to Tar's halter so he could graze without straying. Then he fried bacon, halved some biscuits and made sandwiches. After he'd eaten he spread a blanket on the cool grass, lay down, and stared at the sky. Someone nearby was playing the military favorite, "Lorena," on a harmonica. It was a time for reflection and James knew that every man on that ridge was deep in thought. It took no imagination to know what the next day would bring. They had all seen it before: when the shooting stops you just sort of look around and take note of who is still there and who is gone. For it seemed that a blood sacrifice was the only thing the gods of war would accept; and each battle carried with it a pre-determined list of who would pay.

James could not help wondering why men could not resolve their differences with words instead of weapons. Of course, everyone would say that they tried and failed. But if it were so, the men would not have to worry about being on the next day's list. They could just get up in the morning and go home, and that was all they really wanted to do. But it would not happen that way, James thought. They would get up in the morning and kill each other.

On the overcast morning of July 1st, the Union troopers rolled out of their blankets in time to swallow a hasty cup of coffee. By seven a.m. they had mounted their horses and ridden five hundred yards farther west. There, they were ordered to dismount and were then deployed by General Buford. James was in the 1st Brigade commanded by Colonel William Gamble, which was placed along the east bank of a sluggish little stream called Willoughby Run. Their line extended for a thousand yards from a rail bed south across the Chambersburg Pike. James grabbed his breech loaded carbine and was preparing to take his place in line when an unmistakable voice called his name. He spun around, and there stood General Buford. James knew enough not to salute lest an advance enemy scout should see it and take aim at the general. He ran over to where the commander stood. "Yes, sir," he said.

"Very soon now, Major General Henry Heth's division will be coming over Herr Ridge, about nine hundred yards out in front of us. It will be your responsibility to give the command for this brigade to open fire. When the Confederates are in range, Lieutenant Calef's battery of horse artillery will open on them. That will be your signal. After the first salvo, give the command. I have sent an urgent message to General Reynolds to come up fast with reinforcements. It will take time. We have less than three thousand troopers spread out thin across this line. General Heth's strength is estimated at over seven thousand. We must hold here until support comes up."

"We will keep them entertained, General," said James. Buford clapped a hand on James's shoulder in an avuncular gesture, mounted his horse and headed back to Seminary Ridge.

James took his position and fixed his sight on Herr Ridge. It was just past seven thirty. He was geared for action, anchored by the words of General Buford. The phrase "Must hold here," echoed through his mind. This fight must not turn out as previous engagements had. This time, the Army of Northern Virginia had dared to encroach upon Northern soil. They must not get a foothold here, James thought; they must be whipped.

At eight a.m. Heth's division came into view and marched boldly down Herr Ridge toward Willoughby Run. The Union troopers could see their bayonets shining under the sun, now breaking through the overcast. Without turning his head, James called words of encouragement to the men on his left and right.

"Steady, boys, steady. Every shot drops a man. Here they come now."

Suddenly the Confederate lines were staggered by a blast of artillery fire and at the top of his lungs James yelled, "Fire!" Thousands of rounds tore through the Confederate ranks as the Federals fired furiously. For a full two hours, Buford's dismounted cavalry held up Heth's advance.

By ten o'clock, James's comrades were beginning to give way as the enemy tried to push them back across the little stream. But the young lieutenant was determined to hold his ground. Men on both sides of him were falling but he was not deterred. Finally, Sergeant Patrick McClure came up from behind and grabbed him by the arm. "Look, Lieutenant, look yonder." James turned and saw two brigades of Brigadier General Wadsworth's 1st Division running toward the Union line. "We did it, by God, we did it!" James shouted.

As more fresh troops arrived, General Buford's cavalry was ordered back into reserve. For the remainder of the day, the troopers rested while fighting raged in nearly every direction around the town of Gettysburg. It was difficult to ascertain if either side was gaining the upper hand until the afternoon of July 3rd, when that uncertainty disappeared.

The Union army still held the high ground; Big Round Top, Little Round Top, and Culp's Hill. The center of the line was Cemetery Ridge. At eleven a.m. the fighting on Culp's Hill came to an end. An oppressive silence fell over the field creating a striking contrast to the sounds of battle that had dominated the previous two days. The withering

191

summer heat and the smothering humidity, as well as the fighting, had beaten down the soldiers.

Then, at exactly one p.m., the roar of artillery shattered the silence as one hundred and seventy rebel cannons began firing from a point approximately a mile across open ground from Cemetery Ridge. For an hour and a half, the magnificent cannonade pounded the Union defenses. In the woods behind the line of artillery, fifteen thousand Rebel infantry were forming their lines of battle.

At two-thirty the firing ceased, and at three o'clock, the attacking forces stepped out of the trees. What followed next was perhaps the most shameful waste of veteran soldiers since the ill fated federal assaults against Marye's Heights at Fredericksburg

The Confederate ranks were first decimated by long range artillery fire. When they reached Emmitsburg Road, more than five thousand Union infantry cut down huge numbers with small arms fire. All of the Rebels who breeched the Federal line were killed or captured, and when the battle was over, the Northern army had finally achieved a decisive victory. Although the cost was high on both sides, the difference would prove to be the inability of the South to replace their losses. The following afternoon, in the pouring rain, the Army of Northern Virginia, in a column that stretched for seventeen miles, headed back to Virginia. The Confederate army never invaded Northern soil again.

TWENTY-ONE

Shot by a Dead Man

Although General Meade had performed well at
Gettysburg, like his predecessors, he, too, possessed the
same talent for raising the ire of President Lincoln. Meade
was exhausted from ten days of sleepless nights, no
regular food, and high mental stress. Lincoln was pleased
by the great victory but he wanted the army to move
against Lee and destroy his army before it could cross the
Potomac River. Meade was in no hurry to comply. On July
4th, the Army of the Potomac was enjoying a well deserved
rest and taking its time preparing to head south after the
Confederates.

Following morning mess, James rode out across the
field where the last Confederate charge had been made to
survey the carnage. Everywhere, the wreckage of battle
covered the ground: broken limbers, dismounted guns,
torn and tattered equipment, rifles, sabers, bayonets, bent
and twisted by the mayhem, dead horses swelling in the
summer heat, and covering everything, hugging the ground
like a fog, the nauseating stench of decaying soldiers. The
wounded had walked, crawled, or been carried from the
field, but the dead remained, almost disrespected or
unappreciated now that they had given their all. Who
would care for so many and would their families ever know
from where they never returned? James realized that the
task of burying the dead was monumental. Perhaps at
least to an extent, the problem would be for the citizens of
Gettysburg to solve.

James had seen enough. He turned his horse and
started back at a walk. The look see had taken him as far
as the woods from where the Confederates had begun their
advance. When he got back to the area that had been
occupied by the Rebel artillery, he stopped, listening. Was
it a muffled voice or had he just imagined it? Then he

heard it again. Someone was asking for water. About ten feet to his right was the wreckage of a cannon and limber. Six or eight bodies were strewn around the emplacement. One man was underneath the ammunition box, which had been knocked free from the wheels of the limber and was propped against the axle forming a lean-to. James dismounted, and as he walked toward the broken limber he saw the man beneath the wreckage move a leg.

He went back to his horse, retrieved his canteen, and then walked around behind the limber so he would be near the wounded man's head. At the sound of footsteps, the injured Rebel opened his eyes. James could read the terrible pain on the soldier's face as he knelt down beside him, lifted his head, and gave him water. Underneath all the dirt and powder smoke, it was obvious that the man was really just a boy; a boy he seemed to recognize. It was not easy for the soldier to take the water because it made him cough, and when he coughed he spit up blood. His wound was in the stomach and it was serious. Then the young soldier in the uniform of the 59th Georgia cried out that his insides were on fire and the sound of his voice sent a shock wave through James's whole body.

"My God!" he said out loud. "You're Jefferson Langdon."

Jefferson was his Uncle Joseph's youngest son and he was only about seventeen by now. The young man seemed to be resting a bit easier. James feared he was dying.

"Jefferson."

He opened his eyes again when he heard his name.

"Jefferson, it's James . . . your cousin, James."

A slight smile parted his lips.

"James, is it really you?"

"Yes, Jeff, it's really me."

"But . . . you're a Yank. My cousin, James, couldn't be a damn Yank."

The surprise was obvious but he did not speak with anger in his voice; it was rather matter of fact. "My father told me once that he didn't think that you would ever fight for the South. He said that you were a nigger lover at heart. But none of us thought you would ever join the Yankees."

"Let's not talk about that now. I've got to get you to a doctor."

"No! No, James, don't move me. It hurts too much and anyway, I'm gut shot. You know nobody survives if they're gut shot. Just stay with me, James. If I have to die I don't want to die alone. Stay with me and keep me company."

Going against his will and better judgment, James said, "OK, Jeff. I'll stay with you."

With great difficulty, Jefferson insisted that he be allowed to talk. James listened intently but much of what he heard was not good.

"My brother Franklin and I joined up in June of '61. Neither of us was old enough. Mother was against it but father said the war wouldn't last long and he wasn't going to deny us our moment of glory. You can see how glorious it turned out. Franklin lost a leg at Manassas and he's been home ever since. Uncle Stanley's boys, Clark and Jessie, were with A.P. Hill's Corps at Antietam. Clark was killed near Burnside Bridge and Jessie was wounded. He was home for a while, and then he went back. No one has heard from him since. I saw your parents some months back when I was home. Your father is near crippled with his bad leg and can't get around without a crutch. And your mother, James . . . your mother is not so good. She's confined to bed. Your sisters are taking care of her, but she isn't well. I'm sorry the news is bad. Nothing is turning out like we figured; all this stuff about glory. There isn't much glory in seeing a man with his guts hanging out. It's all going to hell on us no matter which side you're on."

An hour earlier James would have given anything to know how his family was doing. Now he thought he would give anything if he could just forget. For a long time he had worried that his parents' health was not good. Now he knew for sure. He felt sick inside. He felt like he was being punished for his beliefs. But, he also understood that war meant sacrifice. No matter what he had done, his cousin Clark would still be dead, Franklin would still be missing a leg, his mother would still be sick, and Jefferson would still be lying in front of him, dying. Jefferson started to cough again; his blood sprayed James's face. He fell silent; James thought he was dead. He pressed a finger to his cousin's throat. His pulse still felt strong. He had only lost consciousness. James was in a panic. He shouldn't have waited as Jefferson had insisted. Maybe there was still time to get him to a doctor, he thought. James hurried to his horse, paying no attention to the other Rebels. The moment James's backside hit the saddle, a shot rang out, and a bullet knocked him to the ground. He hit hard and rolled three times, ending up on his back. He laid there in shock, confused as to exactly what had happened. At the very edge of his memory was the suggestion that he'd heard a gunshot. There was an awful pain in his head and he could not bring his eyesight into focus.

About a hundred yards away, a sergeant who was out on the field looking for souvenirs as soldiers often do, heard the shot and galloped over to where James had fallen. The sergeant jumped off his horse with a revolver cocked and ready. He quickly checked the area then bent down over James and said, "Lieutenant, can you hear me?"

The voice came to James's ears as if in a dream. His head was pounding and his vision was so blurry that the sergeant appeared to be at least three people hovering over him. Again the sergeant said, "Can you hear me, Lieutenant?"

"I hear you but I can't see you clearly. What happened?"

"As near as I can tell, you've been shot by a dead man. There's a Reb lying over by the wheel of that limber. He's dead but his body is warm and the pistol in his hand was just fired. He must have had enough left to pull the trigger and that was all."

"Another man," said James, "under the limber. My cousin, Jeff . . . needs a doctor."

The sergeant went over to the wreckage for a moment then returned.

"You're right, sir, there's a live one over there. His belly wound looks bad."

"Needs a doctor," said James. "Got to get a doctor."

"You need a doctor, too, Lieutenant. That bullet plowed a furrow on the right side of your skull. I'll get you to the field hospital and tell them to send help for the Reb. Let me get you up now."

The sergeant, fortunately a husky fellow, pulled James to his feet. His knees were weak and he could hardly lock them to stand up. With some difficulty, the sergeant heaved him into the saddle and grabbed a fistful of his jacket, holding on until he could steady himself. "I'll lead your horse, Lieutenant. "Can you hang on?"

"I'll try."

They had only gone a few steps before James slumped forward and wrapped his arms around Tar's neck.

By the time they got to the hospital he was unconscious and it took two orderlies to loosen the grip, made tighter by reflex, and pull him from the horse.

Nearly forty-eight hours passed before James awoke to a world of complete darkness. The bandage started above his hairline and weaved its way down to his chin. All around, he could hear the sounds of wounded men in agony. The sounds and the pain in his head, added to the visual blackout, made James believe that he must surely be in hell. His head throbbed and he was tormented by a burning thirst. He attempted to collect his thoughts, hoping that he would remember what happened, but he could not put it together and the frustration only added to his misery.

At length, he raised his right hand to try to get someone's attention. In a few minutes he felt a hand on his; a smaller, softer, feminine hand. Then he heard an angelic voice say, "I'm happy to see that you are awake, Lieutenant. How are you feeling today?" After a few hard swallows down his parched throat he managed to say, "May I please have some water?"

"Certainly, Lieutenant, I have water right here." He felt an arm slide under his neck and lift slightly, and then a cup was put to his lips and cool water poured into his mouth. After a satisfying drink he thanked his benefactor and asked, "Where am I?"

"You are at St. Francis Xavier Catholic Church in Gettysburg. We've set up a hospital here to assist with the care of the wounded. I am Sister Dorthea. What is your name, Lieutenant?"

197

"James. Lieutenant James Langdon."

"James is a fine name. I have always been partial to it. Are you hungry, James?"

"No, Sister. I don't think I could eat right now."

"Are you sure? Perhaps just some clear broth? You haven't had anything since you were brought in."

"How long has it been?"

"Two days now."

"Nothing right now, Sister. Maybe in a little while. My head is very sore."

"I am certain of it," said Sister Dorthea. "You have a very nasty gash on the right side."

Then after a moment to summon the courage James asked, "Am I blind, Sister?"

"I pray not, James. You've received a number of stitches in your scalp and many times a head injury can disrupt a person's vision for a while. The sight is blurred and the strain of trying to focus can cause additional headaches. That is why we covered your eyes for the time being, to let your optic nerves relax. We'll remove the full bandage in a couple of days and keep only your wound covered."

"I am very grateful, Sister."

"You are most welcome, James. When you are ready to eat something, just raise your hand as you did before. I will see it."

Five days after the shooting, the bandage covering his eyes was removed. He was instructed to keep his eyes closed until the wrap was taken off and then to open them very slowly. At first, the sun streaming through the stain glass windows of the church was so bright that his eyes immediately began to water. They were gently mopped dry with a clean cloth, and little by little, things began to come into focus.

However, it soon became evident that his eyesight had not been restored to normal. Sometimes he would see double images causing him to bump into a wall when trying to go through a doorway. In addition, there was still a great deal of swelling around the wound and he had not entirely gotten rid of his headaches. He was also having trouble with his memory. He knew who he was and he knew, for example, that he had a wife and son, but his short term memory seemed to be erased. He could not remember events that had occurred shortly before being shot.

Ten days after receiving his wound, James was visited by the ranking military surgeon, Major Denton Wilcox. Major Wilcox had stayed behind when the army moved out to supervise the care of the great number of wounded. After conducting a thorough examination, the major explained his thoughts and opinions to James.

"I am sure that you can understand, Lieutenant, that any head would is considered to be serious, even in your case where fortunately the skull was not penetrated or even fractured. With a wound such as yours, there can still be temporary and sometimes permanent damage to the brain, which can affect eyesight or perhaps motor skills. It is my considered opinion that your condition will continue to improve until you are completely back to normal. The downside is that it is going to take time; how much time is impossible to calculate. Therefore, it is my recommendation that you should be relieved from duty until such time as you are cleared by competent medical authority to return. In other words, we are sending you home."

"I suppose I should be happy about that, Major, and I guess I am. But it is with reluctance that I leave my post. I assume that a soldier always feels that way."

"Just the good ones."

"Thank you, sir. I assure you that as soon as I am able, I'll be back."

"In the meantime, Lieutenant, take care of yourself." James saluted his superior and said goodbye.

Three days later, he was on the train from Gettysburg to Mapletown. Major Wilcox had supplied him with a letter and a copy of his medical record to be given to his doctor at home. From that point on, Dr. Pierce would see to his care.

As the train was leaving the station, an old man in the seat behind him was talking to his wife. Apparently they had come to Gettysburg to visit a relative, a Union soldier who had been wounded in the battle. Said the old man,

"What can a man do when he's lost both arms? What is to become of my poor cousin, Jacob?"

Cousin! The word triggered something in his mind. Suddenly it was all coming back. James had found his cousin, Jefferson, on the battlefield. He was badly hurt and possibly dying. He was telling James about the folks back home. The news wasn't good. James was about to go for help when he was shot in the head. Then someone came to his aid; maybe it was sergeant something or other. He remembered being helped onto his horse. Didn't the sergeant say he'd send help for the Reb?

The train was miles from the station now. There was nothing he could do. Did Jefferson live or die? At that moment James wondered if he would ever find out.

TWENTY-TWO

The Price of Commitment

As the train chugged westward, James's thoughts were about the sudden turn of events. There was not enough time to send word to Polly, save for a telegram, and he was worried that a messenger at the front door might frighten her. By the same token, she would not be prepared for James to suddenly show up at home either. At least when he did, she would see immediately that he was alive and in one piece, then he could explain things in person.

He tried to enjoy the thought of soon being in the company of his family . . . and he did. However, the fact that he was going home because he'd been wounded again, did detract from it; not to mention the concern about how well he would recover. The double vision plagued him and his head was still sore. Half of his hair had been shaved off, adding a gruesome appearance to his physical problems.

When the train arrived at the station in Mapletown, James decided to visit Dr. Pierce before going home. He thought it was important to see the doctor as soon as possible and his office was just a short walk from the station. It was necessary now to move around very carefully lest he fall or run into something and further injure himself. Major Wilcox had supplied him with a cane, and although he hated having to use it, he soon found out that it did come in handy.

Fortunately, when he got to Dr. Pierce's office, the doctor was in. When the door opened, the doctor looked up from a journal in which he had been writing, saw James, and hurried to his side. "James, what's happened? Here, let me get you seated." Dr. Pierce took James's arm and helped him into a large stuffed chair. He pulled another one alongside and sat himself.

201

"I just got in from Gettysburg," said James. "I got in the way of another bullet."

"Yes, it was a terrible battle. I read about it in the paper. What is the extent of your injury?" James handed him the letter and the report he was given by Major Wilcox. "This will explain better than I can."

Dr. Pierce read over the paperwork very carefully, and then he said, "You've had a very close call."

"Yes, a little too close. Do you agree with Major Wilcox about my chances for a full recovery?"

"I wish that I could give you a definite answer, James, but I can't. It is simply too early to tell. We'll have to wait for the swelling to go down completely before we can expect much improvement. I can give you something for the pain if you need it and I will change the bandage regularly. You needn't come here. I will visit you at home. Does Polly know you're here?"

"Not yet. I didn't have time to send word. I'm afraid of how this will affect her. I haven't heard from her lately. The army moves around so much that it is difficult for the mail to keep up. Is she well, and my son?"

"They're fine, James. I stopped by just last week. Little James is growing like a weed in a spring garden. They will be happy to see you."

"I am anxious to see them, too. I just hope I don't scare them away. I don't look so good with half my head shaved."

"Nonsense, your hair will grow back quickly, and when everything is healed you'll only have a scar on your scalp. Just be patient. I'll go hitch up Sally and bring the buggy around front. I want you to be home taking it easy."

The reunion with his family was the best medicine he could have received. For Polly, it was joy mixed with an unsettling concern that she obviously tried very hard to hide. Dr. Pierce was very helpful explaining what had happened and what to expect as James convalesced.

When the doctor was gone she took James's hands in hers and cried, "My dear husband. What is all of this doing to you? I have endured the loneliness. I have kept my faith in God and in the government to end slavery and pull the country back together. But it grieves me so to see you hurt again. Is this the price of commitment? God help me, but the price may be too high." At that point she broke down completely.

James stroked her soft blonde hair until her weeping subsided. "I have struggled with this issue myself," he said. "When I woke up in the hospital in Gettysburg I was in total darkness. I couldn't remember what had happened and I was terrified. Then I found out that I was in a house of God and I was being ministered to by a nun named Sister Dorthea. Her voice was so kind and comforting that my fear disappeared. For what purpose I was wounded, I cannot exactly say. But God *was* with me and the fact that I am here with you proves it."

Then James told her the story of how he had been wounded. He told her about finding his cousin, Jefferson, on the battlefield and about everything he'd learned before Jeff lost consciousness.

"I don't know if Jeff survived or not. I do know that my parents are not well and that other members of my family have suffered a loss. That is why this terrible conflict must end. I know it doesn't make any sense, but the only way for it to end is to keep fighting. I remember how you explained it to me the last time I was home and you were right. We must carry on, not just for our sake, but for our son's generation as well."

"Forgive my weakness, James. It is only because I love you so."

"There is nothing to forgive. Please don't think of yourself as weak—it isn't true. I am guilty of having the same feelings as you. We will find our strength in each other and not allow what we have to be destroyed."

"And your family in Georgia . . . what can we do for them?"

"We can pray."

The conversation was interrupted by a baby's cry from upstairs.

"Your son is awake," said Polly. "He probably knows that his courageous father is home. I will tend to him then bring him down for a visit."

James eased back in the chair and closed his eyes. It really was good to be home no matter how it had come to be. When Polly came downstairs, James took his son and held him for hours. Even at seven months he was the image of his mother: fair hair and the same blue eyes. James hoped that one day he would take the boy to Georgia and show him his ancestral home.

By January, 1864, James was showing vast signs of improvement. His wound was completely healed and his eyesight was nearly back to normal. He still suffered from headaches, but they were less frequent. Dr. Pierce was still unwilling to release James from his care. Like Reverend Pyle and his wife, Dr. Pierce had become a very close friend. After all, it was the good doctor who had saved his life the first time he came to Mapletown. It was he who had delivered little James and taken care of Polly.

Now James harbored the suspicion that perhaps the doctor did not wish to see him return to the war. Maybe he thought that if he withheld the release long enough the war would end before he could return to battle. Even if James could prove his suspicion he would not be angry—he would be grateful. The doctor's idea, if it were true, *would* hold a certain degree of promise. During his time at home, James had read every word the paper printed about the progress of the war. He knew, of course, that Gettysburg had been a great Northern victory. What he didn't know at the time was that the Confederate stronghold at Vicksburg, Mississippi had fallen the same day to General U.S. Grant and his army. A turning point had been reached and the more optimistic people in the country might be willing to say that light could be seen at the end of the tunnel.

The beginning of 1864 also marked the one year anniversary of the acceptance of blacks into the Union army. James remembered thinking how wonderful it was that the black man was finally getting the chance to fight for his freedom. Although the privilege had been denied from the outset of the war, principally because no one thought that the blacks would make good soldiers, once given the opportunity they had been expedient in proving the naysayers wrong.

Many battles had been fought since Gettysburg and each one drained more men, more resources, and more resolve from the Confederacy. Then, in March, it was clear that the U.S. Government had settled once and for all upon the general who they felt could squeeze the remaining will to fight from the South. The Senate confirmed General Grant's nomination to Lieutenant General. No one had held the rank since George Washington. Along with being the highest ranking officer, Grant would assume the title of General-in-Chief of the Army of the United States.

It was now a matter of time and James thought often about how he would like to be on hand to see the end. However, it was exceedingly true that being at home with Polly and little James was more appealing than the prospect of seeing his native homeland in ruin. But, James knew that war is an indiscriminate monster that destroys everything in its path and he would have to take the bad in order to see the emergence of the good.

So he was torn, as torn as the nation itself, between staying home with his family and returning to the struggle. He wished he had no control over the situation. He knew that he could resign his commission for health reasons. Dr. Pierce would be only too happy to support him in that decision. He knew he could get his old job back at the bank in Mapletown. With his business education he could aim even higher. There were many opportunities for an educated young man, especially in the larger towns and cities. But he could not separate himself from the voice of his conscience; constantly being reminded of his beliefs and of the promise he'd made in 1861.

One afternoon in October, James went to see Dr. Pierce. As he approached his office, the doctor was just coming out to get into his buggy. When he saw James, he sat his bag on the seat and said, "You look like a man who has made up his mind about something."

"Is it that obvious?"

"Yes. When you've been a doctor for thirty-five years, you come to understand people pretty well. I know the look of determination, especially on you, James. I got to know it the first time you came to town. I am one of the few people in whom Reverend Pyle confided about the underground railway station. Sometimes the Negroes who came to his church needed medical attention. I knew from the start what you were doing, and it takes, among other things, a great deal of determination to risk your life for so unselfish a reason. That's how I know what you're doing here today. When are you leaving?"

"Next Monday, November 12ᵗʰ. I sent a telegram to the War Department in Washington. I requested an assignment that will put me under the command of General Judson Kilpatrick. He commands the 3ʳᵈ Division, Cavalry Corps, and Military Division of the Mississippi. That means he's attached to General Sherman's army. General Sherman is in Georgia, and that is where I want to go. My request was granted. All I need is a release from you."

"I see. I would give you a final examination, but it isn't necessary. You have completely recovered. In fact, you have completely recovered and then some."

"I understand, Dr. Pierce, and I thank you for all you've done and for all you tried to do. It will be mighty hard to leave, but I believe it will be the last time."

"I truly hope so, James. I will send a wire to the War Department right away telling them that you are able to return to active duty. Take care of yourself, son." He offered his hand and James shook it firmly. Without another word he turned and walked away.

That night, James had a long talk with Polly. The emotions that were present were not what he might have expected from his wife or himself. The conversation was much the same as if they were discussing what should be planted in the garden next spring. The Union armies were everywhere down south, pressing the Rebels at every point. There was scarcely a person, Northern or Southern, who couldn't see that the end was near. Consequently, James and Polly took the position that he was going away to finish a job; that he would be back soon, and for good. Tar had been left behind in Gettysburg. James would have to take the train to Chattanooga, Tennessee and secure another mount from Quartermaster Corps and receive his orders from U.S. Army Headquarters stationed there. Then he would ride to Georgia and join Kilpatrick.

On November 12ᵗʰ, James, Polly, and little James walked together to the train station. James hugged and kissed his little family and climbed aboard. As the train pulled out, he stared at them through the window as they waved from the platform. In spite of everything, at the last minute he felt an almost overwhelming urge to jump off the train and run back to the station. But he kept his seat as he remembered those immortal words, "The price of commitment."

TWENTY-THREE

Rejoining the Fold

Early on the morning of November 13th, the train pulled into the station at Chattanooga. After finding a place to have some breakfast, James reported to the headquarters of Major General Andrew J. Smith. General Smith's adjutant, Captain Blanchard, informed him that word had reached the general's office concerning his new assignment. "You will have to wait a bit, Lieutenant, while my clerk types a copy of your orders. Is there anything else you'll need?"

"Yes, sir, I need a horse. My last mount was left in Gettysburg after I was wounded." The captain stroked his mustache for a moment.

"I was not aware of your need for a horse. Let me see what I can do. Come back in two hours."

James walked out a bit irritated at having to wait. He had already eaten and there was nothing else to do. A walk around town was the only remedy for boredom that he could come up with.

In front of a feed store he saw a wagon, a rotund, middle-aged white man sitting in the seat. The front door of the store opened and a black man came out laboring under the weight of a large sack of grain. He was struggling mightily, and when he got his load to the wagon the grain sack came down with a jolt that jerked the wagon, startling the horses. The heavyset man calmed them down with no harm done, still he was angered over the slight spooking of the animals.

He climbed down from the wagon, grabbed a post that supported the roof of the store and pulled himself up to the boardwalk. He brandished a whip in his right hand. Not waiting to see what would happen next, James positioned himself between the black man and the irate farmer and said, "What do you think you're going to do with that whip?"

"What business is if of yours, blue belly?" he said. Intending to throw a scare into the man James replied, "I'm Lieutenant James Langdon, attached to the Provost Marshal's Office in Chattanooga, and if you so much as raise that whip I'll have you jailed."

"On what charge?"

"Assault." The big man was apparently not looking for trouble. He tossed the whip into the wagon and said, "OK, Lieutenant. I lost my temper. It ain't easy to get used to."

"What do you mean?"

"I mean a man's world being turned upside down. Yankee occupation army controlling the town, niggers are free men now. I even have to pay them to work for me."

"It's only fair," said James.

"Maybe you think so. Nothing seems fair when it's forced on you."

"Things change. Just accept it; you'll be a better man for it."

"Damn your Yankee advice. I obey the law. I don't have to agree with it." Then he nodded his head toward the back of the wagon and pointed a finger at the black man. The man got in the wagon and sat down beside the grain sack. The disgruntled employer heaved himself into the seat and started off up the street. As James stared after the wagon, the black man raised his hand as if to thank him for his concern.

James started down the boardwalk thinking that few things in the world are more difficult to change than the human mind. The war was proof of that. You can muster a large army and you can defeat an adversary but you cannot change his way of thinking. The new law said that the black race was now and forever free. James knew it would be a long time before it did them much good. It was not just the people of the South who believed the blacks were inferior. The illustrious forefathers of the United States were to blame with all of their ambiguous talk of freedom. When a race of people is introduced to a new land wearing shackles and chains they are branded from that day forward. After over two hundred years of being slaves, how, James wondered, could the black man ever appear as an equal in the eyes of the whites?

When two hours had passed, James returned to General Smith's office. Tied to the hitching post out front was a mule wearing a saddle blanket and a bridle. He went inside; Captain Blanchard was waiting for him.

"Here are your orders, Lieutenant. I guess you noticed the mule outside?"

"Yes," said James in a wary tone.

"It's the best I could do. You will join up with General Kilpatrick's Corps in Atlanta. Procure a better mount when you get there. That is all."

James couldn't believe that not a single horse was available. How unpleasant it would be to ride the whole way to Atlanta on a mule, and without a saddle to boot. It would be a dangerous trip. If he ran into Confederate cavalry he wouldn't stand a chance. He knew it would do no good to argue or complain. He took his orders, tied his things to the back of the mule as best he could, and rode out of town.

By nightfall, James was only about ten miles south of Dalton. It was very slow going on the mule and more than a little uncomfortable. The only way he could prevent falling off was to keep his legs wrapped tightly around the animal's belly. He decided to get off and walk for a while. He was leading the mule down the road when he noticed a faint flicker of light in a stand of Oak trees a short distance ahead of him. When he was within a hundred feet of what he could at that distance recognize as a campfire, he tied the reins of the mule's bridle to a tree branch and crept toward it, revolver in hand. From behind a tree not far from the center of the campsite he could see a lone figure dressed in a ragged Confederate uniform. The man was stretched out by the fire with a bedroll under his head and a slouch hat covering his face. His fingers were laced together over his stomach and his musket stood against a nearby tree. What interested James the most was the big Bay horse tied to a picket pin near the edge of the firelight. Apparently, the Reb still felt that Georgia was a safe enough haven that he didn't need to bother putting out his fire before going to sleep. If he had, however, James never would have spotted his location.

He waited for a few minutes, watching closely for any movement. When he heard an audible snore, he knew it was time to act. Stepping from behind the tree, he cocked the revolver and stood beside the sleeping man's feet.

"Wake up, Johnnie," he said. The snoring stopped suddenly and the Reb slowly moved his right hand up and pushed back the slouch hat. He sat up looking both sleepy and disgusted at the same time. "*Damn* Yank. I reckon you walk through cemeteries at night wakin the dead."

"Not as a rule. But I need a horse and I *would* wake a sleeping man and help myself to his."

"You mean ya'll is gonna leave me on foot."

"Nope. There's a good young plow mule tied up just down the road and you're welcome to him."

"A plow mule for a good horse? That ain't no fair trade."

"Well, I'm also leaving you here alive."

"I reckon that does even things up some."

"Which way are you heading?"

"Back home to Virginia," said the Reb. "I was with Hardee in Atlanta. What a hell of a fight that was. The whole time I was fightin I says to myself I says, if you don't get kilt in this here battle, you bes go home while you still can. A man of few wits can see where this war is headin so what's the sense of dyin for nothin? When it was over, the army headed south and I headed north."

"Where did you get the horse?"

"I stolt him from a farm las night."

"Well that makes me feel a little less guilty about stealing him from you."

"You got a sense of humor, Yank."

"I'm glad you think so. Now roll over on your belly and put your arms straight out." The Reb did as he was told. James carefully checked him for weapons. All he found was a large bowie knife; he tossed it away. Then he picked up the musket, pulled back the hammer and removed the percussion cap from the nipple. He threw the cap and the musket into the darkness." You can find that in the morning. Now get up and saddle that horse." Again he did as he was told. Enemy or not, James felt a little ashamed.

This worn old campaigner obviously wanted no trouble. He just wanted to go home; a feeling shared by many.

When the horse was saddled, James climbed up and said, "Wait until you hear me ride by, then go down and get that mule. I do hope you make it back to Virginia."

"Thanks, Yank. I'll think a you when I do the spring plowin."

James tipped his cap and rode out through the trees. He wasted no time getting his gear off the mule and tying it behind the saddle. Then he raced by the stand of Oak trees; the Reb's campfire was still burning.

The big Bay was a welcome change from the unenthusiastic mule. On through the night James kept an easy but steady pace, and by daylight he was just twenty miles from Atlanta. Coming up on a long, sweeping bend in the road, he could see dust clouds being raised ahead of him. A little farther and the strains of "Battle Hymn of the Republic" came back to him on the morning breeze. A large body of Union troops was also heading into Atlanta. James spurred the big horse and galloped up to the rear of the column. "What army is this?" James called out.

"Why, it's Uncle Billy's of course," was the reply.

"Do you mean General Sherman?"

"None other. We're his farm boys from Ohio, Illinois, and Indiana. We're headin to Atlanta to help the fellows finish her off and then we're gonna burn a path to the sea.

James waved and veered off the side of the road to get out of the dust. He pulled up, had a drink of water and a thick slice of beef jerky. His emotions were running high. After more than two years he was back in Georgia. So huge was the temptation to bypass Atlanta and keep riding until he reached his childhood home. How wonderful it would be to see it again, he thought. Then a dark cloud loomed on his mental horizon. Things would not be the same. How would he be received? Certainly not joyously—not while wearing a blue uniform.

There was, however, one thing that gave James great satisfaction. The road was crowded with the newly liberated. Scores of black people, ex-slaves, were on the move. With the presence of the Union army there was no more need to escape. Individuals, couples, and entire families were walking away from the plantations. Some carried their belongings on their backs, others had mules and carts. None could probably say exactly where they were going but they were free to go and that was enough for now.

James wondered if Langdon Plantation had been abandoned as well. It would depend upon whether or not the Federals had occupied the area. He thought about Farley Tabor, his father's abusive overseer. How it would pierce his dark heart to see his subjugated workforce drop their burden and walk away.

James shook himself from his place of deep thought and continued on to Atlanta. From five miles out he could see that the sky was nearly blocked out by heavy black smoke. When he reached the edge of the city he was met by a scene of unbelievable destruction. Many homes in the residential areas were still standing, but the business and industrial districts were in ruins. Railway stations, warehouses, and factories had been leveled. Fire had rampaged through an oil refinery igniting a warehouse next door that contained a large supply of gunpowder. The gunpowder had exploded, sending a shower of sparks into the sky, setting other structures on fire. Many of them were still smoldering.

The soul was being torn out of a graceful city, thought James. He remembered traveling to Atlanta with his family several times as a boy. He wouldn't have believed he would ever see it like this. Hundreds of Union soldiers filled the streets, their spirits, in contrast to James's, were lively and boisterous. To them it was more like a circus than a wasteful, destructive act of war.

Turning away from the sad spectacle, he located the headquarters building and reported to Major Henry Hitchcock, General Sherman's Assistant Adjutant General. The major told him where he could find the cavalry bivouac. "Eat hearty and get some sleep tonight. Tomorrow we march and the cavalry will be leading the way."

"Are we really going all the way to the coast, Major?"

"All the way."

James had no trouble finding the cavalry encampment, and for the second time that morning he reported in. This time it was to General Judson Kilpatrick. James had read quite a lot about the general but had never seen him in person. In his opinion, Kilpatrick was an ugly man with a square jaw and bushy sideburns the color of sand. He was an authoritative figure and arrogance was his persona. Although he was a very formidable opponent, many thought him to be a reckless daredevil. The general was understandably very busy and he was short and to the point with James. "Be ready to ride in the morning," he said.

When James was dismissed, he stripped the saddle and blanket off the Bay and gave him a thorough rubdown. Naming his horses had always been an absolute habit and so he dubbed the big horse Goliath. He was bent over checking Goliath's hooves when he heard a voice say, "What do you think of old Kilcavalry?"

James looked around and there stood a trooper perhaps a few years older than him with curly dark hair, brown eyes, and a perfectly trimmed chin beard.

"I beg your pardon," said James.

"What do you think of Kilcavalry? That's what they call him, you know."

"I don't believe I've ever heard that."

"Well it *is* a sobriquet he's just recently earned."

"If you would indulge me, how did he earn it?" asked James.

"Well you see, he has this bad habit of running his troopers and their horses to exhaustion on long rides, then getting them killed in careless charges."

"Sounds like a man with a flair for the dramatic."

"That's a nice way of putting it."

"So do you think we are in for a bad time?" James questioned.

"Have you ever heard of Fighting Joe Wheeler?"

"Yes, I have."

"Well, we'll be seeing him soon. They say he's the roughest one hundred and twenty pound man in the South. His men are no better. I've heard that they are so undisciplined that they sometimes scare the Southern civilians more than we do. By the way, I'm Lieutenant Alvin Mitchell, Mitch to my friends."

"Lieutenant James Langdon." The two men shook hands. "Where you from, Mitch?"

"Pennsylvania, near Philly. You?"

"Georgia, near Macon."

"I sort of thought so but I didn't say anything because I didn't want you to think I had a problem with it. I don't."

"It's OK. Others have asked. No one has given me a bad time yet."

"You're lucky. I've run into some pretty narrow minds in the army. You know you're likely to see home tomorrow."

"What makes you think so?"

"I'm a staff officer so I know a little more about what's going on. But I might get in Dutch for talking too much so keep it under your hat."

"Sure."

"General Sherman has four corps. He is splitting them into two wings with two corps each. The northern wing will be commanded by General Slocum, the southern wing by General Howard. They'll travel on parallel routes for a week or so then turn towards each other and meet at Milledgeville. Kilpatrick's five thousand troopers will ride ahead of Howard's wing to screen the advance. When we ride tomorrow we'll be heading in a southeasterly direction towards Macon."

"Are we to take Macon?"

"Not from what I've heard. We will make an assault on the city but it's only meant as a feint. The idea is to camouflage our real objective. Howard's wing will turn northeast."

"Then I won't see home," said James. "My father's plantation is south of Macon."

"I'm glad, James. It could be pretty rough on you. But you should still prepare for the worst."

"What does that mean?"

"Have you noticed the mood of the men in this army?"

"Yes. They act as though they're on a holiday."

"Exactly. That's because they plan on filling their pockets."

"I don't follow you."

"The wagon train will only carry enough supplies to last about twenty days. After that we will have to live off the land. Each day every regiment will send out foraging parties, about twenty to thirty men under an officer. There job is to gather supplies, but from what I've seen they'll do more than that. General Sherman is a very good military commander but he believes in making war on civilians. He's issued orders forbidding the men to trespass in dwellings. They have also been ordered to discriminate between rich and poor and in either case to leave enough food to maintain the family. But Sherman will not enforce the rules. Once those bummers get started they will pillage and plunder. They'll take what they want and destroy the rest. I've seen it happen right here in Atlanta. For a lot of these men this march will be something of a sport. I just want to warn you, James. You may find it difficult to watch."

James did not know how to answer. He was still naïve enough to be appalled at such conduct and even more so that the high command did not restrain their men. Apparently he was not grasping the concept of total war. And what about the Southern command, he wondered. Were they not yet willing to admit that they had made a mistake? Everyone knew from the beginning that most of the fighting would be on Southern soil. With very few exceptions, this had been the case. Did they not know what to expect if they failed to drive the Yankees off? Was it worth all the waste and all the destruction just to keep a race of people in bondage? God forgive me, thought James, they must be evil.

"Thank you for the information, Mitch, but I have made my bed and I *will* sleep in it. My father taught me that . . . maybe he can be proud of me for something."

TWENTY-FOUR

The March Begins

On the morning of November 15th, 1864, the cavalry, with General Kilpatrick in the lead, rode out of Atlanta. It was not long before they encountered veteran troopers in faded gray. General Wheeler's men threw up roadblocks at East Point, Jonesboro, Stockbridge, and Lovejoy's Station in an effort to slow the advancing Federal army. But the Rebels were simply overwhelmed by numbers and continued to retreat to Macon.

General Wheeler had massed about two thousand men to defend the city. Four miles from the outskirts of Macon, the dismounted Confederate cavalry were dug in behind earthen barriers, waiting for an attack. Inspired by the spirit of their commander, the Yankee riders charged Wheeler's position. James was out in front, bent low in the saddle to make less of a target, firing his army revolver and yelling like a madman. Men on both sides of him fell from their horses; some dying instantly; others were trampled to death by accident. When the Union troopers reached the Confederate line they split left and right then made a half circle and headed for the rear.

After making the turn, just ahead of James, a comrade was hit in the shoulder and slumped forward in the saddle. The wounded man tried to hang on at least long enough to get beyond range of the Confederate rifles. He may have made it except for the fact that another bullet struck his horse in the lower neck causing animal and rider to slam to the ground. James was almost past the motionless soldier, moving at a full gallop when he realized that it was Lieutenant Alvin Mitchell.

Not knowing if Mitch was dead or alive, he wrestled Goliath to a stop, wheeled around, and rode back to where he lay. He jumped to the ground trying to hold onto the big Bay who was wild with fear. Thinking quickly but not necessarily clearly, James tied the reins to his belt. He reached down for Mitch while Goliath tried to drag him away from the shooting. The bullets that screamed past were most uncomfortably close. Two rounds thudded into Mitch's dead horse. After what seemed like eternity, James got Mitch to his feet. He was dazed and bleeding but his survival instincts took hold, and with James's help, managed to climb up onto the rearing Bay. James leaped at the horse's rump and clawed for a handful of saddle. He pulled himself up behind Mitch, reached around him, and took the reins. Goliath needed no urging to race for the rear. It wasn't until they were safely out of range and until the adrenalin stopped coursing through his veins that James realized his left trouser leg had been nicked by a bullet; his right shoulder insignia had been shot away.

After the attack, Kilpatrick retreated and the wounded that were able to make it back, including Lieutenant Mitchell, were taken to the main column for medical attention. Before Mitch was taken away, he held out his good arm and said, "I owe you, James. Your father would have to be proud."

Howard's wing circled northeast as Mitch said they would; Slocum's wing approached Covington on its feint towards Augusta.

Immediately after Slocum's wing passed by the town of Covington, the liberated slaves began to follow the army by the thousands. They waited along the roads and at every crossing. They would crowd into the camps at night carrying information, food, and most of all, gratitude. The joyous slaves told the soldiers stories of how they were whipped and beaten, often having salt rubbed into their wounds. They talked about the bloodhounds that were used to hunt them if they tried to escape. James felt a twinge when they mentioned the dogs, remembering the dog pen that was attached to Farley Tabor's quarters. He also remembered a time hearing the yelping himself when he was leading runaway slaves North from Tennessee. The Union soldiers developed a special loathing for such dogs because they knew that they were also used to track fellow soldiers who escaped from Southern prisons. Whenever they got the chance the men killed the bloodhounds.

Again, the mixture of emotions made it difficult for James to sleep, whenever he was afforded the opportunity. The stories that came from the slaves reinforced his belief that he was doing the right thing. Unfortunately, Lieutenant Mitchell's predictions had been correct about the foragers. They were like outlaws in a territory where there was no one to stand against them. It was free will and free reign; whether the men came back with useful supplies or women's dresses they had stolen, it was all the same to the officers. To James it was largely a desire to steal and destroy disguised as retribution. And it *was* difficult for him to watch frightened civilians trying to pack a few possessions and flee before the approaching army. As in every circumstance, the innocent were being punished with the guilty without a care as to which was which.

More and more the ability of the Confederacy to oppose the Union army was showing signs of desperation. Old men and young boys were all that was left to fill the ranks of local militia. The days of brilliant Southern victories were gone and every attempt to stem the tide ended in a defeated effort.

Near Griswoldville, an inexperienced general named P.J. Phillips attacked a single brigade of Union infantry under the command of Brigadier General Charles C. Walcutt. The Confederates outnumbered the Yankees two to one, but the advantage was offset by one regiment of the Union brigade, who carried Spencer repeating rifles. Bravery proved to be no match for firepower and the Confederates fell in waves before the fast-shooting weapons. When the battle was over, James rode out across the field. Among the Southerners who lay dead or dying, not one was of a legal age for recruitment.

At Milledgeville on November 22nd, the two wings of the army merged as planned. By afternoon, the capitol building was flying the flag of the 107th New York. The stop at the state capital was merely part of the journey, not the destination, and after a short stay the army moved on.

Once again the two wings separated and moved along on parallel routes. The speed of the march was slowed to allow more time to gather the needed supplies. It also made possible the destruction of more resources that supported the enemy. Railroad tracks, rolling stock, and grist mills were reduced to rubbish.

Nearly half the distance to Savannah was covered in ten days with only Wheeler's cavalry amounting to any real opposition. James was not as experienced as most of his comrades; still, in his opinion, the clashes with the Confederate troopers were no small thing. For three days straight, the Yankee riders fought a series of skirmishes that together became known as the Battle of Waynesboro. On two occasions, General Kilpatrick himself was nearly captured.

Then one day, James witnessed something that would remain pressed into his mind forever. The incident occurred at Ebenezer Creek, a muddy stream about one hundred feet in width. Brigadier General Jefferson C. Davis, in charge of XIV Corps, had lost his patience with the cumbersome crowd of refugees that had come to be an unwelcome hindrance to the army. His corps was last in the column of Slocum's left wing. The 58th Indiana had assembled a pontoon bridge across the creek. Davis crossed his men but gave orders denying the ex-slaves access to the bridge. James had been dispatched with twenty-five troopers to cover the crossing because Wheeler's cavalry was not far behind.

When the soldiers and the cavalry detachment had crossed, Davis ordered the bridge cut loose and the slaves were stranded, cut off from the protection of the army. Terrified at being left on the same side of the creek with the Confederates, the panic stricken mob pushed forward to the edge of the bank, toppling those in front into the water. Some were lucky enough to overcome the swiftly flowing stream and swim across. But many, mostly women and children, were pulled under and drowned.

As the drama unfolded, James sat on his horse in disbelief when the temporary bridge was taken away before the eyes of the refugees. He jumped off his horse and began to yell at the engineers, but their orders had come from General Davis and he was ignored. Then he ordered some of his troopers to grab axes, cut trees, and push them into the creek. He paced the bank in a panic as in a bad dream where he was being chased, tried to run, but couldn't. With complete disregard for his own safety, thinking only of saving lives, he dove into the water. James was a good swimmer but the current was strong and he struggled to keep his head above water. Two small children, a boy and a girl, were drifting straight toward him. Just before they were within reach they went under. James dove down, flailing blindly with his arms, trying desperately to locate the children. Suddenly he felt a leg and then another. Pushing for the surface, he brought both children, who had been hugging each other, up from the murky water, coughing and gasping for breath. While kicking mightily, he managed to get the young girl on his back and hold the boy with one arm as he tried to swim with the other. He was in mid-stream and it looked to James that safety was a mile away. His strength was nearly gone and he harnessed every bit of what was left, but his burden was too great, the current too strong.

Just when he felt himself about to sink to the depths, something struck his arm. He realized that it was a rope with a large loop on the end. He slipped the loop over his head and under his armpits, still keeping the children's heads above water. Then someone on the other end started to pull.

When they reached the bank, James was able to grab onto enough roots and grass and hold on but he was exhausted. A pair of hands came down and lifted the girl from his back. Likewise, the boy was lifted out, then a hand was extended to him. For the first time, he looked up and there was Lieutenant Alvin Mitchell.

"Where did you come from?" asked James.

"I was riding in a wagon at the end of the column. I saw you kick off your boots and dive into the creek. I grabbed a rope and came running; I was afraid you'd be swept away."

"I owe you, Mitch. If not for your quick thinking I would have sunk to the bottom with those children still clinging to me."

"You don't owe me, my friend, we're even."

James sat on the bank of Ebenezer Creek while the deadly fiasco continued. Mitch sat down beside him and put an arm across his shoulder. "You did all you could,

James. These poor souls would rather die as free men than live as slaves."

The army marched away toward Savannah. Mitch got James to his feet and back on his horse. Then he climbed up behind him to get a ride back to his place in the wagon. About a hundred yards from the creek they heard the sound of gunshots behind them. Looking back they saw that Wheeler's cavalry had appeared on the far bank and they were herding the remaining refugees back into slavery. "They won't go back for long," said Mitch. "These Rebs are living off their last breath. They will have to surrender soon"

"I hope you're right, Mitch."

He gave James a reassuring slap on the shoulder. "Let's go, James. Savannah is only twenty miles ahead."

After the death of Corporal Thomas Milroy, James promised himself he would never befriend another man as long as the war lasted. But after the incident at the creek, he changed his mind.

TWENTY-FIVE

Surprises in Savannah

When Sherman's army pulled up four miles from
Savannah, it looked as though, in all probability, a bloody
conflict would be necessary before the city could be taken.
Ten thousand men under the command of General William
Hardee were inside. The city had been well prepared with
formidable earthworks bolstered by artillery. To Hardee,
Sherman issued an ultimatum to surrender without delay
or suffer the consequences, but Hardee refused.

General Beauregard, who had entered the city before
Sherman arrived, ordered Hardee to build a pontoon bridge
across the Savannah River so that his men could escape to
South Carolina. Beauregard did not want to risk capture of
the army, as it would be needed if Sherman himself headed
north toward the Carolinas.

Consequently, by December 19th, the escape bridge had
been completed. To confuse Sherman, Hardee commenced
a bombardment on December 20th and continued the
shelling while his army evacuated Savannah. When the
last Rebels crossed over, the bridge was cut loose and set
adrift in the river. Not only was the city taken without a
shot, but even more surprising was the reception the army
received from Mayor Richard Arnold. Understanding the
better part of valor, the mayor favored welcoming the
Union troops to having his city destroyed needlessly. It was
a feeling shared by most of the war-weary citizens. Even
though it still had to be taken with a spoonful of sugar to
get it down, most of the people humored the invaders with
Southern charm and hospitality.

Sherman reciprocated by keeping his men in line with
drilling, inspections, and parades. In addition, small
cavalry patrols of three troopers roamed the streets day
and night to make sure that the peace was maintained.

One evening, shortly before dark, James was on patrol along the water front with two other men: Sergeant Watson and Corporal Reeves. Looking ahead as they walked their horses along the street, James could see what looked like an altercation between a soldier and a female. The woman was making dramatic gestures with both hands, and as James got closer he saw the soldier push her against the wall of a house and pin her there with his body. Spurring his horse and urging his companions to do the same, he galloped down the street and stopped abruptly at the scene. He climbed down from Goliath's back, ran over, and pulled the soldier backwards, knocking him to the sidewalk. The soldier, who was intoxicated, struggled to his feet and threw a roundhouse right at James's head. The punch was easily avoided and as the ruffian's momentum carried him almost one hundred eighty degrees from loss of balance and missing his target; James put him face down in the street. While the troublemaker squirmed, cursed, and pleaded his case, Sergeant Watson clapped a set of manacles on his wrists. Then the sergeant, with the help of Corporal Reeves, hauled the unruly drunk to his feet. "Take this man to the guardhouse, Sergeant," said James. "Make him walk ahead of your horse."

"Yes, sir," Watson replied. "He can walk off some of that popskull."

"Go along, Corporal. I'll catch up to you later." The troopers saluted, mounted their horses, and started the prisoner up the street.

James turned back to offer apologies to the young woman who had been accosted but she had already walked away. After checking left and right, he saw her about two blocks up the street moving at a brisk pace. Darkness had fallen and the street lights had been lit. Perhaps, thought James, he should offer to escort her home.

He mounted his horse and rode up the street, stopping a few yards ahead of the young woman. As she came abreast of him he began making his apologies for the rude behavior of the intoxicated soldier when his words suddenly failed him. Almost simultaneously the young woman's mouth dropped open and she stood transfixed and speechless. James was the first to recover his faculties and in a tone of astonishment he said, "Kate!"

On the list he could have written of things he wouldn't have expected, near the top would have been finding his youngest sister in Savannah. When her initial shock had passed, she, too, found her voice. "James?"

Their family bonds ran deep, and commanded by her natural inclination, she wrapped her arms around him and squeezed harder than James would have thought possible. Then she backed away and he knew that Kate was appalled by his uniform. "It's true," she said. "Everyone hoped and prayed that somehow it wasn't, but it's true. You're a Yankee. The South is dying, your friends and family are dying, and you are on the side that is killing them."

James had no idea how to respond. Even if he had been given a week to prepare, he still wouldn't have known what to say. But he knew he had to think of something quick lest she turn and run away. "Let me try to explain, Kate. I beg you to let me try to explain."

Tears were already filling her eyes. He feared she was going to reject his plea, but she said, "I'll listen. What is it that you want to say?"

"My words and my actions are controlled by my heart and by my conscience. They dominate so completely that I am powerless against them. Ever since I was old enough to understand the meaning of the word, I could not condone the institution of slavery. I always knew in my heart that it was wrong and my conscience would not allow me to forget it. No man has the right to take the life of another man. That is why murder is illegal. So how can it be right to take a man's life by robbing him of his freedom? Without freedom there is no life, just existence. How is it right to work that man without mercy day in and day out; to beat him and sell his wife and children? The crime of murder pales in comparison to forcing a man into slavery, in fact, it might be considered merciful. I learned something else that I didn't realize when I was growing up, something that is even worse than slavery itself. Those who believe in it not only see the Negroes as being unequal to whites; they do not recognize them as human beings. Do you

understand what that means, Kate? It means that they
have taken it upon themselves to play God. Where did they
ever find such audacity? As people, the black race may
have a different skin color, a different heritage, and a
different culture. As a species, they are the same as whites
or Indians or Chinamen. They have the same feelings,
needs, likes, and dislikes.

"I feel like a fool now for believing, but Father had me
convinced that the Negroes on our plantation worked for a
share of what they produced. Should I be blamed for
trusting my own father? But he kept all of us miles away
so that we could not see what was really going on. He even
deceived Mother. On my eighteenth birthday I found out
the truth. I broke the rules and rode to the compound to
see him. Without his knowledge, I witnessed the savage
whipping of a black man named Bo Sampson. He had been
caught trying to escape. Farley Tabor started the
punishment and then . . . father took his turn with the
whip. I saw him in a way I'd never seen before. I was
sickened by the sight of it. I left for home without seeing
him. He caught up to me on the road and admitted
everything. I don't know what I would have done if the war
hadn't come. I *do* know that I would never have let him
turn me into a slave owner. When the war did come, I knew
that I could never fight for the Confederacy. So I deceived
Father as he deceived me. For over a year after leaving
home, I helped slaves escape and then took them north to
freedom. After President Lincoln issued the Emancipation
Proclamation I joined the Union army because the war
became a struggle for the freedom of all men. My fight has
been against slavery, nothing more."

James held his breath and waited to see how Kate
would respond.

She said, "Why did Father keep it a secret?"

"He said that Mother's family never owned slaves. You
know how sensitive Mother is."

Kate winced; James continued. "I believe that he knew
it would be difficult for her to be a party to slavery. I know
now that it also concerns an experience that I had when I
was seven years old. I guess like slavery itself, he started
something and held on to it, knowing that it might one day

explode in his hands. I am sorry for the way things turned out. Maybe someday Father will be sorry, too. Sometimes we must apologize for what we are. Can you understand my reasons?"

James had nothing more to say. Now it was up to Kate. She was silent for a time. The meeting had taken them both off guard. Maybe it was all too overwhelming for a girl so young, only seventeen. Then she took her turn to speak and James slowly realized that she was no longer the giddy, immature little sister he'd left behind.

"I do understand, James, and I want you to know that I do not hate you. I never did, even when the whispered rumors began. As you said, Father kept us away from the harsh realities of slavery. I suppose that he was following a way of life that started generations ago. Sooner or later that way of life had to be broken either by war or by someone as conscientious as you. I despise the war and what it's done to the South. I despise the wasteful destruction that's been done to human life and property. I understand the concept of slavery, even if I didn't see it at home. Like you, I do not condone it and I suffer a certain sense of shame that the South has kept such a despicable crime as part of their way of life. The time has finally come for retribution and it has come with a vengeance.

"When our cousin, Jefferson, came home from the war, we found out that you were with the Union. I'm sorry I reacted badly when I first saw you, James. No matter what my feelings are about slavery, it is still difficult to see you in what is considered here to be an enemy uniform. Father had already had his suspicions but when Jefferson came home, we knew for sure."

"I'm glad that he survived," James interrupted. "I found him on the battlefield at Gettysburg. I was going for help when I was shot. I never knew what happened. He told me about Franklin, Clark, and Jessie. He also told me that Mother and Father were not faring well."

"Father took the news about you very hard. I think he lost a part of himself that day. Mother grew weaker and more distraught from worrying about him and worrying about you. She wouldn't eat. As the war news got worse, so did both of them. Ashton and I tried to care for them; by that time, all of the women of the house were gone. Husbands and sons died in the war and one by one, the women just went away.

"Ashton was close to breaking down. Without telling anyone, she married an Englishman, a blockade runner she'd met in Macon. He had come here after the start of the war to make his fortune as a smuggler. She had only known him for a week. It was Ashton's hope that he would take her to England, at least until the end of the war. But he only took her as far as Virginia. One night his vessel was attacked by a Union warship and he was killed. Now she lives alone somewhere near Winchester. We haven't heard from her in almost a year.

"When Lincoln freed the slaves, the plantation collapsed. All of the white men who worked for father were taken for the service and the Negroes started running away. Soon after, all that was left was Uncle Stanley, Uncle Joseph, and Father. They were ruined. It was all they could do to farm a small plot of land to raise food for their tables." Then Kate stopped for a moment. James knew she had more to say but the further she went, the more difficult it became.

"Then one morning about six months ago, I prepared a bit of breakfast to take up to Mother. Father had already gone to the field. I opened her bedroom door and called to her but she did not answer. I sat the breakfast tray on the nightstand, rattling the cup and saucer, but Mother was asleep. I pulled a chair over by the bed and sat down. I sat there and I sat there, and I waited and waited but . . ." Kate suddenly grabbed James by the arm as if she might draw strength from it. James put his other arm around her and pulled her close, muffling her sobs. He knew the rest. He could feel his heart pounding beneath his heavy wool jacket. Then in a broken voice Kate said, "Oh James . . . Mother wasn't sleeping."

At that point she broke down and James could not help from doing the same. His mother was gone; that sweet gentle woman, his first love. Guilt covered him like a shroud. How much had he contributed to her early decline? How had he not made it possible to see her in more than three years, especially when he was told that she was not well?

James guided Kate to the front stoop of a nearby house. They sat side by side and consoled each other. When Kate regained her composure she said, "I sat in that chair until Father came home. I heard him call to me when he came in but I couldn't answer. He found me in the bedroom with Mother; as soon as he walked in, he knew. It broke him, James. It broke him completely. I got up and helped him into the chair. When I went in the next morning, he was still there. It was difficult to get him to understand that Mother needed to be taken care of. I didn't think he was going to allow her to be buried. I sent for Dr. Mead and he came; along with Reverend Tobias, they helped me with Father. I wrote to Ashton but I never heard from her. With the war going on, I can't be sure she ever received my letter.

"Father sat like a stone for days after the funeral. I wondered where you were. I wished you were there. Finally, he regained his senses. He told me that the war was heading for our front doorstep. He didn't want me in harm's way. I didn't want to leave but he was so distraught that I didn't want to argue with him. I don't know if you remember Mrs. Melanie Hunter. She grew up with Mother in Macon then moved to Savannah after she got married. People still call her Mrs. Hunter even though her husband died many years ago when the ship he was working on was lost at sea.

"She would visit Mother once or twice a year; back then, you were usually away at school. She has a fine house and she lives alone. She didn't have her husband long enough to have children and she never remarried. Father wrote to her and asked if I could stay with her for a while. A month later, Father received a letter from her. She said that I could come and stay as long as I wanted, so Father sent me here. Mrs. Hunter has been good to me, but when the war is over and Father sends word, I'll go home . . . if home is still there."

It was well after dark now. James told Kate that he would walk her home. As they made their way to Mrs. Hunter's house, James told her about his life since leaving home. She was both surprised and sad when he told her about Polly and little James. She told James that she hoped to meet her sister-in-law and nephew someday. James promised her that the day would come. "I hope someday soon we will all be together again, Kate."

"Before your hopes become too high, James, please understand that a reunion with Ashton may not be possible. After Jefferson told us about seeing you at Gettysburg, Ashton denounced you and she swore an oath that she would never speak to you again. She blames you for a great deal, even for the death of her husband. Her wounds may never heal."

When they reached Mrs. Hunter's home, James hugged his sister again.

"I can't tell you how good it is to see you, Kate. I believe the army will be here for a couple of weeks. I will visit as often as I can while I'm here. I intend to speak to my commanding officer before we pull out and ask for a short furlough. I'd like to visit home before I leave Georgia. I must see Father and try to explain myself to him."

"Maybe it would do him some good," said Kate. "But I really don't know."

"I have to try," he replied. "I'll say goodnight now, Kate. I need to find a quiet place to think and to pray."

TWENTY-SIX

The Best Laid Plans

The following weeks were very difficult for James as he did his duty and mourned his mother's death. It did not help knowing that his oldest sister, Ashton, hated him, and quite likely, his father as well. The bright spot, of course was not only finding Kate in Savannah, but more importantly she did *not* hate him. In fact, each opportunity he had to spend time with her made the relationship seem more as it had been before the madness all began. He wrote Polly a long letter bringing her up to date about his family.

A week before the army was ready to leave Savannah, James requested permission to see General Kilpatrick's Chief of Staff concerning a leave of absence. At first, Major Jennings was reluctant to acquiesce to his request. He explained that while he could appreciate the fact that James had been away from duty for over a year and a half because of a serious wound, still he had only been back on active duty for a short time. However, when James told the major about his mother's death and that home was relatively close by, the major relented, granting him three days.

On January 21st, the army was prepared to move out and head north into South Carolina. For James, it was very hard to say goodbye to Kate. He promised he would write to her after he'd visited their father. He further promised that he would be in touch with her after the war. "I'll bring my wife and son to Georgia. I am very anxious for them to meet you."

"Please take care of yourself, James, and tell Father that I am well and ready to come home whenever he thinks best."

"I'll tell him, Kate, goodbye."

231

James climbed up on Goliath and headed out of the city toward Macon. It was true that he was shadowed by trepidation at the thought of confronting his father. He was also filled with some queer sort of anticipation, helplessly hoping that the visit would turn out better than he expected. The day before leaving Savannah, he purchased some civilian clothes that he intended to wear for the visit. He would not insult his father by wearing the uniform of whom *he* thought of as the enemy. He could hardly believe that he was finally on his way.

In spite of James's preoccupation with his family problems, there was still a war going on and a soldier must never forget that, especially in enemy territory. So absorbed was James in his preparation for the visit, that he did not realize he was being followed. When the first bullet whistled past him, the Confederates were just a few hundred yards behind and bearing down fast. Quickly assessing the situation, he could see that there was no cover anywhere close. Even if there had been, the odds were just too great. Accepting the fact that he had made a costly mistake, he did the only thing he could do. Reining Goliath to a stop, he dismounted, dropped his weapons and put his hands high in the air.

In about a minute he was encircled by a dozen gray-clad riders. A tall, rough hewn sergeant got off his horse and checked to be sure that James had completely disarmed himself then he said, "One a Sherman's boys ain't ya? You get lost from the herd?"

"No. I was heading home."

"Where's home?"

"Macon."

"Macon? In that Yank uniform? You tryin to be funny?"

"No. My home is near there." James immediately regretted his blunder. What could have been worse than admitting to the likes of these men that he was a Southerner, especially since he was learning to disguise his accent so that it was not as recognizable? If only he had changed into the civilian clothing he'd purchased, before leaving Savannah. Ever since hearing of his mother's death, his ability to think clearly had suffered. Two serious mistakes in a row equaled the unfortunate result.

"So you're a traitor," said the tall sergeant. "That's twice as bad as a regular Yankee. Least they's fightin for their side. You is fightin agin your'n. You is a dirty son of a bitch." One of the other soldiers, a private with dirty yellow hair and a nose like an eagle's beak said, "Let's shoot this turncoat scum."

"I got me a better notion," said the sergeant. "We'll take this bastard to Andersonville. Captn Wirz jes loves traitors. He'll see to it that this prick suffers proper fore he dies. You wouldn't wanna cheat this boy outta some Andersonville hospitality would ya?"

"I reckon not," said the private.

"But Andersonville is for enlisted men, Sarge," said a third captor. "This back stabber is a lieutenant."

The sergeant took a knife from his pocket and carelessly slashed James clean of all insignia. "Now he looks just like a private."

The rest of the Rebels enjoyed the laugh and added their agreement to the whole idea. Once again, fate had dealt him a cruel blow. There wasn't a soldier in the entire Union army who didn't shudder at the name Andersonville.

James knew that the guards at the prison would go much harder on him if they found out that he was from the South.

The sergeant stripped Goliath of his saddle, then with the help of another man, hoisted James across the back of the horse face down on his stomach. Then they passed a rope underneath and tied his hands and feet together.

"Jake," the sergeant said to the big nosed private. "You and Ladge deliver this garbage to Andersonville. Then head to Macon. We'll catch up with you there." Then to James the sergeant said, "Have a nice ride, traitor. We'll say howdy to everyone in Macon for ya."

Camp Sumpter, as it was officially called, was located on a rail line that connected Macon and Albany, about sixty miles southeast of Macon. It was twenty-seven acres of bare ground enclosed by a stockade of squared tree trunks. At the prison's inception, it was the intention of the authorities to build a barracks. However, by February 1864, the flood of prisoners was so overwhelming that the shelters never materialized.

When James reached the prison with his captors he was in agony. His insides ached from miles of bouncing on his stomach and his wrists were raw and bleeding from the rope that bound them. He had not been given as much as a mouthful of water during the entire trip. Twice he was plagued by the need to relieve himself and did so, which increased his discomfort.

When big nose Private Jake cut the rope and shoved him off Goliath's back, James laid on the ground too stiff and sore to get up. Undeterred by James's condition, Private Jake and his comrade Ladge, each grabbed an arm and dragged him to the commandant's office, letting him drop on the front porch. The door opened and a Confederate captain came out to investigate the noise.

"What have we here?" inquired the captain in a voice heavily laden with a Swiss accent. The two troopers saluted and Private Jake said, "Beggin your pardon, Capm. This here is a present from General Sherman that we ketched outside a Savannah. He's a Yankee traitor from Macon. Some a the boys wanted to shoot him but then we figured he'd a might rather spend some time in your stockade, sir." Captain Wirz looked at James lying in a heap on the porch.

"Stand him up. I want him to show me some respect. Stand him up."

Like lifting a sack of grain, they hauled James to his feet and threatened to beat him if he didn't stand up straight. "You are from Georgia but you fight for the Union?" said Wirz. James did not answer so Private Jake stomped on his right foot almost hard enough to break bones. "Can you answer now?" said Wirz.

"Yes, sir."

"Why did you turn your back on your country?"

"I didn't, sir, the Confederacy did."

"That is a good answer. I don't like it, but technically it is a good answer. We did pull out of the Union; we felt we had the right. Do you believe in human rights?"

"I believe in the rights of all humans."

"All humans?"

"Yes, sir, all humans white and black."

"Again a good answer. Again, an answer I do not like, but technically good. But we are the Confederate States and we are at war. You are not only the enemy, but as you like technicalities, we also see you as a traitor. I have the authority to hang you if I wish but I believe *that* punishment would be insufficient so I will let you rot in my stockade. Should you make any trouble for me I will hang you straight away. Take him to the front gate, soldiers, and have him admitted."

TWENTY-SEVEN

The Deadliest Battlefield

The gigantic main gate swung open and before James was the living hell that all referred to as Andersonville. For as much as he had heard about the place, even from men who had spent time there, it was still far worse than words could describe. It was a huge open mud pit covered by thousands of tents constructed from sticks and scraps of canvas or blankets. Beneath many of the tents, the ground was dug out, resembling something like a gopher hole. The stockade held an enormous collection of withered, emaciated creatures covered with long hair, beards, and the tattered remains of a uniform.

Most of the inmates seemed to be milling around aimlessly as if they had no earthly purpose. But even if they had the strength, what was there to do? The only true activity was waiting; waiting for liberation or waiting to die. It was a fact that more men died of disease than of battle wounds.

James felt a pang of anger toward General Sherman; he had been so close. The army had marched two hundred and seventy-five miles from Atlanta to Savannah with no real opposition except for Joe Wheeler's cavalry. Why didn't they swing a little further south and open the gates for these poor forgotten souls? Was Sherman too busy hunting glory? Would he have looked upon these helpless, starving men as a burden like the thousands of slaves that followed after him? Certainly it would not have been difficult to overpower the small Confederate force that guarded the prison.

For a time, James simply stood and stared at the inmates as a man might stare at any tragic scene. The awfulness of it grabbed his attention making it difficult to pull away. The men could have been categorized by stage of health and appearance, ranging from those recently captured to those who had been there for many months.

Eventually he was approached by an inquisitive corporal who, from the looks of him, had been there for some time. "Welcome, friend. I'm sorry to see you here," said the corporal.

"No sorrier than I am to be here," James replied.

"You think you're sorry now, just wait til you've been here for a couple months. This ain't no prison. It's a death camp. Ever since they stopped the prisoner exchange, the Rebs just lock you up in here and take bets on how long you'll last. It would be more humane to shoot us than take us prisoner. If the war doesn't end soon, we'll all die in here. I guess it really comes down to the individual; some will just naturally last longer than others. There's no safe water to drink except rain water, when it rains. There's no proper medical care and no decent food. Unsifted corn meal filled with husks and eaten raw is every man's daily portion. Every single day we carry out the dead. Most die of disease and malnutrition, some give up hope and cross the dead line."

"Dead line?"

"Yeah. See that single rail fence running the whole way around, a few feet from the wall?"

"I see it."

"That's the dead line. Cross it and they'll shoot you down."

"How long have you been here, Corporal?"

"Name's Tim Fallon. Been here four months now. I got here just before they hanged the raiders."

"My name is James Langdon. Who were the raiders?"

"A bunch of scum who banded together and survived by robbin and killin the new boys when they got captured. There was about a thousand of them; mostly misfits and bounty jumpers. When new boys came in, they usually had full haversacks. The raiders would attack em, steal their food, clothing, blankets, everything. They ate good while the rest of us starved. Anything they stole and didn't need they would trade to the Rebs for things they wanted, like whiskey. They killed quite a few men in the doing. One day the boys decided they'd had enough. They attacked the raiders and rounded up the leaders. That bastard Wirz actually agreed to let us put them on trial. We had a prosecution and a defense; we had witnesses and a jury, just like in a regular courtroom. We found them guilty and hanged the six ring leaders. After that, things got more peaceful in here if nothing else."

"What are the chances of escape? I know that some have managed it."

"Now and then a lucky few are able to tunnel their way out but it ain't easy. The digging's hard and if you *do* get outside the wall you better be sure you can give yourself a good head start. The Rebs got themselves a pen full of bloodhounds and they will track you down if you don't have a lot of distance on them. Besides that, the son of a bitch in charge of trackin escaped prisoners is a real crackerjack at his work. They say he used to be an overseer on a big plantation and he's got a lot of experience runnin down escaped slaves. He's not only good at his job, but if he catches you, he don't bring you back until he's enjoyed dealing out his own brand of punishment. Sometimes he don't bring back the men he catches at all. As long as no one gets away, Wirz don't ask for explanations."

"Yes," said James. "I've heard terrible things about this place. It has quite a reputation. Now that the Confederacy is so near to collapse, I suppose that our suffering is all they have to look forward to each day."

"You really think it will be over soon?"

"Yes, Tim, I do. I was with Sherman before I was caught. I saw what he did to Georgia, now he is headed for the Carolinas. Grant is closing on Richmond and when Sherman gets to southern Virginia they'll have the Confederates in a vise. It can only be a matter of months."

"That sounds mighty good. If a man could just stay healthy it might be possible to wait it out now. But that's easier said than done. If only there was a little food. I think I could put up with the boredom and the other hardships if I just had something to eat."

"Are you married, Tim?"

"No, I'm not, thank God. My ma died when I was born so it's just Pa and me. I worry that he's thinkin that I was killed maybe. I always wrote regular so he has to know by now that something has happened. You have to bribe the Rebs to get a letter mailed and not too many have the price. I feel sorry for the men that *do* have wives and children."

"I wrote to my wife a week ago. I hope it isn't an eternity until I can write again. This war has got to end soon . . . it's just got to."

"Listen, James, my tent mate died a few days ago. It's just a hole in the ground with an old piece of canvas over top but if you want to share it you're welcome."

"I'm much obliged."

Tim led the way between two rows of gopher hole shelters and when James got a look at his new home, the reality of his capture sunk in deep. He had no tolerance for self pity but he had finally gotten to the point where he had to ask God why he had come to the end of the earth at Andersonville. Maybe his luck had completely run out. He climbed down into the five-foot deep cavern, sat down, propped his elbows atop his knees and let his face drop into his hands.

"It happens to everybody in the beginning, James. I'll leave you alone for awhile."

James didn't answer or even look up. Tim disappeared beyond the top of the hole. One word entered James's head, lodged there, and took root; escape.

For the next two months, he spent the daylight hours walking the perimeter of the stockade for two reasons. The first was for the exercise and the second was to search for some weakness that he could exploit. He knew that time was working against him, tapping his strength, diminishing his chance of finding a way out. His tent mate, Tim, had fallen to the next stage of his incarceration. Sores dotted his thin body; teeth fell from rotten gums. He rarely left the hole anymore except when chased by his dysentery; sometimes he didn't even bother then. He was decaying before James's eyes and there was nothing James could do but watch him die. He knew that the same would eventually happen to him. By now his face was covered with beard; his hair was touching his shoulders and he was filthy from living in dirt. He had long since traded the brass buttons from his ragged uniform for a few small bites of something edible.

One small thing James did to help keep his sense of awareness intact was to follow the days and the months on a crude calendar carved into a piece of wood. On the morning of the last day of March he awoke from his usual restless sleep. Waking up in Andersonville, merciless as it was, proved even worse on that particular morning; first because he had been dreaming about having breakfast at home with his family before the war, and second, after looking across the gopher hole at Tim, James realized that his friend was dead. Another life carelessly thrown away, he thought, another young man who should still be alive but was not.

Tim was from New York. He had lived there with his father on a small dairy farm. Now he was just filler for another unmarked hole in the ground hundreds of miles from home. James made a mental note, optimistically promising to someday write to Tim's father so that the man would at least know what had become of his brave soldier.

He scrounged a scrap of paper and wrote Tim's name and home state on it. Then he took part of a shoestring from the dead man's dilapidated brogans and tied the tag to a protruding toe. After the minimal preparation, he recruited another man to help bear Tim's body to the dead house, which was right outside the stockade wall. As usual there was a line of men, two live with one dead in between, waiting for the guards to open the gate. Carrying out the dead was the only time a prisoner ever saw the free side of the stockade wall. Once, James watched a man who had helped carry out a body, lose his head at the sight of the open field and take off running. The Rebs shot him to pieces.

When the gate opened, the procession moved out toward the dead house. After delivering Tim's body, James was on his way back when three men on horseback came across the bridge spanning the filthy creek that ran through the prison. Two of them were soldiers and the third was a coarse looking man in civilian clothing who was carrying a sawed off shotgun in his right hand.

Waiting for the horses to pass in front of him, James stared at the civilian as if drawn by something familiar. Suddenly he knew what it was; the eye patch. The man wore an eye patch; the former overseer, the villain Tim had told him about. It was Farley Tabor.

As Tabor passed by, he stared back at James with a look of genuine hatred in his expression, but James did not know if Tabor recognized him. It had been over four years since they had seen each other and James looked very different now in his unkempt, undernourished condition. Seeing Tabor at the prison was unexpected but certainly not surprising. In fact, if James had held the responsibility of finding a place in the war that was suitable for Tabor, he couldn't have thought of one better. With the slaves gone, he undoubtedly needed someone else to abuse.

James went back to the gopher hole and sat in silent resignation. He felt that he was ready to succumb to his circumstances. Even the thought of Polly and little James was failing to strengthen his will to go on. In spite of his lackluster spirit, he believed that any day the war could end and how sad it would be to die just before the final shot was fired.

TWENTY-EIGHT

Nine Lives

Just when hope had all but expired, a desperate opportunity came from the most unlikely source that James could have imagined. Late in the afternoon two guards entered the stockade, walked up and down between the rows of tents, peering into each one as they went. When they came to James's hole they stopped. "Would you be Langdon?" asked a skinny farm boy in gray who was no more than sixteen. James nodded without looking up. "Come up outta that hole."

"What for?" said James, still looking at the ground.

"Commandant sent us to fetch you." That was odd, James thought. There was never any reason for Wirz to send for a prisoner, no reason at all. The Reb repeated the order and tapped James's shoulder with the bayonet on the muzzle of his rifle. Passing on the notion to refuse and force the guard to shoot him, he crawled out of the hole and walked toward the gate ahead of his escort. When they got outside, there was Farley Tabor, sitting on his horse, grinning like Satan on Judgment Day. James saw something else he recognized: a coiled bullwhip hanging from a leather strap on his saddle.

To the farm boy Tabor said, "Get yourself a horse, Private, you'll be comin with me." Then he spoke to James, "Captain Wirz is tired a eatin army rations. I promised him squirrel stew for supper tonight. I ain't got time to sit and wait for em so you're gonna climb some trees and shake a few outta their nests."

James knew immediately that it was all a lie. Prisoners were never let outside the wall for any reason except to remove the dead, and even if it were true, he was certainly in no condition to climb trees. James knew that wherever Tabor intended to take him he wouldn't be coming back.

The farm boy soon returned with a mount. James was ordered to walk ahead of the horses, down the road, and into the woods. Glancing toward the treetops he saw many squirrel nests, but they passed them by. He kept on walking and before long, they had covered perhaps two miles.

Finally, Tabor called a halt and James turned to face him and the farm boy private. The black-hearted masochist lounged in the saddle and stared down at James as if he were setting the stage for a big performance. At length he said, "I got a little story to tell you, Private. I worked for many years as the overseer on Langdon Plantation. The owner was John Langdon, a good man and a good Southerner. Like all good men, he put his family first; gave them everything they needed and everything they wanted. He had this son that he treated like a king would treat a prince. He taught him all the things a boy needed to know to grow into a fine gentleman. He saw to it that the boy had a good education. Because of John Langdon, his son would one day inherit a wonderful future. Now you would think that this boy would repay his father with loyalty and respect. You would think he would give his life before turning against his family."

"I reckon I sure would have," said the private.

"You and me both," Tabor replied. "I never even knew my old man and my ma raised me in the same room of the Louisiana whorehouse where she did business, and I still stood by my homeland when trouble came. But this rich boy, this ungrateful son of a bitch, he turned traitor to his family and his country. He sided with what should have been his nigger lovin enemies. He ran out on his father when he was crippled, which, by the way, worried his mother into an early grave."

Tabor was trying his best to get at James's insides and he was succeeding magnificently. Technically, much of what the man said was true; deep in James's heart, it was not. Still, it hurt and he wished that if Tabor was going to kill him that he would just shut up and do it.

"What would you do with a piece of shit like that, Private?" said Tabor.

"I reckon I'd shoot him," was the reply.

"You ever shoot a man, Private?"

"No, sir. I only been in the army for a year. They stuck me here as a guard. Never got a chance to fight at the front."

"Then I guess it would do you some good to shoot this traitor, rid the South of one more enemy." The young man hesitated for a moment before saying, "Yes, sir." He didn't sound sure.

"Problem is, a bullet would be too quick and easy. I heard that the soldiers who caught this lowlife wanted to shoot him, too. Then they got a better idea. They brought him to Andersonville. Well now, *I* got a better idea. Seeins how he sides with the niggers, I figure he should be punished like a trouble makin nigger, and a trouble makin nigger gets this." Tabor untied the leather strap and held the bullwhip out for James to see. "I'm gonna whip this traitor and if there's anything left when I'm done, you can put a bullet in it." Tabor got down from his horse and rummaged in his saddle bag for a length of rope. The farm boy sat his horse with a rifle across his lap.

James knew that he could not survive a whipping and even if he did he'd be finished with a bullet. Tabor advanced toward him. "You got anything to say before I carry out the sentence?"

"I won't defend myself to the likes of you. Do what you will and get it over with."

Tabor was not satisfied. He obviously wanted James to plead for his life. Maybe there was some advantage in that. "I think you talk so much because it helps you to forget your cowardice, Tabor."

"What did you say to me?"

"You heard me. Beating on someone whose hands are tied makes you feel strong. Hunting an unarmed man with guns and dogs has you convinced that you're brave. But you're just a gutless coward. That's why *you* are not at the front. That's why *you* weaseled your way into that human pigsty, to fight against men who wouldn't have the strength to fight back."

The ploy worked. Tabor lost his self control and his judgment. He stood six feet away, chest heaving, nostrils flaring. Suddenly he threw his right fist into James's jaw.

The blow knocked James to the ground. By now it was dusk and very nearly dark in the woods. As James lay in a heap, Tabor drew back the whip. He snapped his wrist; the crack sounded like a gunshot, but it missed its target by a foot. Cursing profusely, he cracked the whip again. This time it struck James's right hand but before Tabor could pull it back, James grabbed the end, wrapped it around his fingers and held on tight. With all his reserve, he yanked the whip and Tabor, whose grip also held firm, stumbled forward. A dead tree branch got tangled between his heavy boots. At least sixty pounds overweight, Tabor fell hard; face down on the ground. Ignoring the farm boy, James crawled on his hands and knees as fast as he could, climbed on top of the prostrate man, and wrapped the whip tightly around his throat.

Tabor kicked wildly and dug his fingers into the ground but the fall had knocked the wind out of him. If not for that, he could have rolled James off his back easily. Unable to fight back, in just minutes, he died by the whip he had lived by. James quoted the bible, saying, "The light of the wicked shall be put out." The night was all dark for Tabor now.

James sat back and relaxed his grip. It was only then that he remembered the farm boy. He looked over and saw him silhouetted against the night sky. He was sitting perfectly still. Why hadn't he joined in? Why hadn't he shot James, saving Tabor's life? James stood up and waited a moment for his knees to stop shaking. As he walked over to the silent soldier, he heard something hit the ground. The young man had dropped his rifle. "I hope you won't kill me, mister."

His voice quivered and James was pretty sure he was sobbing. "Of course I won't kill you but I can't help wondering why you didn't kill me."

"I couldn't do that. I guess I'm the coward here. I ain't never shot a man and I never want to. I was forced to join the army, that's why I'm here. I just talked tough earlier because Tabor expected me to. I'm glad it didn't come down to him makin me shoot you."

"Not wanting to kill doesn't make you a coward. It proves that you are a decent human being and that is

something far more difficult to find these days. I'm very
sorry that I had to kill Tabor."

"He didn't give you much choice. Maybe he had it
comin. I seen him do some terrible things to the prisoners.
My pa always said you reap what you sow."

"Where are you from, Private?"

"Just outside Chattanooga. Pa and I raise hogs."

"Well I am very thankful that I met you," said James. "I
consider that you saved my life. I have to get out of here.
I'm taking Tabor's horse. I'm afraid that I have caused you
trouble though. What will you tell them when you get
back?"

"I'm not goin back, I'm goin home. The war's over. We
get news every day. Gen'ral Lee is expected to surrender
any time now. I reckon they won't send anyone lookin for
me. Why don't you ride with me? You can stay with Pa and
me til you get your strength back." James thought it over.

"That's a kind offer, Private."

"You can call me Ely, Ely Anderson."

"You can call me James. But the war isn't over yet and
you're in gray and I'm in blue. That might cause a
problem."

"I got a flannel shirt and a pair of work britches in my
saddle bag. You're welcome to em."

James realized that God had not abandoned him after
all; proven by his escape from Andersonville. Meeting Ely
was also a blessing. He changed into the civilian clothing
and the two of them headed west. Hopefully, it would be
some time the following day before Tabor's body was
discovered. By then they would be a long way from the
prison. James was in desperate need of decent food and a
bath, but the fresh air of the outside world was a vast
improvement. They did not see a single soldier, blue or
gray, during the ride to Chattanooga. It seemed like the
war was already over.

TWENTY-NINE

Endings

It was mid-afternoon when they reached the farm where Ely lived with his pa. It was a modest little place but very well kept; even the hog pens sported a fresh coat of paint. Compared with much of the South, the farm seemed to have escaped the ravages of war.

Ely and his pa were good Christian folk and quite generous with their hospitality. Mr. Anderson was about the same age as James's own father. He was a sinewy man with callous hardened hands and gentle blue eyes. But what impressed James the most was the older man's reaction when he found out that his son had aided and abetted a Yankee soldier.

"I never did believe in secession and I don't hold with slavery," he said. "I am sorry for the man, Tabor, but my boy tells me that he would have killed you, James. You're welcome here for as long as you like."

It wasn't hard to understand Ely's temperament after meeting his pa. James found himself wishing that his own father shared some of Mr. Anderson's qualities. He had always believed that his father was a God fearing man but he also knew that the bible says man cannot serve two masters. That, James concluded, was the mistake John Langdon had made.

After a week of resting and eating to the point of feeling guilty, James was able to throw a respectable shadow again. He pleaded with the Andersons to allow him to work off his debt, but they would not hear of it. He relaxed on the front porch and wrote a long letter to Polly, which Mr. Anderson graciously offered to take to the post office.

On the 10th of April, after a hearty country breakfast, the Andersons set out for town to purchase supplies. By this time, James had become quite attached to his benefactors. As difficult as it was, he decided that when

247

they returned, he would tell them he would be moving on. He had no idea where Sherman's army was but he knew he needed to find it and rejoin his outfit.

James was in the barn tending to his horse when he heard the wagon coming down the road. Then he heard something else that made him hurry to the doorway to investigate. The horse and wagon were racing for the house like a fire engine heading for a blaze. Ely and his pa were whooping and hollering and raising enough dust for a stampede. James ran out to meet the two excited men without an idea as to what might have set them off.

The wagon had not come to a complete stop before Ely jumped off waving a newspaper, then holding it out so that James could see the front page. "Lee surrenders army of northern Virginia", was the headline. James could hardly believe it was real. A warm, wonderful feeling came over him as he took the paper and read the whole story. Lee had surrendered to General U.S. Grant at a place called Appomattox Court House in Virginia. The ceremony had taken place at the home of Wilmer McLean. There were still Confederate armies in the field, the story related, but they were expected to capitulate soon. The Confederate Government, Jefferson Davis, and members of his cabinet had fled south and were being pursued by Union troops.

The war, in effect, was over. James tossed the paper into the air; there were handshakes and back slapping all around. Then Ely's pa called for a moment of silence and the three men prayed for the many that had not lived to see that happy day.

Eventually, the momentous excitement subsided, but a peaceful feeling remained in the aftermath. James decided to stay one more night with the Andersons. The following day would hold a brand new beginning. The first thing he would do was go into Chattanooga and resign his commission. He wanted no more to do with the army. After that, with no fear of any more obstacles, he would go to Langdon Plantation and see his father. Finally, he would go home to Mapletown and promise Polly that he would never again leave her side.

It was not easy getting to sleep that night. The next morning he was awake before daylight. Fortunately, the

Andersons were early risers. James was far too restless to stay in bed any longer. He dressed quickly and went to the kitchen, received morning greetings, and returned the same. He shoveled another delectable breakfast then prepared to be on his way. "I have no means to repay you for all your kindness. I owe my life to all that you've done."

"It was our privilege to be of help, James," said Mr. Anderson. "You're a fine young man and we'd be pleased to hear from you when you get resettled. It would be repayment enough to know that you are safe at home with your wife and son."

"I assure you that I will keep in touch. God bless you both." Driven by a spontaneous need, James embraced Mr. Anderson and then Ely. He felt no less than if he were saying goodbye to family.

Leaving the army was as easy as signing some papers and collecting some back pay; rather unceremonious after all he'd been through. Still, he felt that it had all been worthwhile. It had brought him to the day when he believed, at least, that all serious tragedy was in the past.

Of course, once again, he was contemplating the reunion with his father. But James still felt a great deal of love for the man, and if his father cared for him the injury to feelings *could* be overcome.

It would be a long day's ride to Macon but James did not feel like pushing hard on this trip. He decided, in fact, to ride as far as Atlanta; spend the night, then continue the following day. After four years of high anxiety and low depression, punctuated by physical injuries, he just wanted to relax his mental posture. He didn't feel like hurrying anything. He imagined that most of the people in the country felt the same way. It was time to catch their breath before getting on with their lives. With the fighting nearly at an end, accounting and accountability were at hand. It was time to welcome home the men God had spared and sing dirges for those he hadn't. It would be many years before the wounds would heal and many more to carry the scars.

James tried hard to consider himself lucky and could have if not for the loss of his dear mother. Now that he was at the end of his mission, she was the one he'd miss the most. If only he could see her one more time. Her death so very much increased the importance of making peace with his father.

Atlanta by every definition was a busy city. The inhabitants had rebounded quickly. The post office was operating, newspapers were being printed, and rebuilding was taking place everywhere one looked. Considering the progress that had been made, it was hard to believe that Sherman had been there just five months earlier. It was, thought James, so good to see construction rather than destruction.

That evening he lay on his hotel bed thinking about the next day. Over and over again he pictured the house as it had been when he last saw it. He could see Mrs. MacGruder tending the lovely flower gardens and George Lynch repairing a wheel on the family carriage. He thought of Olivia Jones; a wonderful cook and a wonderful person, Millie White, Lucy Sipe . . . where were they now? Darcy Davis's son, Tyler, had gone to war . . . did he survive it? Kate told him they were all gone.

In 1860, James lived in what he believed was a perfect world. What would he see tomorrow? What would he picture in his mind four years from now?

At about noon on Thursday, April 13th, James was on the road, only about seven miles from his childhood home. By the direction he'd traveled, he would reach the old compound first. As he approached the lane leading back through the woods an irresistible urge to see it came upon him. He remembered his eighteenth birthday, the day he defied his father by riding back to see the place for himself. He also remembered watching by the wood's edge while his father and the late Farley Tabor whipped Bo Sampson for trying to escape. How very long ago it seemed.

When he broke into the clearing, the first thing he noticed was that the field office and the overseer's quarters had burned to the ground. He wondered if the slaves, as an act of reprisal, were responsible. The rows of slave cabins still stood but were silent and weather worn like old markers in a cemetery. The barns that once hummed with activity had the distinct look of abandonment; the corral that held hundreds of mules was empty and half knocked down. Here and there sat a wagonload of rotting cotton; a true testament to the death of Southern economic power. If James had believed in ghosts, surely, he thought, they would inhabit such a place; restless for vengeance against the human suffering inflicted there.

It was a dismal beginning to his return home. He wondered why triumph was never purely free of concessions. He had spent four very hard years doing what he could to help eradicate slavery. His reward was the realization of his dream. Now he would have to learn to live with the price that was paid. Not for himself, but for his father who had spent a lifetime building his world: Did he regret seeing it in ruins? Why did his family have to lose everything? James could only surmise that the larger the sin, the more severe the punishment.

Of a sudden, a compelling urge to reach the house put an end to his procrastination. He spurred his horse to a hard gallop, and soon he could see the south side of the roof above the trees. He nearly wrenched his horse's neck as he came to a stop in front of the house. Before him was a vision so familiar yet so different that he could not recall spending his early life there. The neglect, dilapidation, and damage of war did not agree with persistent memories of parties, celebrations, and reunions. What once stood as a symbol of elegance was now marred by chipping paint, broken windows, and missing roof slates. Two of the tall columns supporting the roof over the veranda had been shattered by artillery shells, leaving the left side of the roof hanging precariously. As far as James could see, the lawn was overgrown, reaching to the bottom of the first floor windows, and the flower gardens were choked with weeds. The frame of the big barn still stood with its roof intact, but most of the exterior boards were missing. The Union army had apparently paid an unwelcome visit as it had to so many homes.

Scanning the surrounding area, his gaze came to rest on a spot on the other side of the driveway. The family cemetery was bordered on three sides by large Cypress trees. It was the final resting place of his grandparents and now . . . his mother. He had been dreading the sight of the grave, as it was final proof that she was really gone. Now he was drawn to it because in the midst of all the ruin, the little cemetery was still pristine in its appearance. The wrought iron fence stood perfectly straight and had the look of recent paint. The grass was neatly trimmed and all of the graves were adorned with fresh flowers.

James climbed down from the saddle, leaving the reins to trail in the dirt. He walked over to the cemetery, opened the gate and stepped inside. He knelt before his mother's grave and spoke silently to her, believing in his heart and soul that she could hear him. He told her how much he loved and missed her; he told her what a wonderful mother she was. He told her about Polly and about her grandson; he told her she would meet them someday when all God's children were together.

When the visit was over, James was both surprised and very grateful for the genuine feeling of peace he felt inside. He sensed that his mother was close by; his feeling of loss was not as great.

Finally he went up to the house, climbed the steps to the veranda and opened the door. When he went inside, his initial shock returned. The furniture, nearly every piece, was smashed and scattered over the floor. The wallpaper hung in tattered shreds; the fine rugs were slashed and dotted with cigar burns. Mirrors had been shattered, once beautiful oil paintings had been run through with bayonets, rifle butts, or boot heels. The destruction had been out of pure vengeance; there was no other purpose for it.

James stood quietly and listened, he heard not a sound. If his father was in the house he must be sleeping. Slowly he walked down the hallway toward the office. The door was closed. He reached for the knob and turned. He gave the door a push; it swung open, revealing the same scene of deliberate damage. Books lay in piles on the floor; papers were everywhere, nothing had been left untouched. The desk was upside down in the middle of the room and a high back chair was next to it facing the outside wall. James was about to walk away when he heard a quiet sound like someone clearing their throat. Then the high back chair began to turn and he realized that it was occupied. His father pivoted the chair around until he was face to face with his son. James was not prepared for what he saw. The man in the chair had aged four years since his last visit but he looked older by ten. The deep creases in his face looked more like scars from a knife; his eyes were puffy and bloodshot. James could remember his father as a physically strong man with the resilience of an Oak tree. Now he looked feeble, shrunken, and vulnerable; the brace on his bad leg added to that impression.

John Langdon was not yet fifty years old but he would need evidence to prove it.

"Hello, Father."

"Hello, son. It's been a long time." He managed a weak smile. "Find something to sit on, son. I have to talk to you." James found a chair from which the arms had been broken but still sturdy enough to sit on. He sat facing his father.

"I heard you ride up, James. I knew it was you. I knew you'd come eventually. I'm glad. Did you visit your mother?"

"Yes, Father. I loved her very much, I will miss her."

"I know. We will all miss her. I always hoped that I would leave this earth before her. Life does not always let things happen the way we want them to. Sometimes we don't even get the chance to say our goodbyes. But sometimes we *do* get a chance to make things right, a chance to say things that need to be said. If you will be patient with me; if you will sit and listen, I will take advantage of the opportunity."

"Of course, Father. I will listen for as long as you wish to speak."

James was more than willing to sit and listen. He was nothing short of grateful for his father's demeanor. He had long feared that the man would not want to speak to him after all that had happened. Apparently, the events of the past four years had had a profound effect on more than just his appearance.

"I've had a pretty clear understanding for some time of what you've been doing since the day you first left home, but none of that is important now. For a period of time, I reacted much in the way that you would expect. I was hurt, I was angry, and I considered you to be very ungrateful.

253

"I like to think that I was blind back then. I was blinded by the fact that I followed in my father's footsteps and never questioned anything about the way we lived. I never saw any wrong in it. I became a plantation owner and an owner of slaves, and you were *my* son. I felt that you owed your loyalty to me as I had to my father.

"Even when I fully understood that you did not share my point of view on slavery, I believed that you should and would turn out to fit the mold of what *I* thought a Southerner should be. As I said, I was blind. I did not realize then that a man needs more than fine clothes, a good education; material things. A man also needs understanding, a right to his own conscience, and the freedom to do what *he* believes is right. No man should think that he can buy that away from you, not even your own father.

"When your mother passed away, so did my blindness. The last thing she said to me the night before she died was, 'Someday, when you see your son, give him your understanding. He is doing what he believes is right.' Then she went to sleep. For days after she was gone, I studied about that. I realized that she knew more about what was going on than I'd thought and she knew more about me than she'd let on.

"So many things came clear to me. I finally understood it didn't matter that I was following in my father's footsteps; carrying on with tradition. What we were doing, owning slaves, was something you could not accept. I depended on your loyalty, but I understand now that you could not give it. You had a deeper sense of loyalty; to God and your fellow man. I am proud of you, James, and I always will be; proud that you had the courage to go against all that you were raised to be because you were right. I only wish I'd seen it sooner; or maybe I did and just didn't have the guts."

James was thoroughly astonished. He was filled with an elation that was unparalleled. For so long he had been haunted by what he thought to be irreparable damage between him and his father. A relentless guilt had plagued him every day since before he ever left home. Now it was all washed away, knowing in the end, that they were on the same side.

Nothing could destroy the happiness that James felt at that moment. Then his father said, "The South paid for her mistake, son. She paid with many lives, much property, and the time it will take to recover. I do not mourn my material losses. Maybe because of it, I will owe my maker less when I die."

James noticed something that made him feel uneasy. He could not make sense of it but somehow his father's voice had taken on a different tone. He sounded like a man who was disoriented, waking out of unconsciousness, not really sure where he was. He wore a strange half-smiling, half-woeful expression. He kept talking, but he wasn't as coherent. "We deserved what we got . . . made my peace with God . . . miss your mother terribly . . . glad I saw you, son."

Then he reached behind his back with his right hand and scratched himself for several minutes with a slow deliberate stroke. His eyes were fixed and unblinking; he brought his hand from behind his back. The pistol appeared from thin air. He put it to his head and squeezed the trigger. It sounded like a cannon; still James heard his own voice, "No!!!"

THIRTY

Epitaph

The smoke from the gunshot hung in the air like a dark cloud. The smell was acrid and irritating to the nose. The body was slumped in the chair, almost to the point of sliding to the floor. What had happened? James didn't know.

An hour later he looked at his father; lying on the floor, covered with a blanket, and wondered how he'd gotten there. Everything since the gunshot had been erased. James felt incapacitated. He could not think and did not know what to do. A partial bottle of whiskey lay on the floor near the wall, no doubt overlooked by the ransacking soldiers. James pulled the cork and put the bottle to his lips. He was not a whiskey drinker, but that didn't seem to matter. He took a long pull from the bottle. It burned all the way to his feet and he coughed as the heat of the liquor nearly choked him. For good or bad, it seemed to bring him back to reality and he broke down, crying like a child.

When he could cry no longer, he pulled himself together and grasped the responsibility before him. He went out to the big barn's skeletal remains and found a spring wagon that was still in serviceable condition. There were no horses except the one he'd been riding since Andersonville; the late Farley Tabors'. In a few minutes he had the wagon hitched and ready to go. He wrapped his father's body in blankets and placed it in the bed of the wagon. Then he began the slow, reflective drive into Macon.

There were a number of travelers on the road, both black and white. Most were laden with household possessions, heading for a new home, and hopefully, a better life. James acknowledged no one and no one bothered him. One look at his stoic expression and a glimpse of his unmistakable cargo afforded him a great deal of understanding.

James and his family were well known in Macon. He wondered briefly how he might be received by the locals. The war was over but grudges would remain for years to come. He decided that he didn't care.

He felt no angry stares boring through him as he drove down the street, but he did seem to be drawing some attention. Men tipped their hats; women bowed their heads and crossed themselves. James kept driving.

When he reached the undertaker's, he drove around to the rear entrance where the deceased were carried in. Mr. Templeton was sweeping the back porch when James arrived. It took him a moment, but James saw the flash of recognition in the man's face. He set his broom against the wall and hurried down the steps.

Mr. Templeton was a gentle, caring man, well suited to his profession. James knew him best as a member of the same church his family attended. Once, when Reverend Tobias was down with consumption, Mr. Templeton substituted for him. He proved to be a fine orator. James climbed down from the wagon and shook hands with the undertaker.

"James, my boy, I didn't know you were home. What has happened?"

"Can I speak to you inside?"

"Yes, of course. Please come in." He led the way to his office and offered James a seat.

"I must rely upon your discretion, Mr. Templeton. My father shot himself."

"Dear God, why?"

"The war ruined him. There is nothing left of the plantation, but I believe that my mother's death was more than he could bear. I got home early this afternoon; we talked for a short while. He was visually worn down from all he'd been through, but he seemed rational. Then all of a sudden, something about him was different. Thinking back now, it was as if he'd made up his mind. I believe that he was only waiting to see me again. He wanted an opportunity to speak to me. I didn't know he had a pistol hidden behind his back. He shot himself before I knew what was happening."

"Tragic," said Mr. Templeton. "No one could have ever predicted the cost of this terrible conflict. You're father is among many others who were ruined by the war. I know of two other men who took their own lives. I knew your father well, as you are aware. Please accept my most profound sympathies. He will be sorely missed by the entire community, and you may rest assured that you can rely on my complete discretion."

"I'm grateful, sir."

"There is something else, James, something you probably don't know. Maybe it isn't my place to tell you this but your uncles, Stanley and Joseph, are gone. They sold out and moved away. I don't know where they went. They tried to get your father to do the same but he would not agree. You're right about one thing though; he *was* waiting for you to come home."

When James would have bet he could hear nothing more that could make a bad time worse he was wrong. He knew all too well how much the alliance with his uncles had meant to his father. Losing their support was tantamount to losing the war.

Before the shooting, James thought that his father seemed to be in a rational state of mind, but now he wasn't so sure. Had he really concluded that slavery was wrong or was he just trying to make peace with his only son? James would never know. Even if the latter were true, he would still be forever able to take comfort in his father's last words. And he did have one solid consolation: knowing that there were many factors contributing to his father's final actions. There was no reason for him to believe that he alone was responsible for his father's death.

When he had finished making the final arrangements with Mr. Templeton, James asked for a total of the expenses. "There will be no charge, James. I would deem it a privilege to handle this for your father and his heroic son."

"Heroic?"

"Indeed. I suppose that war secrets are of no importance now. Not more than two months ago your father told me all about your bravery, working for the Confederate Signal Service. He told everybody. Of course he couldn't give us details but we all know how you risked your life for the Southern cause. We are all grateful, James and the hope is that you will rebuild your father's plantation and stay around Macon."

James was both amazed and confused, not only by Mr. Templeton's words but by his father's deception. Was he trying to save the reputation of the Langdon family name or was he protecting his son? Again, James chose to believe the latter. And if he had any immediate thoughts of telling the undertaker the truth, he soon forgot them. He would not disgrace the memory of his father by having him exposed as a liar.

James drove back to the house and made the necessary preparations at the cemetery. His father's body would be transported to the cemetery the next day and he would be laid to rest beside his wife. Mr. Templeton would deliver the eulogy and James would be the only other witness to the burial. That was the way he wanted it. He did not want a flock of well meaning citizens showering him with undeserved praise. James wished that Kate could be present but there wasn't time. As for Ashton; he had no idea how to reach her.

The following afternoon at one o'clock, the hearse rolled up to the gate of the little cemetery. Mr. Templeton, dressed in a fine black suit, climbed down. They lowered the coffin into the grave, and then prayed that Almighty God would welcome their dear departed brother into heaven.

When the brief service was over, Mr. Templeton said, "It is a dark day, James; not just for you but for the entire nation. We are all in mourning now. President Lincoln was shot last night at Ford's Theater in Washington. He died this morning at seven twenty-two. They say the actor, John Wilkes Booth, was the man who shot him. There is a massive manhunt underway."

"I had hoped that the killing was over," said James. I fear the bullet that killed the president has done more harm than all the bullets fired during the war. Mr. Lincoln wanted to heal the nation. Who will do that job now?"

The two men walked away from the cemetery in silence, Mr. Templeton to his hearse, James, to the house. He needed to write a letter to Kate. He walked back to the office and without really knowing why, started cleaning up the mess left behind by the intruders. He put books back on shelves and straightened furniture. There was much that needed repaired or replaced, but when he was finished, it gave him a strange feeling of satisfaction. As he was going through the desk drawers, he came upon his father's will. In accordance with his last wishes, and taking into account the passing of James's mother, the plantation now belonged to James. There were, however, certain provisions for Ashton and Kate.

As he read the words penned by his father's own hand, he realized how important it was to his father that Langdon Plantation should live on after his death. To let it disappear would be the same as rubbing the memory of John Langdon from the face of the earth. James was in a quandary. He had never planned to stay in Georgia; he did not feel that he had any right to stay. His plan had been to go back to Pennsylvania to live when the war was over. Now he was having second thoughts. Maybe he was being given a second chance to honor his father. If he rebuilt the plantation he would be fulfilling his father's wishes. He could run a business, he knew that . . .

James sat back in his chair and took a long look around. Suddenly he knew what he must do, it was all very clear. He would write to Kate and tell her to come home. He would find Ashton, somehow, and convince her to do the same. He would go to Mapletown, pack up his family and say farewell to a wonderful town and some wonderful people. No matter what was necessary, Langdon Plantation would flourish again, this time without slavery. James could almost envision his parents looking down from heaven . . . and they were smiling.